Avery spoke softly in a velvety low voice that sent shivers down her spine. "As I recall, Miss Braddock, it was you, not I, who became 'overly excited' and had need of deep breaths in the solarium at the Richardson's ball."

Linney flushed a very becoming shade of bright pink and snapped her fan shut. She tugged to take back her hand, but Avery refused to let it go.

"It is *most* ungentlemanly of you to bring that up, my lord. It was a single incident and, as I was rather tired, I was overly susceptible to your rather limited charms. I dare say it will not happen again."

Lord Hammond arched one eyebrow at her words and waited for her to fully meet his gaze. When she at last stopped looking about and focused on him, her constantly changing hazel eyes flashed a determined green, reflecting the silk gown that so perfectly outlined her figure.

Avery ducked his head to whisper in her ear. "Challenge accepted, my lady."

With a glance over his shoulder at the euphoric crowd, Avery pulled Linney into a secluded bower of hydrangeas at the edge of Lady Haversham's rose garden and behind a rather large Grecian column where they were sheltered from prying eyes. The determined look on his face did not bode well for Linney.

"I warned you not to tease, Miss Braddock. Now you must pay the price."

Praise for Carolina Prescott

THE DUKE'S DECISION was a winner in the Historical Romance category in the 2019 Fiction From the Heartland contest of the Mid America Romance Authors in Kansas City.

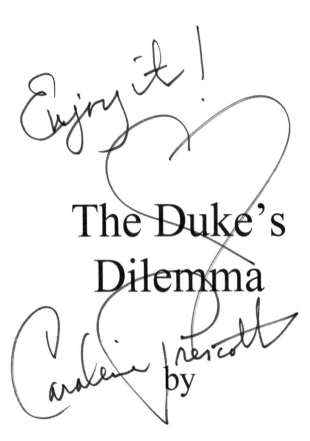

Enjoy it!

Caroline Prescott

The Duke's Dilemma

by

Carolina Prescott

Dukes in Danger:
A Haversham House Romance
Book 2

The Duke's Dilemma

Cover Art by *Debbie Taylor*

The Wild Rose Press, Inc.
PO Box 708
Adams Basin, NY 14410-0708
Visit us at www.thewildrosepress.com

Publishing History
First Edition, 2021
Trade Paperback ISBN 978-1-5092-3785-2
Digital ISBN 978-1-5092-3786-9

Dukes in Danger:
A Haversham House Romance, Book 2
Published in the United States of America

Dedication

For Linda, who left too soon

Chapter 1

Haversham House, late August, 1815

"Oh, for heaven's sake, Vivian, stop fussing!"

Miss Linea Braddock, cousin, confidante, and maid of honor to the soon-to-be Duchess of Whitley, batted at her cousin's hand and continued to adjust the silk underskirt.

"You look beautiful, but I must say it's a good thing the current fashion is high waists, short bodices, and gathered skirts. No one can tell your condition just from looking at you, although..."

"What?" The almost-duchess narrowed her eyes at her cousin.

"Well, it's just that the way you look at your duke and the way he looks at you, I doubt anyone will be surprised when your little one makes an early appearance."

Linney twitched the train of the exquisite gown of *Poussiere de Paris* satin. It was the exact creamy color of *café au lait* and had been encrusted with patterns of seed pearls on the bodice and around the hem.

"There. That's perfect. You have the glow of a bride with just the slightest undercurrent of being in anticipation of a happy event." Linney stifled a chuckle and shook her head as the bride tugged once more at the snug bodice.

"Stop laughing," said Vivian crossly. "You and I have always been blessed with an abundance when it comes to our *décolletage*, and I knew I would become more…abundant, but I had no idea it would happen so quickly. Madame Augustine let out the bodice just this week at my final fitting. How can it already be so tight?"

"It's penance for anticipating your vows," proclaimed Linney with a decidedly superior sniff.

"I didn't anticipate them all by myself," muttered Vivian. "I don't see Whit suffering any consequences. In fact, it's just the opposite. He's embarrassingly ecstatic about what he calls my 'blossoming' figure."

"Of course he is. He's a man. He has eyes, and he is fond of using them to enjoy the female form—especially yours. I think it's sweet."

Turning away from her cousin's answering glare, Linney picked up the bridal bouquet of bachelor buttons, Queen Anne's lace, and honeysuckle, and tightened the blue ribbon holding the flowers.

The spacious dressing room looked out over the famous formal gardens at Haversham House. The estate—just outside London—was the location for many of the most talked-about *ton* gatherings, most notably the infamous house parties given by the effervescent Lady Haversham. Today it also had the happy honor of being the site of the most unexpected and most romantic wedding of the London season as the eleventh Duke of Whitley was joined in holy matrimony with Lady Vivian Rowden.

As Linney observed, whispers ran rampant about the source of the bride's glow and about the groom's uncharacteristic but decidedly dear manner toward his fiancée. And although the official reason given for a special license and hasty nuptials was the duke's required presence in Paris to help negotiate the peace after Napoleon's defeat at Waterloo, many a dowager would be counting the months until the appearance of the duke's first offspring with a knowing smile.

"You can tell me how sweet it is when *your* breasts are overflowing your stays and tender to the touch," said Vivian, continuing her grumble. "I all but snapped Whit's head off when he…"

She stopped abruptly. "Never mind. That's probably something I shouldn't be discussing with you." She glanced over at Linney, but then smiled broadly at the rosy blush coloring her cousin's cheeks. "Oh, I see. Has Lord Hammond spoken to Uncle Will yet?"

"No." Linney poked out her bottom lip. "Actually, he hasn't even spoken to me. It is the *most* annoying thing in the world. I do hope he's not waiting to ask me until after he speaks to Papa. Lord Hammond can be rather stubborn and old-fashioned at times. This whole marriage business puts me in mind of two farmers bartering over a milk cow."

"Don't say milk. Or cow. Or… Just use some other analogy, please."

With another tug at her bodice, Vivian studied her reflection in the looking glass, turning and looking over her shoulder to see a back view of the gown. "They do get a bit medieval when talking about their women, don't they?" she mused. "Perhaps they think about it as a rather large transaction that needs all sorts of contractual safeguards. Truly, I don't know what comes over them."

"I love Avery," said Linney, "and I was under the impression that he loves me, but now I'm starting to wonder. Why doesn't he just ask me? Do you think it's because I have no title and he's an earl and will someday be a duke?" She held out the pearl-and-diamond earrings that were a wedding present to the bride from her duke.

"What I *think* is that you are overthinking it. Just be patient. Men can sometimes make very simple things quite complicated—much more complicated than they need to be."

"Maybe…but what else could it be? I don't have a huge dowry or any property to negotiate. And even if I did, the undeniable fact is that everything I have—up to and including my very person—becomes his when we marry."

"It *is* rather antiquated," agreed Vivian. "Although Whit did insist that my widow's portion and all the income from V. I. Burningham's puzzles be set aside in a separate account of my own. I thought that very forward thinking of him."

Linney groaned and leaned back against the bed post. "Oh, you're right. If I think too much about it, I become terribly insulted, so I'll just bury my head in the sand like the proverbial ostrich. But really, what is he waiting for? Did you talk to the duke about your vows? What did he say?"

Vivian smiled. "When I told him I would not promise to obey him unless he promised to obey *me*, he just closed his eyes and shook his head. But later he told me he talked Bishop Wren into leaving it out of my vows."

"Good for you! Now I can use you as my example

when it's my turn—if it ever is."

"Avery is reportedly not on good terms with his father. Perhaps that's the issue," offered Vivian.

"I suppose…but if that were the case, wouldn't it make sense for him to just say so?" Linney fluffed Vivian's skirt one last time and took a step back. She sighed at the picture her cousin and best friend made in her wedding gown.

"Perfect. You look exquisite, Vivian. Truly, you do."

Linney carefully hugged the woman who had been like an older sister to her since an early age, trying to forestall the tears that threatened. "Shall we go down? Papa is waiting, and you're already late—such a trial to a man like the Duke of Whitley."

Laughing, the two linked arms and made their way to the top of the grand staircase. With a final kiss to Vivian's cheek, Linney took a deep breath and started down the stairs toward the waiting crowd.

Most of the thoughts swirling in Linney's head as she descended the curved marble staircase were about wishing Vivian and Whit a lifetime of happiness together, but at least one or two were spent wondering if *she* would ever be making that same bridal journey.

As she reached the last step, her eyes met those of Avery, sixth Earl of Hammond and heir to the Duke of Easton. Her heart skipped a beat as he held her eyes and slowly smiled that slightly dangerous, velvety smile that brought color to her cheeks and a tingling warmth to other parts of her body.

And while everyone else watched the Duke of Whitley's lovely bride process to the altar, Lord Hammond only had eyes for her.

Chapter 2

"It was a lovely ceremony, don't you think?"

Linney looked up at Lord Hammond as she put her hand on his sleeve. "Vivian and the duke are perfect for each other."

"It was," agreed Lord Hammond, "and they are, but I still say it should have been *my* wedding, not Whit's."

He tucked Linney's hand under his arm and led her away from the merry crowd spilling out from every open door onto the Haversham House terraces. Congratulations were on the lips of every guest, each one quick to offer an opinion on the glorious day, the beautiful bride, the smitten groom, or some other aspect of the ducal nuptials.

"You don't want a very big wedding do you, Linney?"

"Oh, Avery, Avery…how very little you know of women."

"Why do you say that? I dare say I know a little something about them—especially ones wearing soft green gowns that cling to their rather delectable curves."

Linney shot him a scolding look before continuing. "Every girl dreams of a fairy-tale wedding, my lord. Of walking down the aisle wearing the most beautiful gown she's ever worn. Of meeting her prince in front of friends and loved ones in a church festooned with thousands of flowers. The prince then proclaims his undying love for her and they live happily ever after." Linney sighed dreamily at the vision she'd created.

"I should think something without all the waiting would be more desirable," countered the earl. "Perhaps a special license and a quick exchange of vows in front of a vicar?"

Linney frowned at his proposition and he quickly dissembled. "Think how, uh…romantic it would be. An intimate moment shared only between the lady and her…er, prince."

"I should think that would depend entirely on the prince and how he presented his offer of marriage," she replied. "As far as *I'm* concerned, it is a moot point in that I've declined all offers from those who have asked and, as of yet, have no other offers to consider."

Linney was madly in love with the earl, and had every intention of marrying him, but a girl does need to be asked. It would not do to encourage Avery's undesirable and rather arrogant tendency to assume things that had yet to be firmly established. Even as often as he alluded to matrimony and weddings when they were alone together, the cold hard fact was that Lord Hammond had not yet offered for her hand, and Linney felt the absence of such a request keenly.

Avery scowled at Linney's words and continued his litany of grumbling as he all but hauled her down the path that led toward the far end of the rose garden and a rather excellent statue of Diana, goddess of the hunt.

"I don't think Whit quite appreciates the sacrifices I've made for him." Avery frowned at a lizard daring to dart across his path. "Against my own wishes, but out of deference to my older brother, I let his wedding take precedence over mine."

"Well, he *is* a duke, so I would think he could get married pretty much whenever he wanted to. And as much as I hate to beleaguer the point, my lord, you have no betrothed to marry—unless…perhaps Lord Haversham's cousin has caught your eye?"

Avery stopped suddenly and snorted. "Lady Smythson? Surely you jest."

He narrowed his eyes as Linney danced ahead on the path, smiling at him over her shoulder.

"And what do you mean you've declined all offers from those who have asked? How many offers of marriage have you had?"

He walked slowly toward the waltzing, fairy-like creature in front of him. "I caution you, Linney. I am in no mood for teasing. I've had to postpone all my plans simply because my half-brother has no control. If he and Lady Rowden—excuse me, I mean *her grace*—had exercised some restraint during their courtship, or taken a few precautions, I could have been down to Terra Bella and back by now, and I would be the one eagerly anticipating a honeymoon with my bride. It was quite enough to stand up as Whit's best man with the knowledge that my own matrimonial plans are gathering dust, but the man was near bursting when Vivian walked down the aisle—it was embarrassing."

Linney halted in the middle of the path and blinked owl-like at him. "You're jealous."

Avery stopped just in time to avoid running into her. "Of course I'm jealous! I am tired to death of waiting for everyone else. I want what Whit has."

"You want to marry Vivian?" Linney looked at Avery, batting her eyelashes in false confusion and shaking her head sadly. "I must tell you, my lord, I do not think my cousin shares your feelings. She is much enamored of her new husband."

Avery narrowed his eyes again. "Are you deliberately trying to provoke me, Miss Braddock? I have given you fair warning that I am not to be trifled with this morning. You ignore my words at your own peril."

"Goodness, my lord," said Linney, plying her fan as she gazed up innocently at Avery, "you *are* in a mood. How will you *ever* find a young lady to marry you when you sport such a thunderous countenance?"

"Linney..."

But the beautiful Miss Braddock had skipped on ahead, disregarding both the earl's words and his glare in her direction.

"You know, my lord," she called back to him, "it is not good for men of your very advanced age to get overly excited. Such stimulation—especially on a warm day such as this—can be very bad for your constitution. You should follow my example and adopt a more calming mien, which would bring you a more serene outlook. For example, in spite of the many queries that have been put to me this day about the status of my own marital aspirations, I remain *sans souci*—without care."

"I speak fluent French, Miss Braddock, thank you."

"Perhaps if you took deep breaths of fresh air, my lord. Try it. In...now out...now in..."

Avery grabbed Linney's hand. His eyes met hers as he pressed the delicate trophy to his lips. He spoke softly in a velvety low voice that sent shivers down her spine. "As I recall, Miss Braddock, it was you, not I, who became 'overly excited' and had need of deep breaths in the solarium at the Richardson's ball."

Linney flushed a very becoming shade of bright pink and snapped her fan shut. She tugged to take back her hand, but Avery refused to let it go.

"It is *most* ungentlemanly of you to bring that up, my lord. It was a single incident and, as I was rather tired, I was overly susceptible to your rather limited charms. I dare say it will not happen again."

Lord Hammond arched one eyebrow at her words and waited for her to fully meet his gaze. When she at last stopped looking about and focused on him, her constantly changing hazel eyes flashed a determined green, reflecting the silk gown that so perfectly outlined her figure.

Avery ducked his head to whisper in her ear. "Challenge accepted, my lady."

With a glance over his shoulder at the euphoric crowd, Avery pulled Linney into a secluded bower of hydrangeas at the edge of Lady Haversham's rose garden and behind a rather large Grecian column where they were sheltered from prying eyes. The determined look on his face did not bode well for Linney.

"I warned you not to tease, Miss Braddock. Now you must pay the price."

Linney laughed as she reclaimed both of her hands and set them on her hips. "And what, pray, is the charge for merely stating the incontrovertible fact that you, to the best of my knowledge, have no fiancée to whom you might be wed today?"

Never taking his eyes from hers, Avery took a step closer, making it necessary for her to look up to maintain eye contact. He cocked his head slightly and, with a knowing smile, commandeered Linney's left hand, turning it to display a bare wrist exposed by her short lace gloves. He raised her wrist to his lips and smiled when he felt the quickening of the underlying pulse.

In a low voice he murmured, "What of you, Miss Braddock? Is there no one who has won your heart? No one to whom you have given yourself in theory, if not in fact?"

Linney gulped, but defiantly looked away with an air of *ennui*. "No, my lord, there is not. I had once hoped I might draw the attention of a rather homely earl, but it is said he is under the spell of a family heirloom—a ring, I believe it is—without which he is unable to offer for any maiden."

"Excellent! Then I needn't worry about challenging anyone's claim when I take possession of this soft bit of shoulder here."

The very tall, very dashing Earl of Hammond very delicately touched his lips to the bare skin where Linney's graceful neck met her exposed shoulder. She shivered from head to toe, as she stubbornly reiterated, "No, my lord. No one."

The earl released her wrist but trailed one finger back up her arm as he moved behind her. He put a hand on each of her shoulders and placed a kiss on the nape of her neck, dislodging a stray curl that fell just short of the back edge of her lace-trimmed bodice. The tip of his tongue traced the form of the curl down her spine and Linney trembled again.

"Are you chilled, madam? I thought the day rather warm, but you are shivering."

"Yes. I mean, no. I am quite warm, thank you, my lord."

With a bird's-eye view of her *décolletage*, Avery bent to whisper in her ear. "Ah, yes. I can see that now. Your lovely skin is flushed. Your neck... Your shoulders..." His lips followed the direction of his words, and his hands molded the sides of her gown. "And that same lovely pink is kissing the tops of your breasts. I wonder...might I be afforded that same privilege?"

She gasped as he caressed her flushed skin with his forefinger, slipping it just beneath the front edge of her bodice. For an instant, his big hand cupped the breast that had been pushed up by her stays, and then that same forefinger brushed across the thin fabric straining across her breast, finding and circling the nipple until it tightened into a hard bud.

"Are you certain you are not chilled, Miss Braddock? I must say, I see evidence to the contrary."

Linney stood motionless under his spell. The wicked words he whispered in her ear flushed not only her cheeks and her breasts, but sent a warmth to her very core. Avery put his arms around her waist, pulling her against him—close enough for her to feel the hard length of his arousal against her backside. She closed her eyes and relaxed into his embrace.

"Do you remember the last time we had this conversation, Miss Braddock? It was in the Richardson's solarium. You were flushed with that same delightful soft pink. Your lips were a darker pink from my kisses, and your bottom lip was pouty and full because I had stopped. Do you remember why I stopped, Linney? Was it because you asked me to?"

Linney shook her head.

"Did you want me to stop?"

"No," she whispered.

"Then why did I stop?" Avery's kisses were everywhere now, spaced between his soft words.

"You stopped because… You said you wanted…" Linney couldn't get her mind to concentrate on anything except what Avery was doing to her with his hands and his mouth. How could he do all of these lovely things and still hold a conversation?

"What did I want, my love?" Avery traced the outline of her ear with his tongue and then nipped at her earlobe as he growled his command. "Tell me why I stopped, Linney."

"You said you wanted to know if…" Linney gasped as he plucked at the hardened tips of both breasts through the thin, green fabric. He caressed his discovery with the pads of both thumbs as he cupped the soft weights in his hands.

"Tell me, Linney. What did I say as I covered your breasts with my hands, like this, and teased the budding tips, like this?"

Linney ached for more. Breathlessly, she answered, "You asked if they were also pink."

"If what was pink? Not just your breasts, my love. I knew they were pink, I could see the color disappearing down the front of your frock as it does now. What did I want to know, Linney?"

"I don't know," said Linney, frustrated because she wanted only to feel, not talk. "I don't remember."

"*I* remember." Avery's voice was so low she could barely hear it. "I wanted to know if the nipples I was teasing were the same dark pink as your lips. And were they, Miss Braddock?"

With a moan, she turned to face him, pushing him back against the garden wall as she put her arms around his neck and pulled his mouth to hers, answering him between kisses.

"Yes, my lord. They are the same dark pink as my lips. I remember because you pulled down my bodice and I watched you touch my breasts. And when you touched them with your tongue they grew harder and turned an even deeper rose. But only when you took one into your mouth did it become the dark pink of my lips. Are those the words you wanted to hear, my lord?"

Avery's mouth had made its way down to the tops of Linney's breasts, showcased beautifully by the square-necked bridesmaid's gown. With one hand he supported Linney while with the other he tugged at her bodice, pulling the material down her shoulder to expose one perfect breast. He touched the dark pink peak with his tongue, and Linney moaned. As he drew the nipple into his mouth, his hand caressed down over her hip and began gathering up the material from her skirt.

Linney whispered his name, arching her back to offer more of herself to him. He was already crushed against her, but it was not close enough.

"Are you certain you want a big wedding, Linney?" he said. "With a special license we could be married by the end of next week."

All rational thought was fleeing Linney's head at an alarming pace. "I haven't a care about the wedding, my lord," she said with one last heroic effort at talking, "but you...you haven't...you haven't asked me to marry you."

Avery stopped in mid-kiss. "So *that's* what you meant when you said I had no betrothed and no fiancée?"

Linney slowly refocused on his face, frustrated with the sudden cessation of his lips. She closed her eyes and took a deep breath to compose herself.

"Yes, my lord. *That* is what I meant. Am I mistaken?"

When he did not reply, she took a step back and out of his arms, adjusting her bodice to cover herself. More than a little out of sorts, she continued.

"Perhaps there has been pressure from your father to make a more appropriate match? A titled lady, perhaps, or one with a better connected family or bluer blood?"

Avery frowned. "No. That's not the case at all. I told you I wanted to wait until I had the Easton engagement ring, and obviously I had to postpone my trip to Terra Bella because of Whit's wedding. I just assumed you knew we would be married."

"Why would I assume that, my lord?"

"Linney, we have been...intimate. You have allowed—"

Linney put a finger on Avery's lips. "Perhaps you *should* marry someone else, my lord. I seem to have very loose morals, and you certainly could do better than the daughter of a lowly solicitor. But in either case, I don't think you should assume anything."

"I have taken liberties, Miss Braddock, and I am a gentleman who honors his obligations."

"So now I am an obligation? Do you really not understand the difference between honoring an obligation and asking me to marry you?"

"The result is the same, is it not?"

"Not necessarily, my lord," said Linney crisply. "For example, if you were to ask for my hand in marriage because you love me and you want us to share a life together, then I would say 'yes.' But, if you were merely offering to make good on a societal expectation, then I would courteously decline your offer."

"Surely you jest. You would be ruined in the eyes of society were our intimacies to be made known."

"You wish to marry me simply because I allowed you to take certain liberties?" Linney's eyes flashed a brilliant green.

"That's reason enough, is it not?"

"Not in my book."

Avery scowled. "Are there others whom you have allowed such liberties, Miss Braddock?"

"Perhaps you should have made such inquiries sooner, my lord. It seems you don't know me as well as you think you do."

"What the hell does that mean?"

"It means, my lord, that as you and I are not betrothed, you do not get to ask me those types of questions."

Turning her back on him, Linney stalked ahead on the path. She bent to pluck a sprig of lavender and brought it to her nose. The warm sun brought out the fragrance from every tiny spear, but, unfortunately, it reminded her of the masculine version of the scent favored by Lord Hammond. Annoyed, she threw the sprig to the ground, and then turned back to face Avery with a bright smile.

"Now that Vivian is married and Napoleon has surrendered, perhaps I shall go abroad and continue work on my portfolio. Vivian and I went all over London, and I've drawn all the interesting buildings the city has to offer. Maybe now is the time for me to visit places I've always longed to see. I understand the Parthenon in Athens is not to be missed. They say it has no straight lines—did you know that? Every column has a slight curve to maintain the building's symmetrical appearance. I would so love to draw it. Or perhaps the Taj Mahal in India. Have you ever been to India, my lord?"

"Do not attempt to change the subject, Linney. It is beneath you." It was not Avery who spoke to her now, but rather the haughty and arrogant ducal heir. "You know I want to marry you and—"

"What I *know*, Lord Hammond, is that, of the several offers of marriage I have received, *none* of them have been from you. So, as of this moment, I am not betrothed or engaged or spoken for or promised to anyone—and specifically not to you." She tipped her chin up in a defiant gesture. "But who knows? Perhaps there is an offer forthcoming this very day. One that I might be wise to accept."

"I do not find this at all amusing, Linea."

Linney narrowed her eyes to look at the man whom she loved not wisely, but too well. Even when he frowned he was beautiful. His burnished-brown curls were the color of autumn and cropped shorter than the tousled look inspired by the fashionable Beau Brummel. She could easily imagine a statue of him as revealing as the one of Diana—a statue that showcased a broad chest and muscled arms as well as the shapely backside and strong thighs of an avid horseman. And between those thighs? Well, the breeches Avery wore with his morning coat did little to conceal the aroused male that he was. No doubt *that* aspect of the statue would be impressive as well.

"Did you think to marry me without ever asking for the honor, my lord? That would be quite presumptuous—even for you."

"What exactly does that mean, Miss Braddock?"

Without waiting for an answer, he stepped closer. He took her hand in his and guided it to his shoulder as he placed his other hand at her waist, running it down her side and around to caress her bottom. He covered her lips with his own, reveling in their softness, and then he deepened the kiss as he pulled her impossibly close, nipping at her full bottom lip and demanding entrance. After a few more moments, he pulled back to look at her.

"Certainly I did not expect to win your hand without a proper offer, Linney, but I *was* under the impression we had an understanding. Am I wrong? *Do* we have an understanding?"

Linney opened her eyes and saw him looking down at her with such fire in his eyes that she caught her breath.

"Linney, there is no one else for me. Please tell me there is no one else for you. I will pledge my whole life to making myself worthy of you, my love. You will be my countess and, eventually, my duchess. We will have strong sons and beautiful daughters, and we will live happily ever after—to the vast astonishment of the *ton*."

Linney shivered and rested her forehead upon his chest before answering. "Oh, Avery, I do love you...you know I do. And I don't need an old family heirloom on my finger before I agree to be your wife.

Why will you not just ask me?"

Avery sighed and rested his chin on top of her head, which happened to be at just the right height. "Linney, listen to me. When I offer you my hand in marriage, I want to do it as I give you the Easton engagement ring to wear—not just as a symbol of our engagement, but because it's a blessing from my family. Starting all the way back with the very first duke, every Easton bride has worn that engagement ring. It's a beautiful ring—the center stone is rose quartz, a stone that stands for never-ending love and happiness. On both sides of the center stone are two diamonds representing the engaged couple. The larger stones are surrounded by smaller, perfectly matched diamonds that represent each generation. After our first son is born, I will add another diamond to the ring so it will be ready for him to give to *his* bride."

Linney slipped her arms around his waist, her ear on his chest, where she could feel as well as hear his heart beat.

Avery continued. "My father and I have not always been on the best of terms, Linney, but I want him to pass the ring to me just as my grandfather passed it to him to give to my mother. It's important to him…and to me. I want us to have the blessing associated with the ring, Linney, and I want my father's blessing as well, but both are at Terra Bella. I've already written to him that I am coming home to get the ring, but…"

He took a step back so he could look into her eyes. "Linney, you must understand. Until I have the Easton ring, I will not ask you to marry me. Now do you understand why I have been so frustrated at the delay caused by Whit and Vivian's wedding?"

Linney stepped back into his arms and nodded into the front of his morning coat. "Thank you for telling me this. I…"

"What is it, my love?

"Nothing. Never mind. It's silly."

Avery set her back from him and ducked down to see her face. "Linney?"

"I understand now, Avery, really I do. And I look forward to your return from Terra Bella with all my heart."

"But?"

"No. There is no 'but.' " She hesitated again.

"Linea?"

"It's just that, right here, right now, there is nothing except my starry eyes to show your intentions. I want so much to tell someone—everyone—that you love me and how very, *very* much I love you. But I'm afraid to acknowledge your love—even to myself. I'm terrified that I will wake and find this was all a dream."

"I told you…"

"Yes, you did. And I do understand, I just wish…before you leave, I mean…could you not just *ask* if I might *start* to think about *considering* your suit?"

Avery smiled as she plowed ahead nervously.

"If you did, then, of course, I would tell you that I could *never* make such an important decision without a great deal of thought and that I would need days and *days* to think about it before I could possibly give you an answer and…"

Avery laughed, and Linney stopped her chattering. She looked down at her slippers, embarrassed by her vulnerability.

With a fingertip, Avery raised her chin. "Would it mean so much to you, my darling? Would it ease your mind if I asked you to wait for me while I travel to…"

"Oh, yes," said Linney eagerly. "I mean, of course I will need time to think on it, but—"

"Wait," said Avery. Taking Linney's hand in his own, he drew off her glove and kissed her palm, and then, holding her eyes with his own, he knelt before her on one knee. "Miss Linea Priscilla Braddock, mere words can never convey my feelings for you. I cannot imagine my life without you and every day I pray you feel the same. Please tell me you will—"

"Aaaave-ry! Oh, Aaaave-ry!"

"Avery, where are you? Is Linney with you?"

"Linney, do you hear us? You must come right away. Vivian is ready to throw the bouquet, and you must be there to catch it!"

Avery came hastily to his feet just as the bushes parted and three small girls in identical white dresses with apple green sashes swirled around them. "The Furies" Whit had dubbed the trio—ages nine, nine and three quarters, and ten—who bore the floral names of Rose, Lilly, and Marguerite.

"Why are you standing behind the bushes, Linney?" asked Rose, the eldest and usual leader of the three.

Lilly, the one who missed nothing, narrowed her eyes and frowned up at Avery. "Why is there dirt on your knee, Avery? Were you looking for something on the ground?"

Marguerite, the most impulsive, simply grabbed Linney's hand and pulled her toward the path. "Come on! We have to go *now*. Vivian is going to throw her bouquet, and all the other unmarried ladies are already there. Hurry!"

With a helpless backward glance at Avery, Linney allowed herself to be herded toward the terrace of Haversham House where, in the oldest of bridal customs, the new Duchess of Whitley was preparing to throw her bouquet to fend off the celebratory crowds.

As she was swept away by a wave of small, chattering females, Linney forlornly waved her ungloved hand at Lord Hammond, still partially hidden behind the hydrangeas.

Chapter 3

Dusting the specks of dirt from his knee, Avery looked up to see his half-brother, the Duke of Whitley, striding toward him. He frowned. "Why aren't you getting ready to leave on your honeymoon? The Furies just kidnapped Linea to catch Vivian's bouquet."

"Yes, I know. I sent them down here to fetch her. I thought it would be less embarrassing for her to be found in a compromising position by three little girls than by her future half brother-in-law, the duke. You really must be more careful with the young lady's reputation, Avery. I am not the only one who noticed that the two of you had disappeared down the proverbial garden path."

"If you're here to lecture me about propriety, your grace, you can save your breath. Unless, of course, you plan to apologize, and then I *might* be inclined to listen."

"Apologize? For what may I ask?"

"Do you deny that your need for a hasty wedding has delayed my own matrimonial plans? If you had demonstrated a bit more control over your primal desires, I would have been to Terra Bella and back by now. Linney would have the Easton engagement ring on her finger, and she and I would be discussing the merits of eloping versus hosting a large society event. And let me assure you that after having spent a mere ten minutes with her behind the hydrangea bushes, eloping would have won the day."

Whit chuckled. "It's good for you to wait, brother. It builds character." He glanced over at Avery's stormy face. "Or am I making an unmerited assumption about the waiting?"

Avery glared at his half-brother. "That is none of your business, your grace."

"To the contrary. May I remind you that I am now the young lady's cousin by marriage? I will not look kindly upon your taking chances with her reputation, Avery."

"Why are you still here, Whit? Go. Go on your honeymoon with your duchess and leave me alone. Go bill and coo like the two besotted turtledoves you are, just don't do it in front of me. For God's sake, I introduced the two of you just two months ago and now you're married!"

"To be precise, Alexander from the bookstore introduced us, but patience, old chap. Your time will be here soon." Whit's face turned solemn. "Maybe sooner than you wish. Here. This came for you." He held out a folded piece of paper sealed with the Easton ducal crest. "The messenger is waiting for a reply. I rather think he's been told to bring you back with him. I wanted to see if you had need of me before I escaped with my bride for a week of marital bliss."

Avery broke the seal and unfolded the message. It was not in the familiar hand he expected.

"Is it your father?"

Avery furrowed his brow as he scanned the paper. "It says the duke was in an accident. The doctor attending my father advises all haste in getting there."

"An accident? What kind of accident?"

"Some sort of carriage mishap."

"Where?"

"This says it happened on the Great North Road when he was on his way to Scotland."

"Scotland? I thought the duke never left Terra Bella—especially since Mother died. Isn't that why Charlotte insisted on bringing the Furies to London?"

"That was my understanding as well. Obviously he got out of the castle more than we thought."

"What the bloody hell was he doing in Scotland?"

"Evidently, getting married. This is signed by the Duchess of Easton."

Whit's eyebrows shot up. "Well, I *am* surprised. I was under the impression his grace was in a perpetual state of mourning for our mother."

"The last I heard from him, he was. Something's not right, Whit. I should leave for Terra Bella right away. Help me find Linney, will you? I want to let her know what's happened. I was just telling her I would be traveling soon to Terra Bella to get father's blessing on our engagement and retrieve the ring, but I didn't think I would be leaving today."

Turning back toward Haversham House, the two men were met with the sound of rising excitement heralding the appearance of the bride and the throwing of the bouquet.

Whit put a hand on Avery's arm, nodding toward the throng gathered on the terrace. "If you go back up to the house, it will be hours before you can get away. Your friends will be ribbing you about your disappearance with Miss Braddock behind the hydrangeas, and the young ladies—and their mamas—

will be waiting to press their own suits since you, as yet, have no official entanglement. The messenger has already spent a day finding you here. Go around back and leave from there. I'll let Linney know about the missive from your father. I'll tell her you had to leave immediately and will write as soon as possible."

Avery scowled, but then sighed. "I guess that's probably the best course. I'm sure Linney will understand, and I don't want to spoil Vivian's day."

Whit smiled with brotherly empathy. "I know that look. You've got it bad, Av. If it's any consolation, from what I see, Linney is just as smitten. Vivian agrees." He clapped his younger half-brother on the back. "She adores you, Avery—you can see it every time she looks at you. You're just going to have to trust that Miss Braddock will wait for you to return to her. You know," he added with a twinkle in his eye, "in most societies, being betrothed is as binding as being wed—with all of the benefits. If that doesn't put a spring in your step, I don't know what will."

"I'll tell you what will," muttered Avery, "a special license and my *wife* accompanying me on this journey." He looked at Whit sheepishly. "Perhaps we do not *have* to marry quite as quickly as you and Vivian, but Linney and I... Well, I will definitely be speaking to her father the very minute I return from Terra Bella."

"Excellent to hear, but I caution you to prepare yourself for a lengthy engagement. Linney is a young girl—not a widow like Vivian was. What if she wants all the fuss and pomp that go with a proper *ton* wedding at St. George's? You are an earl, after all, and a ducal heir. You wouldn't want her to miss out on all of that, would you?"

"She did mention a fairy-tale wedding, but then she said she didn't care, although…to be fair, she might have been a bit distracted at the time." He smiled at the memory, but his smile was short lived and immediately replaced by a worried frown. "Tell her I will write as soon as I can. Jeffries and I should be able to make Farnham by dark and then Aylesbury the night after. With good weather we'll be to Terra Bella by nightfall Saturday."

Avery signaled a footman, gave him a message for Jeffries, his man of affairs, and asked for his mount to be brought around. "You'll make my excuses to Lord and Lady Haversham?" he said to Whit. "And be sure to kiss the bride for me."

At Whit's broad smile, Avery rolled his eyes. "Oh, for God's sake, man. Get control of yourself. You're an embarrassment." He shook his head. Then he smiled. "How did the pair of us get so lucky as to find the two most wonderful ladies in the world?"

"I don't know," admitted his half-brother, "but I'll be on my knees every night thanking the Almighty for mine."

They had almost reached the stables when Whit put his hand on Avery's arm. "Avery, there's one more thing you should know. Monsieur Jones is back in England. We tracked him to Scotland and lost the trail, but now there are signs he has crossed back into England."

"Why? What does Napoleon's chief spy want now that *Le Petit Caporal* is safely ensconced on Saint Helena under heavy guard? There is no chance of his escape this time."

"Yes, well, that's what we thought the first time.

Napoleon still has loyal followers on the outside—
Jones is just one of many. However, according to our
sources, the man's whole *raison d'être* now is revenge.
On the Crown, of course, but specifically revenge on
you, Vivian, Edgewood, Camberton, and myself."

Avery wrinkled his brow and cocked his head.
"Camberton? I don't think I've had the pleasure."

"It's not important. Suffice it to say he is also
under my command and in danger from Jones. I tell you
all of this only so you will keep your guard up. You're
traveling with Jeffries as your only companion, and you
will be much in the open."

Avery nodded. "Thank you. I assume this means
you will be taking extra care as well?"

"Yes." Whit's face was grim. "For myself, but
even more for Vivian. Until this man is in custody, we
must assume he will stop at nothing."

Avery smiled ruefully. "And here I thought you
never assumed anything."

Whit's smile was tired. "I will make an exception
in this case. If you need me, just send word. For you, I
will even leave my new bride. She is not feeling well in
the mornings and has expressed reluctance to travel to
the continent. We may yet end up spending our
honeymoon in the comfort of my town house."

"I'll send word as soon as I learn the situation at
Terra Bella."

Whit clasped Avery's hand. "Safe travels, then."
The brothers embraced, and Whit watched as Avery
strode away toward the stables.

****

"What do you mean, he's gone? He was just here.
We were…well, we were talking about…different

shades of pink and…other things."

Linney's face helpfully illustrated her point.

"Whit said Avery received a summons from Terra Bella with the news that his father had been injured in some sort of an accident and he should make all haste to get there."

"Did the messenger say how the duke was faring?"

"No, but I don't think it bodes well that Avery left so suddenly. He asked Whit to tell you he would write as soon as possible. Whit did say Avery was extremely reluctant to leave without talking to you, but time was of the essence." Vivian's face reflected her concern for her cousin. "Oh, Linney, I'm sorry he had to leave so abruptly. The situation must be dire. Do you need someone to keep you company? You could come with Whit and me."

Linney laughed outright through the tears that had suddenly gathered in her eyes. "Of course! I'm sure that is exactly the vision the duke had in mind for his wedding night. Perhaps I should arrange for a trundle bed in your chambers?"

"Very well, perhaps it's not the *best* solution, but I do hate to leave you like this."

Linney gave Vivian's hand a quick squeeze. "Don't worry about me. I'll be fine. Mama and Papa and I are going back to London tomorrow morning. Papa has some drawings he wants me to do for one of his clients, and I have shopping to do. I also have plans for a tremendous mural for my new baby cousin. You, on the other hand, should hurry. Your duke must be chomping at the bit."

Vivian smiled with the cool assurance of a woman confident in the love of a doting husband. She leisurely sat down at her dressing table and gently kicked off her slippers.

"I like knowing he's waiting for me. In fact, I think I'll just let him wait another twenty minutes or so while I fix my hair."

"How can you do that? I would never have the nerve to keep Avery waiting. I would be afraid he might go off without me."

"You mean like he did today?" Vivian's astute comment did not go unheard.

Linney shrugged. "It's different for us. Avery and I are not married or even officially engaged. Obviously we've been keeping company, but he has made me no promises."

"I think promises are made in many different ways, Lin. However, if you aren't sure whether Avery would wait for you, then perhaps you aren't ready to be married to him. Or, perhaps you just don't know him as well as you should." Vivian cocked her head as she scanned her cousin's face in the mirror. "When you're ready, the waiting is not a burden but rather a lovely anticipation of your coming together. For example, I know Whit will always be there for me just as I will always be there for him. There is no question about it. Once that became clear to me, I knew I was ready to marry him."

"And did he know at the same time? Was that when he asked you to marry him?"

Vivian laughed. "He *told* me I was going to marry him several times, but only when he knew he could be the husband I needed did he *ask* me. And when he asked, I said yes."

"You are a very wise woman, Vivian. You and

Whit are going to be the happiest couple in all the world."

A scratch at the door interrupted the cousins' confidences.

"Come in," called Linney, brushing at her tears.

"Your grace," said the upstairs maid, dropping a curtsy in Vivian's direction, "his grace said to tell your grace that if your grace is not down the stairs in two minutes, then his grace will come up and throw your grace over his grace's shoulder." The girl blushed. "Those are his grace's words, your grace, not mine."

"Thank you, Sarah. Please let the duke know I will be down directly."

As the door closed, Vivian grimaced. "It's going to take me a while to get used to all of this 'your gracing.' "

Smiling, Linney watched Vivian carefully remove her hat and place it to one side on the dressing table. Her eyes widened with awe as Vivian casually looked around for another hair pin to insert into her simple French twist.

"You don't think he will come up here?"

"On the contrary. I'm counting on it."

In just a matter of seconds, there was a great commotion on the stairs that could be heard all the way down the hallway, and it featured the voice of the Duke of Whitley grumbling loudly.

Linney grinned as Vivian stood and placed one stockinged foot on the stool beside her chair. She raised her skirts and petticoats to reveal a very shapely leg and then slowly smoothed the fine silk and adjusted her garter.

"Have a lovely honeymoon," whispered Linney,

closing the connecting door to her room just as the door to the hallway flew open. Before she stole away, Linney heard the duke's roaring entrance and the low, throaty response of the duchess greeting her new husband. Linney could only imagine Whit's delight at finding his wife in such an enticing pose.

The silence that ensued spoke volumes.

Chapter 4

"Linney, dear! Oh, here you are at last. I was afraid
you wouldn't see me waving."

Avery's aunt, Lady Charlotte, was hard to miss in
her vivid finery which bore an unfortunate resemblance
to a ripe persimmon.

"Did you get a piece of the wedding cake before it
was all gone, my dear? I saw that her grace tossed the
bouquet in your direction, so we all know you will be
the *next* to marry. Now we just need to know *whom* you
will wed. Before you go to sleep tonight, you must put
your piece of wedding cake under your pillow. Do that
and you will dream about your future mate."

Lady Charlotte leaned in and whispered
confidentially, "I've found it's best to wrap it first in a
handkerchief. That way you won't wake up with a head
full of crumbs."

Most of the time, Lady Charlotte was quite
practical and down to earth, but oh, she did love a
wedding. She would wax on for hours about happily-
ever-afters and dreams coming true, conveniently
leaving behind the less romantic business of contracts
and settlements and family engagement rings. She was,
understandably, the keeper of all the best wedding
traditions, superstitions, legends, and old wives' tales,
and she brought those little bits of magic with her to
every ceremony she attended.

"Yes, Lady Charlotte, I did," said Linney obediently, not knowing how to tell the good lady that she had also already consumed said piece of cake.

"Well, it's probably beside the point anyway, dear. I think we all know who the man of your dreams is." Lady Charlotte's whispered confidences had gained volume, and now she added a little giggle as she tried to look stern. "Where *is* that nephew of mine?"

With any luck, the sudden color on Linney's cheeks might be attributed to a reflection off Lady Charlotte's ensemble. Hoping to bring the lady's remarks back to a more private volume, Linney conveyed her response in a low voice.

"Lady Rowden—I mean the Duchess of Whitley—just told me that Lord Hammond was called away to Terra Bella. Evidently his father has been involved in some sort of carriage accident." She paused for a moment, trying not to instill her hurt feelings into the next part of the narrative. "He didn't have time to make his farewells, so it must be quite urgent."

"Yes, dear, I know he was called away, but Avery did not say goodbye to *you*? How could he leave and not say goodbye to *you*? The two of you are practically betrothed. Whatever was he thinking? Well, you are not to worry, my dear. Everyone knows he is smitten with you—surely he told you so when you were behind the hydrangeas? The two of you were gone for quite a long time. Everyone was remarking on it."

So much for suffering her humiliation and hurt in private. On the positive side, there would be no need to repeat the gossip, nor would there be any discrepancies in the accuracy of the information. Lady Charlotte's voice carried quite clearly to the edges of the crowded terrace. If ever there was a time for the ground to open up and swallow someone, that time was now. And frankly, Linney did not care whether the ground devoured Lady Charlotte or herself.

"Lord Hammond was simply taking me on a tour of Lady Haversham's gardens—I had not seen the roses in full bloom." Linney spoke in her most careless tone.

"It must have been a very *thorough* tour, my dear." Lady Charlotte smiled broadly at Linney. Was that a wink?

"Surely, he had time to make his intentions known to you then? Of course everyone knows that once the Standish men decide on a woman, they are so very tiresomely faithful—just look at his father, the duke. He's practically been a monk since the death of his duchess, my dear sister." Lady Charlotte dabbed at the corner of her eye with her fine lawn handkerchief.

Linney was uncomfortably aware that everyone in the vicinity was now listening with unabashed interest. But, alas, the lady was not done.

"Linney dear, did you forget your parasol on that very long stroll with Avery? You are looking quite flushed. I hope you have not burnt your complexion. It would not do for you to be tan at your wedding. All you want is the faint color of a blushing bride on your cheeks."

Murder would definitely detract from Vivian's happy day, and spontaneous combustion was rather messy, so really there was only one other choice. Linney quickly kissed Lady Charlotte on the cheek and set her escape in motion.

"Please excuse me, my lady. My mother has need of me."

Placing one foot in front of the other, she controlled the impulse to run full speed toward the house as Lady Charlotte called loudly after her.

"I'll come around early next week, dear. It's never too early to start picking fabrics for Lilly, Rose, and Marguerite. I never like to dress them alike, but for Avery's wedding I could…"

Linney held her breath until she slipped inside the huge front door of Haversham House and closed it gratefully behind her. She pressed her burning cheeks against the cool, dark wood as she whispered to the ancient panels, "Oh, Avery, not even a kiss goodbye?"

****

Voices at the other end of the hall caught Linney's attention, and she quickly stepped into an alcove with the hope of avoiding guests who might wonder why the cousin of the bride had tear-streaked cheeks and such a red nose. It was, after all, a wedding, not a funeral. She froze when she heard her name on the lips of the young lady leading the group down the corridor. The shrill laughter that pockmarked the muffled conversation could only belong to Miss Maribel Conway, a young lady whom Linney had met at the beginning of the season and had actively avoided ever since.

Linney was not in the habit of eavesdropping—at least not intentionally—but she was also not without a certain curiosity as to why her name had come up in conversation with this particular group of damsels. Unfortunately, the young lady responding to Maribel— most likely her bosom friend, Lady Sybil Wentworth— spoke in the low, cultured register that aristocratic young ladies were taught, making it almost impossible to hear what she said.

Maribel laughed again. There was little culture in her tinny tone. "She may *think* Lord Hammond is in love with her, but that doesn't mean he will marry her."

A low question was interrupted by Maribel's emphatic confirmation. "I don't just *think* so, Sybil, I have it on great authority that he is simply using her for his amusement. My maid's cousin told my maid she saw Lord Hammond kissing Miss Braddock behind the Venus statue just this morning."

Linney heard a third voice join the conversation.

"Very well, Hester, the statue of *Diana*, then. What difference does it make? No, Sybil, my maid's cousin was not behind the statue. Lord Hammond was there kissing Miss Braddock. And my maid's cousin told my maid that the statue was not the only one with a bare breast."

The squeaks of horror and delight sounded suspiciously alike as the ladies moved closer. Linney withdrew farther into the shadowed recess.

"Oh, Maribel!" Sybil's part of the conversation was now more easily understood. "That is so very naughty!"

"I didn't say it. My maid's cousin said it to my maid. Lord Hammond is the Duke of Easton's heir, so he'll need to wed a viscount's daughter at least. And both sisters of the Marquess of Greer are out this season. Lord Hammond may frolic with Miss Braddock, but he's certain to marry a title—her father is only a solicitor, for heaven's sake."

"I was outside just now and heard Lady Charlotte say Lord Hammond has gone back to his family estate and didn't even tell Miss Braddock goodbye," said Hester.

"She's making a fool of herself by pretending he's in love with her."

"She'll change her tune soon enough when Lord Hammond puts the Easton engagement ring on a real lady's finger."

The muffled reply was too low for Linney to understand.

"I suppose she *could* be his mistress," replied Maribel. "According to my maid's cousin, she certainly seems to be preparing for the part."

The tittering took the trio past the alcove where Linney stood, her face flaming, her heart pounding, and her head telling her that the young ladies were not wrong.

Chapter 5

"So, the Earl of Hammond is on his way to the ducal estate? With only his man of affairs at his side? This is indeed news I wish to know. You have done well, Jane. Did Lord Hammond indicate why such a hasty trip was necessary?"

"The footman told me he heard the earl say to his brother that the duke had been in some sort of carriage accident. He said he also heard the old duke has taken a new wife."

Monsieur Jones wrinkled his brow. " A new wife? That certainly was not part of the plan."

"It seemed to surprise everyone—at least that's what the footman said the earl said when he was talking to the duke. Not the duke, his father, but the duke, his brother—half-brother."

"The one who was just married today?"

"Yes, sir. That one."

"Did you see the bride?"

"Oh, I did, sir. She was lovely. Her gown was a lovely light brown satin and covered with them little tiny pearls and it had flowers embroidered along the—"

"I did not ask for a fashion review," snapped the man, known to Jane only as "Monsieur." "Did the bride and groom leave before you came here?"

"Oh, yes, sir. They was off in a shiny carriage with everyone throwing the rose petals we'd been collecting from Lady Haversham's gardens. We collected them every day except when it was raining, because..."

Jane stopped when she saw Monsieur narrow his eyes. "Yes, sir, they are gone. They waved at everyone, and the duke tossed out gold coins as they drove off. I caught two of 'em!"

"And what of the cousin?"

"Whose cousin, Monsieur?"

"The cousin to the new duchess—Miss Braddock. Was she still there? Was she enjoying herself?"

"Oh, yes, she was still there. She caught the bride's bouquet and was laughing and smiling with everyone, but she weren't as happy as she were when the earl was there. I think she misses him."

"I don't pay you to think, Jane. I pay you to report what you see. What did you see that makes you say Miss Braddock is missing the earl?"

"Earlier in the day, she and Lord Hammond had taken a very long stroll in the rose garden—only they wasn't strolling—if you know what I mean. I saw him pull her behind the flower bushes down there near that statue of the woman with no clothes on. Then, later, after he left, she kept dabbing her eyes with a hankie. It fell when she went to put it into her pocket and when I picked it up, it was damp like it had soaked up a lot of water."

"Do you have it?"

"Beg pardon?"

"Do you have it? Do you have her handkerchief?"

"I...uh..."

"Give it to me, girl. I saw your fingers move in your pocket." He held out his hand. "Give me Miss Braddock's handkerchief, *s'il vous plaît*."

Jane reluctantly took the embroidered square of fine lawn out of her pocket and handed it to the man in front of her.

He smoothed out the square and said softly, "Perhaps while I wait word about Lord Hammond's father, I should see if there is something I can do in London. If Miss Braddock misses the earl, then he most likely misses her. Seeing her hurt or losing her altogether would be very painful for him, don't you think?"

"Why would he lose her, sir? In my opinion, they's more likely to end up married than not—especially if they get caught playing house like they was this morning."

Jones sighed and turned his attention to the problem at hand. "Yes, you're quite right. Thank you, Jane. You have done an excellent job and have been very useful to me. I regret to tell you that I will not be needing your services any longer."

In the woods surrounding the tiny hunting cabin there was no sound and certainly not anything to indicate foul play, so it was not until several days later that Jane's lifeless body was found inside.

Chapter 6

Avery was up before daybreak. Nothing at the Bishop's Inn in Farnham encouraged lingering, so after penning a brief but heartfelt apology to Linney and a promise to write more soon, he franked the letter and left it for the morning post. Then he and Jeffries set out on the next leg of their travels, with a southern breeze hinting of wet roads in the not-too-distant future.

"There's an inn on the far side of Aylesbury that my family often patronizes," said Avery after several hours of silent progress. "They set a decent table and their ale is some of the best you'll find. We're making good time and should get there before dark."

Jeffries, still sleepy from the short night and early departure, grunted in reply.

They *had* made good time. And Whit's advice yesterday had proved sound—Avery was on his way within minutes of bidding farewell to his brother. But now that he was away, he sorely regretted leaving without saying goodbye to Linney. In addition to it being a rather ungentlemanly thing to do, he... Well, he missed her. Already. And more than he liked to admit to anyone, including himself.

Fortunately, the ambitious pace he and Jeffries set meant the two could not easily converse. Unfortunately, the lack of conversation gave him more time to dwell on the past few months and on the fascinating young woman who, in that short time, had changed his life.

Lord Hammond had never met anyone like Miss Linea Braddock. She was charming and witty, and she was beautiful. Her unusual white-blonde hair gave her the look of a Nordic princess and the glow of an angel. She had hazel eyes that changed as quickly as her moods—a golden brown when she was drawing or dreaming and a brilliant green when he held her in his arms. The memory of Linney in his arms had Avery shifting a bit in his saddle. He'd better find another avenue for his thoughts or this trip would become quite uncomfortable, if not downright dangerous to his future plans. Perhaps if he focused on Miss Braddock's faults…

Linney could be quite vain.

Avery grinned. No amount of cajoling could convince her to wear her spectacles at social occasions. Her nearsightedness made it difficult for her to identify people and things. At one soiree, she mistook the Duke of Wellington for a footman and asked him to direct her to the ladies' retiring room. Luckily the national hero was unoffended and knew the location of the room in question. And, it being Linney, she smiled and thanked him prettily enough—even as she continued thinking him a servant in the house.

After that incident, Avery tried to convince her to wear her spectacles, but she airily quoted Shakespeare, declaring, "All's well that ends well."

In addition to being vain, she was more than a little fanatic about her drawing. Although to be fair, that wasn't really a fault. She was an extremely talented artist, and the fault—if there was one—belonged to society for restricting her in ways a man would never have to endure. Such restrictions never seemed to bother Linney, but only because she refused to bow to society's lower expectations and higher standards for females.

Avery smiled, thinking of the countless times when Linney talked to people she shouldn't and didn't speak to those she ought. It wasn't that she actively rebelled against the society matrons who tut-tutted at her behind their fans, it was just that she had better things to do.

Linney was funny and absolutely fearless—which could on occasion be a problem. And she talked all the time. *All* the time. But chatter that would have driven him to Bedlam coming from anyone else was music to his ears coming from Linney's lips. He was enchanted by her unique perspective on people, places, and events, and he loved nothing more than to hear her go on and on about anything—from the best flavor of ices at Gunther's to the problems inherent in the Georgian style of architecture to the latest bill being considered by Parliament. She was...authentic—a refreshing respite from the very predictable daughters of the *ton*. Perhaps it was the artist in her that made her speak so freely and fostered such openness and candor in her demeanor, but whatever it was, it made him love her all the more.

Love? Was that truly what he felt for her?

Based on his past experiences, maybe he wasn't the best judge, but this time seemed different. Perhaps it wasn't prudent for him to choose a young woman in her first season for his countess—maybe he *should* marry a lady with a title and deep-blue blood lines. But his relationship with Linney seemed so easy. So natural. So right. *Could* it be love?

Avery shifted again in his saddle. This train of thought was only making matters worse. He was going to do himself an injury if he didn't redirect his wayward reflections.

Determinedly, he rode closer to his man of affairs. "When is Roberts planning to follow with the carriage?"

"One of the horses threw a shoe," said Jeffries, raising his voice so it would carry. "They were headed to the smithy when I left and planned to leave at first light this morning. They shouldn't be too far behind us."

Avery nodded and shifted again, desperately fishing for another topic of conversation. "Did my aunt say anything to you about the duke's accident?"

"Only that she wished him well."

Avery laughed. "Jefferies, old boy, I think we both know that Lady Charlotte has never said as little as that in her entire life. What else did she say?"

Jeffries grinned. "You're right, my lord. She did mention that she would not be too sad if the duke were soon reunited with your sainted mother in heaven."

"And…?"

"And the sooner the better so you could inherit the title. And then she asked whether you had directed me to oversee any marriage contracts between yourself and Miss Braddock and whether I thought your sisters would prefer pink or yellow dresses for your nuptials."

"That sounds more like my aunt. Were you able to divert her so you could take your leave without too much trouble?"

Jeffries chuckled. He was an amiable fellow and enjoyed the variety and adventure that came with his role as the earl's secretary, valet, confidant, and all-round man of affairs. "Fortunately for me—and for you and Miss Braddock—another lady commandeered Lady Charlotte's attention at that very moment, and I was able to make my escape."

"Well, Aunt Charlotte may end up being disappointed. It seems my father has found happiness on earth again—at least according to the missive I received. I decided there was no reason to mention this theoretical marriage to Aunt until I understood the whole of the situation. She does tend toward theatrics."

Jeffries grinned at his employer's understatement and then fell silent, leaving Avery's thoughts to turn once again to the love he'd left behind and their last conversation—interrupted by his little sisters.

Surely Linney knew what he'd been about to say? After all, it was she who asked about his intentions. He smiled, remembering that, even as she campaigned for him to give her some indication of his intentions, she made it clear she would require time to think on the matter when he did. But surely she knew he was down on one knee to ask her to wait for him. Surely...

Damn Whit and his efficiencies! He should have ignored his brother's advice, found Linney, and had a proper farewell, complete with all shades of rose and pink. Linney was young and, in spite of the love she professed for him, she was an innocent. She did not know the ways of the *ton*...or of men. What if some handsome young swain came along with pretty bouquets and flowery words and swept her off her feet while he was away? She was a female, after all, and he knew first-hand that female hearts were susceptible to posies and poetry. What if some fashionable young swell asked her to drive in the park behind his new phaeton? Or offered her his escort to the shops?

And what about at the upcoming dances? Linney had only recently been given permission to waltz from the society matrons—even *he* had not waltzed with her yet. Certainly she might be swayed while in the arms of some handsome rogue who held her too close and murmured inappropriate things in her ear.

The thought of Linney sharing her first waltz with someone other than him made his blood boil.

"Bloody hell!"

"Is there something wrong, my lord?" Jeffries guided his mount closer.

"What? Oh. No, Jeffries. I was just thinking that I really should have taken the time to say my goodbyes to Miss Braddock. Especially since the length of my stay at Terra Bella is uncertain."

"I'm sure his grace explained things to Miss Braddock, my lord."

"Yes, I suppose he did. I just don't like how I seemed to abandon her—especially after we…I mean I don't want her to think… Oh, never mind."

"If it's any consolation, my lord, my oldest niece is one of the upstairs maids at the Braddock house. According to her, one of the family's worst-kept secrets is Miss Braddock's affection for you. Evidently you often figure quite prominently in the young lady's dreams."

Avery scoffed at his secretary's words with a rather sheepish grin on his face. "Do I? Well, that's rather reassuring, I must say. Although ladies sometimes say one thing and mean quite another. Have you noticed that, Jeffries? Not that Miss Braddock would do that, of course. I don't doubt *her* constancy. It's just that I don't trust any of those pompous young men who seem to flock around her, being recently one of them myself. I was never above pressing my advantage with a beautiful young lady if the opportunity presented itself."

"Perhaps you might send a more lengthy message to the young lady this evening, my lord?"

"An excellent idea, Jeffries, assuming we can get to the inn before that storm." Avery nodded toward the gathering of dark clouds on the horizon and urged his mount forward.

With any luck, the worst of the storm would have passed by morning and they'd have an uneventful ride to Terra Bella. And then, with just a bit more luck, he'd have the Easton engagement ring in his hand before dinner.

Chapter 7

"I *thought* I heard someone in here."

William Braddock strode into his study to find his only child sitting behind his desk, her hands folded upon a blank sheet of foolscap and her mind obviously somewhere else.

"What on earth are you doing up at this hour, daughter? Is something amiss? I didn't expect to see either you or your mother until this afternoon."

"Good morning, Papa," said Linney, rising so her father could take her place in his chair. "I couldn't sleep, so I thought I'd do some sketching. I came down here to see if you had any more paper. I seem to have used up all of mine."

She drifted toward the floor-to-ceiling windows leading to the modest garden outside.

"There should be extra in the second drawer there. Do you need much?" Her father nodded toward one side of the desk as he sat and began to rearrange the papers in front of him.

Hearing no response from his daughter he looked up. "Linney?"

"Yes, Papa?"

"I asked how much paper you needed."

"For what?"

"Your sketches. You said you came in here for paper. Are you sure you're awake? How much do you need? It's in this drawer."

"I'm sorry, Papa. I was thinking about something else. Just a piece or two will do." She came around to the side of the desk and leaned over to kiss her father on the top of his head before opening the drawer. "What are you working on?"

"Actually, something that might interest you. The Society is planning to hire several draftsmen and artists to render a variety of drawings of the artifacts and buildings that fall under our protection. They have asked me to draw up contractual agreements for the positions and assist with the hiring. I've been trying to recall the names of some of the fellows you studied with. I'd like to see their portfolios so I might recommend them to the council. Do you know anyone who might be interested?"

Linney stood up and crossed her arms over her chest. "Do *I* know anyone who might be interested in doing technical drawings and renderings of building facades? Perhaps someone whose work you have seen and admired?"

She tapped an index finger upon her cheek as she pretended to ponder the question. "Hmmm, let me think. If only I knew of someone who had studied for years at the feet of one of the greatest artists of our time and who—aside from being quite the competent watercolor artist—had experience creating drawings that had been accepted as legal documents. If only I knew of someone with those credentials…"

Her father didn't look up from his work, but replied, "That would be ideal. Do you know anyone who has all of those qualifications?"

"Are you teasing me, Papa?"

This time her father stopped his work to look up. "Why would I tease you, Linea? I'm quite serious. This is an excellent opportunity for a young artist. Can you think of no one? Didn't you befriend any of the students when you studied with…oh, what was his name? The landscape artist. I quite liked his work, and you seemed pleased with your lessons."

"Signore Strassoldo, and yes, I was pleased with what I learned from him. And yes, there are several students with whom I still correspond. In fact, there is one who would suit your requirements to a T—if only her father would give her a chance."

"Her?"

"Papa!"

"You are speaking of yourself? Please be serious, Linea. The Society of Antiquaries of London is a professional organization, not a school. We have a significant number of important artifacts to catalog and have just acquired a new property bequeathed to our care. We are in dire need of someone to create scale drawings of each item and to provide record drawings, floor plans, elevations, and renderings of the grounds and façade for the various structures on the property."

"I *am* being serious, Papa. You've seen my portfolio. I was the star pupil in Signore Strassoldo's classes, and I have done many such drawings for your cases—renderings of building exteriors as well as technical drawings of specific items."

"That was different. The drawings you did for me were simply tidying up my sketches. And your lessons were…well, they were *lessons*."

"With one of the most talented artists of our time."

"With a friend of your mother's family who was

happy to indulge her by taking you as a pupil. You are a young lady, Linea, and—as much as I love your watercolors, as does anyone who has seen them—you are in the middle of your first season. You have social obligations that keep you busy doing…all manner of things. This is a position that the Society will keep on retainer—perhaps for years."

"That makes it the perfect opportunity for me. I can do it on my schedule."

"Listen to me, Linney. You will undoubtedly be married soon, and then you will be busy setting up your household, having children, taking care of your husband…"

"Do you think doing all of that means I will give up my drawing and painting? Even if I were to marry and have twenty children, I could never stop drawing. It's part of who I am, Papa. You know that. Do you remember what happened when the headmistress at my first boarding school decided my drawings were unladylike because they were too realistic? When she tried to rid me of the bad habit by taking away my pencils?"

"Please don't remind me of that time, Linea. Your mother and I were terrified when you ran away from that place. We thought we might never see you again. I still say a prayer of thanks every night that you were able to find your way home to us."

"Yes, and do you remember how I made enough coin to get back home? It was because of my drawings. I sold the little portrait sketches I did of people. My talent kept me safe and it brought me back to you and Mama—it is a part of who I am. The man I marry will have to understand and appreciate how important my art is to me."

"No man is going to play second fiddle to a hobby, Linea. If you insist on dividing your time between a husband and your drawing, you will end up an unmarried spinster."

Linney considered her father's words. Certainly his was the view generally held by society. What if he was right and she had to decide between a husband and her drawing—between Avery and her drawing? Which would she choose? She and Avery had never talked about her gift in these terms. He knew that she drew, of course, and had often said how talented he thought she was, but did he, like her father, also consider it to be merely a hobby? Did he think of it as something that a proper young lady had in her repertoire of skills, but something to quickly abandon once society called on her to perform her designated domestic role?

"At least let me apply for one of the positions. If I am not selected, then there will be no further problem."

"The awarding of the positions is not up to me, my dear."

"Even better. Just submit my portfolio to the council as you would that of anyone else. I do not expect preferential treatment because you are my father, but might I not expect equal treatment? I will even use mother's maiden name so there is no connection to you. Please, Papa?"

"I don't know, Linney. I don't think it is a good idea, but I will think on it. I will also speak with your mother about it."

Linney moved to stand behind her father and started rubbing his shoulders. "If you allow me to submit my work, I will give you the names of three other artists who would be excellent at the job."

"That sounds a bit like blackmail, daughter."

"I would never try to blackmail you, Papa. You are much too clever for that."

William Braddock rolled his eyes at his daughter's blatant attempts at manipulation and went on the offense. "What of Lord Hammond? You have been spending a great deal of time in his company. What would he say to your working as a draftsman for the Society? I suspect he would not be pleased, and I would not condone your keeping it secret from him."

"I would not keep it a secret. Lord Hammond and I are friends, and as my friend, I believe he would embrace something that made me happy. Certainly I would embrace what made him happy, were the roles reversed."

Linney drifted back to look out the window. "I cannot tell you with any certainty what Lord Hammond would say on the matter, but it is of no consequence because he and I are not officially connected in any way." She played with the cord holding back the patterned drapes.

"I don't want to offend you, Papa, but men are rather strange creatures. In some ways they are very fragile even though they appear to be big and strong. Sometimes I think they mistake stubbornness for strength and character. Lord Hammond has lately confused me with such strength and character, and I'm finding that I don't always interpret his actions accurately."

"You sound rather annoyed with the gentleman, Linea. Did you and he have a falling out?"

Linney sighed. "There was nothing to fall out of.

He had to leave for his family home in Northamptonshire. His father was in an accident of some sort and he was called home."

"Surely you don't begrudge Lord Hammond traveling to be with his ailing father, do you? My daughter would not be so selfish."

"Oh, no, no. It's not that. It's just that he left without saying goodbye."

"Are you saying he did not tell *you* he was leaving or that he told everyone else goodbye *except* you."

"A little of both, it seems. One minute we were having a lovely time strolling in Lady Haversham's garden, and the next minute he was gone. He told others goodbye, but not me."

"Has he given you the impression that you should be expecting something more? Has he trifled with your affections? I will not—"

"He has not, Papa," Linney interrupted quickly. "I give you my word that Lord Hammond has made no promises to me."

"Very well, then. Perhaps you are simply overlooking something. If his father is injured or ill, he was most likely upset and distracted. You cannot fault him for that. You must go about your business and not fret about the man. There seem to be quite a number of other young gentlemen eager to have your attention."

Linney laughed. "You make it sound so simple, Papa."

"Is it not?" Puzzled, William Braddock turned to look up at his daughter.

With a determined smile, Linney turned back to face him. "Of course it is. You're right, Papa. I simply must find something to take my mind off him."

"Excellent! Do let me know if there is anything I can help with, my dear."

"Does that include allowing me to submit my portfolio to the Society? And if the council selects me, allowing me to take the position?"

It was William Braddock's turn to smile. He sat back in his chair and looked at his incorrigible daughter. "Do not think you can sweet talk me, Linea. I have already given you my answer. I will think on it and I will speak with your mother. That is all I can promise for now."

"Yes, Papa."

Stubborn, thought Linney as she retreated out the door to the garden. Just like all the other men she knew.

Chapter 8

The Dog and Pony's reputation for strong ale and clean, commodious rooms was well earned, so the fact that Avery slept very little that night was the fault of neither the inn nor its keeper.

In addition to the abrupt uncertainty he left behind with Linney at Haversham House, Avery was more than a little anxious about what he would find when he arrived at Terra Bella. Considering that he had been summoned so hastily was reason enough to believe his father's condition was dire. For all he knew, his father was already dead. That the summons had been sent from a stranger claiming to be his stepmother was even more cause for concern.

Granted, his father had never seen fit to keep Avery apprised of his domestic activities—not that Avery could blame him when every topic they discussed turned into a fierce argument. In fact, the last time Avery had been home, he and the duke had argued—loudly—about updates to the family wing of the castle. The only thing they had managed to agree upon was that the roof over the guest wing of the main house was leaking and in need of repair, and *that* only because the large bucket in the hallway allowed no room for quibbling.

Avery and his father saw things differently. For Avery, renovations and modernizations to the castle, the farm, and the tenant holdings were much-needed improvements that increased the value of the land. For his father, they were unnecessary expenditures and intrusions into people's lives.

Avery's previous visit had lasted only two days, and ended with him abruptly leaving in a fit of frustration and anger. The two men had not had any further contact until three weeks ago when Avery wrote to his father saying he planned to marry and asking for the Easton family engagement ring. As yet, he had heard nothing back about his request.

Evidently his father had been too busy entertaining guests and courting a new wife.

When Avery's mother died in childbirth some nine years earlier, he was already away at school. His father sent Avery's three younger sisters to live with his sister-in-law in London, and then the duke essentially dropped out of society. Solicitors handled the family's business in London until Avery finished at university. Merton, the butler at Terra Bella, and Mrs. Chapman, the housekeeper, essentially ran the castle and kept Avery apprised of any problematic situations. His father met with his steward only when necessary, and—other than making regular visits to an attractive widow in the village—the duke received only family and seemed more than content with his solitary life. Avery was vaguely aware that visitors had stopped to see the duke this past spring, but everything else seemed to be going along as usual.

If it was true that his father had taken a wife, perhaps it signaled a softening of his father's self-imposed seclusion. Maybe he was ready to live his life again and take an active interest in his responsibilities as the Duke of Easton.

There was, of course, another scenario—the possibility that an unscrupulous woman had taken advantage of his father's grief and somehow parlayed that into marriage. His father would not be the first in the family to fall into such a scheme.

Tired of the same unhappy thoughts circling like vultures in his brain, Avery arose, dressed quickly, and then woke a none-too-happy Jeffries, who ate a bowl of hot porridge and drank a mug of coffee while Avery penned another letter to Linney. In it, he explained what he knew of the situation at Terra Bella and confessed his uneasiness about his father's condition. He gave the sealed missive to the innkeeper, along with enough coin for it to be dispatched with all haste to London, and then he and Jeffries set out for Terra Bella. With such an early start—and assuming they did not run into bad weather or trouble along the way—they would reach the castle before sunset. And then he would know how his father fared and whether, in fact, he had a new stepmother.

Fear touched his heart as Avery thought the unthinkable—by sunset he would also know if he was still simply Lord Hammond or if he was, in fact, the ninth Duke of Easton.

****

"Was that Lord Hammond what just rode out?"

The two men working their way through a hearty breakfast were strangers to the innkeeper, who responded cautiously, but not impolitely.

"What's it to you?"

Lord Hammond and his traveling party always spent the night at the Dog and Pony when traveling to or from London, and the innkeeper had no desire to jeopardize that patronage.

"We're on our way back to London. Been down to Eastland and Castle Terra Bella on an errand for the duke's solicitors. I thought that was his son, the earl, and thought it interesting that he chooses to stop over at your inn. That's an impressive recommendation for any establishment."

The innkeeper actually puffed up a bit. "What can I say? Quality knows quality. The earl's been stopping here on his journeys to London since he first went up to university. The duke and his duchess always stopped here too—before her grace passed on."

"Well, it's a fine advertisement for a fine lodging, and one I'll surely pass on to my fellows."

"Off to London, you said? Going there directly or have you business elsewhere?"

"Straight to London Town and the duke's solicitor." The man patted his coat pocket. "Got a document right here to deliver to the firm. We're on our way after I finish this cup of coffee. Always preferred tea myself, but your coffee could change my mind."

"Might you be interested in an extra errand? I can pay."

"I suppose that depends on what the errand is, now, don't it?"

"Just deliver this letter for the earl. The direction says Sudbury Street, Mayfair. Is that too much out of your way?"

"We go right by there. No trouble at all—and I'd never turn away a little something extra. Buy the wife some trinket or such. She were none too pleased that I had to up and leave this last time." The man shook his head. "That woman can make my life a misery when she's not happy."

"Have another cup of coffee while I fetch it, then, and my thanks to you. We're already short-handed and you've saved me from sending one of the lads."

As the innkeeper walked away, the first man winked at the second. "And that, my friend, is how 'tis done. Monsieur Jones will be pleased."

Chapter 9

Last evening's storm had washed out a few smaller bridges, and the swollen streams necessitated caution in crossing, but Avery and Jeffries still made good time on their trek. Just as the sun was kissing the horizon, they topped the hill that marked the southern boundary of the homelands for the Duke of Easton.

Terra Bella. Beautiful earth. Never was a place so well named. The setting sun cast a golden glow on the valley before them as they pulled up to give the horses a rest. The castle still lay several miles ahead of them— a gray smudge against the evening sky.

"My best friend, Hill Barbour, lived there," said Avery, pointing at an impressive structure built on a rise to their right. "The two of us played over every square mile of this place—the meadows, the streams, the forests. We fought all manner of dragons and pirates and highwaymen and always prevailed."

He grinned as he recalled his childhood adventures of long ago. "Hill had a twin sister, Henrianna, who sometimes managed to tag along. Of course, we gave her the role of fair maiden to be rescued, but quite often we were unsuccessful and the fair maiden was brutally murdered. We did, however, always make sure to avenge her death. For a while, we let Hen be the dastardly villain. Then one day, she lured us into our own traps. She tied me to a tree and suspended Hill upside down by one foot. It was almost an hour before I got free and cut him down. Hen always did tie the best knots."

"She sounds like my youngest sister," said Jeffries. "The brother I never had."

Avery laughed. "That sounds about right. The three of us went everywhere together—fishing, exploring caves, climbing to the top of those big oaks. Most of the time, Hen wore Hill's old clothes, but when she got older and had to wear skirts, we told her she couldn't play with us anymore because she couldn't keep up. She punched us both in the stomach and went to tell her mother. Unfortunately for Hen, her mother agreed with us. She still slipped out to join us every once in a while, but things changed after that."

Avery grew quiet as the past swirled around him. He and Hill had been sent away to St. Stevens together, but they went their separate ways to attend college and university. Whenever they were both home, however, their friendship picked up right where it left off. Hill knew Avery always had his back, and Avery knew he could count on Hill for anything, but especially to be honest and forthright with him, no matter that Avery would someday control the duchy in which they both lived.

After university, Avery and Hill went down to London together and took rooms in the same part of town. Napoleon's army was already slashing its way through Europe and the two friends talked long and hard about joining the fight. As a duke's heir, Avery was, of course, forbidden by his father to join up—a restriction that Avery took as a personal affront to his manhood and one which added considerably to an already heated antagonism between father and son.

That season's balls, soirees, and garden parties had a special intensity—almost as if everyone knew the future would be colored by the conflict on the continent. Hill and Avery set the *ton* on its ear as they laughed, danced, and flirted their way through London society's finest entertainments, setting female hearts aflutter night after night.

One evening, at a masquerade ball given by the slightly risqué Lady de Pole, Avery met the stunningly beautiful Olivia, Lady Payton. Just out of mourning for her unfortunate husband, who—according to the *on dit*—was not as proficient with a pistol as his wife's lover had been, Lady Payton was actively seeking a suitable replacement for her dear, departed spouse. Before his untimely death, Lord Payton had managed to minimize his wife's inheritance and curtail her income, so the very handsome heir to the very wealthy Duke of Easton was at the very top of the lady's list.

On the night they were introduced, Lady Payton teased Lord Hammond into a darkened parlor and allowed him to take far too many liberties. She then invited him to escort her home and accompany her into her boudoir where, for the next three days, she introduced him to new worlds of sexual pleasure. Completely besotted, he spent every possible moment in the lady's company—or, more specifically, in her bed—until his father finally ordered him home for a reckoning.

The argument that ensued was epic—even for Avery and his father. Lady Payton's reputation was well known, so it was no surprise that the Duke of Easton forbade a marriage between the widow and his heir. He threatened to cut Avery off without an allowance if he married Olivia, but Avery, imagining himself in love, defied his father and vowed to elope to Scotland where he and his beloved would live simply, away from the *ton*. He returned to London and immediately called upon Olivia to tell her the news, but, as his father had rightly surmised, the lady was more interested in Avery's wealth and his place in society than in his love—she wanted to be the toast of the *ton* in London, not a nobody in the wilds of Scotland.

Pleading malaise, Lady Payton asked Avery to call the next day so they could discuss their future, but when he returned the following afternoon, he found Olivia in bed with Hill. Olivia acted contrite, but Avery realized he'd been played for a fool. In his anger, he accused his best friend of treachery and demanded satisfaction. Only the intervention of the Duke of Whitley kept Avery from making a terrible mistake. As he learned later, it was Lady Payton who had lured Hill to her bedside—ironically using Avery as bait. Unfortunately, by then, the relationship between the two old friends was beyond repair.

Avery had not spoken to Hill since that incident some five years ago, but being back at Terra Bella always made him wonder how and where his friend was biding.

"Lord Hammond?"

Avery returned from his reveries to see Jeffries nodding toward a horseman in the distance who, seeing Avery, pulled up to wait for them. Avery recognized the doctor from the village and called a greeting. "Doctor Mohr, good day to you. Have you come from the castle? How is my father?"

"Lord Hammond, welcome home. I wish it were under more pleasant circumstances. I have just left your father, and I'm afraid the news is not good. I'm glad you were able to come. Your father's, uh... Lady Tangier did not want to bother you, but I told her the duke's condition was grave and insisted she send for you."

"Thank you for your candor and for your action, sir. Will you tell me what happened?"

"I can tell you my side of the tale, my lord, but I'm afraid you'll have to ferret out the rest for yourself. This Tuesday last, your father's butler sent for me because his grace had been brought home with severe injuries. In his note, Merton said that his grace and Lady Tangier—" The doctor looked at Avery. "Are you acquainted with the lady, my lord?"

Avery shook his head. "Not that I'm aware of. Please, continue."

"As I understand it, your father and Lady Tangier were traveling to Scotland in the lady's coach when they were accosted by highwaymen. They managed to fight off the attack, and his grace ordered the coach to turn back to Terra Bella immediately. In the middle of all the commotion, your father suffered some sort of seizure, and then the coachman, in his haste to turn the carriage around, broke an axle. The carriage overturned, killing the coachman and injuring the duke. The details are unclear—mainly because your father's injuries take him in and out of consciousness and because Lady Tangier's maid says her mistress is too distraught to answer any questions."

"What do the footmen say?"

"They did not return with the others, so I haven't had the opportunity to speak with them as yet. When I arrived at the castle, his grace had obvious trauma to his head and an injury to his chest which had collapsed a lung. I was able to re-inflate the lung, which eased his breathing, but he was still unconscious. That's when I insisted they send for you. Lady Tangier was reluctant to do so and accused me of all manner of things. She eventually acquiesced when I told her that if she did not send for you, I would. I told Merton to let me know if a message did not go out."

"So the duke has not regained consciousness since he returned to Terra Bella?"

"That's certainly what I was led to believe. I was able to bind his ribs, one or more of which are assuredly cracked, but then I was called away to tend to a family in the village. Before I left, I told Lady Tangier and Merton I would return the next day, but to send for me immediately if his grace regained consciousness. I wanted to assess his condition before I gave him something for the pain I knew he would be in."

"And?"

"I was never called. When I returned the next evening, your father was still unconscious, but it was clear he had been dosed with laudanum."

"Why would someone sedate an unconscious man?"

"It's not something a competent doctor would do, my lord."

"You believe the duke regained consciousness and someone gave him laudanum to relieve his pain?"

"Possibly. But, when I asked who had administered the drug, both Lady Tangier and her maid denied any knowledge of it—even though they claim to be in charge of his care. I asked Merton and the rest of the staff if anyone had given his grace laudanum, and they denied even being in the room."

"Why aren't Mrs. Chapman and Olsen caring for my father?"

"Another thing that was unclear to me, my lord. Unfortunately, over the past few days, I have had an unusually high number of calls from the village—there was a fire at the inn—and I have not been able to spend as much time as I might at your father's side. His injuries are severe, but in my estimation, they are not life-threatening. Of course, it would have been better had he been attended in the vicinity of the accident, but Lady Tangier told me his grace was most insistent he be brought back to Terra Bella."

"So he *was* conscious after the accident?"

"So it would seem, my lord."

The doctor paused for a moment. "Lord Hammond, I have visited Terra Bella three times since your father's accident. The first time I made it very clear that no laudanum was to be given without my express permission. However, in each case, when I returned, it was obvious his grace had been drugged. Lady Tangier and her maid deny any part in it, but it seems to me that someone doesn't want the duke to regain consciousness."

The doctor leaned back in his saddle. "Unfortunately, without talking to his grace it's difficult to ascertain his condition or understand what happened in the first place. This morning when I called in on your father, I asked Lady Tangier if she had sent for you. She said it was none of my business and told me not to return. I am heartily glad you are here, Lord Hammond. I believe your father may be in grave danger from that woman—even though I have no way to prove it."

He'd heard enough. Nodding at Jeffries, Avery said, "Thank you, Dr. Mohr. I believe the best course at this time is for me to hie myself to Terra Bella and see my father. Please call at the castle tomorrow, if you would be so kind. "

"I will call at one of the clock, Lord Hammond. If you have need of me before then, please send word. God speed, my lord."

Avery glanced at the darkening sky as he guided his horse back to the road. It would be after dark when he and Jeffries finally arrived at Terra Bella. He heartily hoped it would not be too late.

Chapter 10

"Did the doctor ask about the laudanum again, my lady?"

"No," said Lady Tangier. She paced back and forth on the soft blue-and-cream Aubusson rug in front of the fireplace. "But he did ask if I had sent word to Lord Hammond about his father. The man had the audacity to say if I had not heard from Lord Hammond by tomorrow, he would write him personally."

"Do you think he knows what happened? Will he tell Lord Hammond?"

"How should I know?" snapped Lady Tangier. "He didn't have the courtesy to discuss his thoughts with me. He simply *informed* me of his intentions. So I *informed* him that he need not come around again to see his grace because I would be sending for my own physician."

"And did you? Send for your physician?"

Lady Tangier looked disdainfully at her maid. "Of course not, you fool. Why would I want another doctor loitering about? Now cease interrogating me—I'll remind you who is the mistress here and who is the servant. And come away from that window. You act as if the King's own army will be riding up at any moment. What can you see anyway?"

"There's still a bit of daylight left, my lady. Even

when it's dark, I can see a rider coming past the lighted gatehouse. Don't you want to know when Lord Hammond arrives?"

"*If* he arrives. Lord Hammond and his father were not on good terms when they last parted. With any luck, when my message finds him, the arrogant upstart will decide to take his own good time to get here. Or better yet, decide not to come at all."

"But if the doctor sends for Lord Hammond and tells him he believes you are dosing the duke with laudanum—"

"To be clear, Agnes, it is you who administered the laudanum, not I."

"Yes, my lady, but you told me to do it. I'm only the one who— Oh, good evening, Lady Genevieve."

"Eve, darling. You look troubled, my dear. Whatever is the matter? That will be all, Agnes."

Eve waited until Agnes had closed the door behind her. "The duke still has not regained consciousness, Mama. He does not respond to anything I say. I am so worried. Do you think we should send for Lord Hammond?"

"I have already done that, my pet. I have been so frightfully worried about my darling Edward that I forgot to mention it to you. The doctor said there was no need to worry, but I sent word anyway."

Lady Tangier put her arm around her daughter's shoulders and walked with her to the sofa, where they sat. "But, my dear, you must remember, they did not get on well. Lord Hammond may decide he does not wish to see his father."

"That would break the duke's heart, I think. He misses his son very much." Eve looked around her.

"These new rooms are much more spacious than your old ones, are they not?"

"It's not about more space or better furnishings, dear. I thought it best to be as close to the duke as possible in case he has need of me."

"I talked with Olsen. He said the doctor thinks someone gave the duke laudanum."

"The duke's valet should not be discussing his grace's condition with you, and obviously Edward's injuries are beyond the expertise of that local quack—which explains why the duke is doing so poorly."

She lowered her voice to a determined whisper. "If Lord Hammond doesn't come soon, I shall have to take over the running of the duke's household. I'm afraid everyone is taking advantage of the poor dear while he is ill. His valet is a gossip and the doctor can't even identify what ails the duke, much less cure him. Why on earth would anyone give laudanum to an unconscious man? Can it even be done? I am so terrified that Edward might not recover." The countess wiped at a supposed tear with a handkerchief embroidered with the Easton crest.

Eve patted her mother's arm. "Don't worry, Mama. I'm sure Lord Hammond will be here soon, and he will take care of everything. The duke told me he thought they were finally going to get back on good terms with each other now that Lord Hammond was to be married. He said Lord Hammond has the look of his late wife, which haunted him when his wife first died, but now is a great comfort. He misses his duchess so."

Lady Tangier abruptly pulled back from Eve and stood up. "I don't see how a man can look like a woman. That doesn't speak especially well for either of them."

She walked over to her dressing table and sat down, watching Eve in the looking glass. "Anyway, the duke has asked me not to speak of his late wife, and he asked me to tell you the same thing. I think he doesn't like to be reminded of her, which, if what you say is true about their resemblance, might be another reason why he doesn't invite his son here very often."

"Do you think so?" said Eve, frowning and moving to stand behind her mother. "The duke told me wonderful stories about when the duchess was alive—his face fairly glowed, remembering. He talked about the house parties and balls and how they had such plans to introduce their little daughters into society when the time came... Did he ever tell you how he asked his duchess to marry him? Evidently there is a magnificent family engagement ring that gets passed down to each heir to give to his bride. The duke hid the ring in a box inside a box inside another box. He said there were seven boxes in all—one for each month of their courtship. Isn't that romantic? I think—"

"Eve, dear, you really mustn't go on and on. No one wants to be around a young lady who chatters so. Was there something you wanted?"

"Just to ask you about Lord Hammond and tell you I am worried about the duke."

"It's not good for you to be shut up in that sick room all day, dear."

"I don't mind, Mother, truly I don't. Since you won't allow anyone else to sit with him, and you have so much to do, he is alone much of the time. For a little while this afternoon I thought he might be about to say something to me. I think it comforts him to have me there, but I wish there were something more I could do to help."

"Just the same, it is not proper for you to be in the duke's rooms alone. From now on, Agnes or I must be with you when you sit with him."

"I know you're both busy. I'll get a maid or a footman to sit with me."

"Very well, but if he seems to be waking up, you must send for me immediately." Lady Tangier unfurled her handkerchief again—this time accompanied by a despondent sniff. "After all, he *is* my betrothed and, for all intents and purposes, we *are* married."

"What?" Eve could not contain her surprise. "The duke asked you to marry him? When did he do that?"

"Really, Eve, I'm sure I told you about the duke's proposal. That's why we went to Scotland—to be married. You must pay more attention, dear. I don't like repeating myself over and over."

"That is so odd."

"Why is it odd?" snapped Lady Tangier, turning to face her daughter. "Do you think I am not attractive enough to merit the attention of a man like the duke?"

"Of course not, Mama. You are very beautiful. Everyone says so. It's just that the duke told me once he would never remarry because he misses his duchess so much. He said it wouldn't be fair to take another wife when he is still so in love with her. I wonder what changed his mind?"

"Eve, darling, you are so naïve." Lady Tangier smiled a sly smile and turned back to her looking glass. "There are many things a woman can do to change the mind of a man—especially a man as virile as the duke. He was interested in…in becoming more intimate, shall we say, and, of course, I told him that, as a lady, I could not entertain his desires outside the bonds of marriage."

"I see. Did all of this happen recently? Because just the week before last—"

"It's difficult to pin down a specific day," said Lady Tangier. "We tried to hide our love, but last week he finally declared himself and begged me to elope with him to Scotland. He made me vow to keep everything secret. I think he wanted to avoid all the fuss and bother of a big wedding—especially because that meddling old bishop would insist on officiating."

"But the duke and the bishop are friends," protested Eve. "They play chess every Sunday after services. Whyever would the duke want to avoid his friend?"

"Men are strange creatures, darling. Who knows what thoughts they harbor and why? I told you the duke wanted to keep our engagement a secret. That's why he asked me to wait before I wore this."

The countess reached into a carved wooden box on her dresser and retrieved a smaller, brightly colored enameled box. Opening it carefully, she showed Eve the contents, a beautiful ring made of rose gold with a pink, multi-faceted center stone surrounded by sparkling diamonds.

Eve gasped. "That's the Easton engagement ring, isn't it?"

"Yes. Isn't it lovely?" Her mother put the ring on the third finger of her left hand and held it out for Eve to admire.

"And the duke gave it to *you*?"

Lady Tangier gave her daughter a black look before taking off the ring and placing it back in the small box. She closed the lid with a sharp snap. "It is an engagement ring, is it not? And as I have just explained to you, Edward and I are engaged. Why wouldn't he give me the Easton engagement ring?"

"I thought...well, the duke told me the ring is given to the duke's *heir* to give to his bride. Why would he give it to you when—"

Lady Tangier stood up and walked away. "No more questions, Eve. You have given me a megrim. I'm sure it is not my place or yours to question the duke's decisions. Please call Agnes to bring me a cold compress for my head. I must lie down."

"But, Mama—"

The countess held up her hand. "Not another word. Once the duke is well again, he will announce our marriage and all the details will be made known. Until then, you should hold your tongue. It's beginning to sound as if you think the duke isn't responsible for his own actions. I don't know why you would say such an unkind thing. Here I am, quite fatigued with worry about my darling Edward, and all you can do is pose question after question. I will not listen to any more talk against the duke."

"Mother, I wasn't..."

"Please leave now, Eve." With a sideways glance at her daughter and a dismissing wave, Lady Tangier sat gingerly and reclined on the chaise. "Oh, Agnes, there you are. Where is my compress?"

Agnes went the basin to wring out a cloth and returned to lay it on her mistress's brow. As soon as the door closed behind Eve, the countess flung the cloth aside and sat upright on the chaise.

"Get that off me," she snapped. "How dare she

question me like that? I should never have let her spend so much time with the duke. I thought it might help if they became close, but it has only served to make her annoyingly curious." Lady Tangier rose and began pacing again.

Picking up the discarded cloth, Agnes observed, "She does get on well with the duke. I've often heard them laughing and talking after dinner. He is very fond of her."

Stopping for a moment to glare at Agnes, Lady Tangier said, "Damn that doctor for insisting I send for Lord Hammond. Once he arrives, all will be lost. If the duke regains consciousness, he will tell everyone the truth about his attack and about what really happened on the road."

"Monsieur Jones can't be pleased with the news that the duke survived. Have you heard anything?"

"I haven't told him yet."

"Oh, my lady, you must tell him at once. You do not want to make him angry, and once Lord Hammond is here, it will be difficult to send out—"

"Hush, Agnes. Monsieur Jones is the least of my worries right now. All he wants is for Lord Hammond to become the Duke of Easton as soon as possible. Why should he care if along the way I become the dowager duchess with a bequest and a place in society? Lord Hammond will still be the Duke of Easton."

"If the duke regains consciousness, he will tell everyone you were never betrothed."

The duchess gave her maid a withering look. "You grow as tiresome as my daughter. We must simply make sure he never wakes up." She took a deep breath and exhaled, patting a stray lock back into her coiffure.

"He's a stubborn old coot, I'll grant you that. I thought for certain he would be gone by now."

"Lord Hammond will surely demand proof of a marriage when he arrives. Won't he ask to see the lines or to speak to someone who witnessed your vows? The footmen with the carriage know you were never married. I don't think Lady Eve is convinced, either."

"Don't be so impertinent, Agnes. It could be days before Lord Hammond arrives. By then the duke will be gone, and no one will question the late duke's actions or think to talk to footmen who are no longer employed at Terra Bella. We have plenty of time yet."

Back at the window, Agnes clicked her tongue. "Perhaps not as much time as you think, my lady. I believe Lord Hammond has just arrived."

Chapter 11

It was late. Avery pushed the glass of amber liquid away from the edge of his father's desk—*his* desk now. His desk, his responsibilities, his duty. His title and everything that entailed.

He and Jeffries had arrived just after darkness fell. Hurrying up to his father's rooms, Avery knelt by the massive bed and grasped his father's hand on top of the coverlet, saying his name. He was certain he'd felt an answering squeeze, weak though it was. He was also certain he'd heard his father whisper "son" and mumble something about Avery's mother. There was another slight movement from the big hand holding his so weakly, and then his father was gone.

He had stayed away too long.

From the looks of things, his father's life had changed dramatically and he knew practically nothing about any of it—nothing about the visitors who arrived months ago and now claimed to be related. Nothing about the repairs and the other work being done in the castle and on the farms. Nothing about the changes in the village. All were suggestions made by Avery and dismissed by his father—only he didn't really dismiss them. He'd listened and he'd started the work without saying a word to Avery. No doubt because every time they talked, they argued.

This trip was to have been the one where Avery

called his father's bluff—the one where they set up a new relationship. During his last visit, Avery had gotten the impression his father actually enjoyed their heated debates—even seeming to bait his son if the conversation became too dull.

Avery was eager to tell his father all about Linney. He wanted to convince the duke to leave Terra Bella and attend their wedding. He wanted to hear his father tell the story of how the Easton engagement ring was made by the first duke for his bride from of a piece of rose quartz found at the heart of Easton lands. And how, when the first duchess had died giving birth to an heir, the duke had added two diamonds to the setting and then kept the ring safe for his son to give to his own bride. He wanted his father to put that family history in his hand and he wanted his father's blessing to marry Linney.

But he had stayed away too long, and now it was too late. Thank God he'd arrived in time to say goodbye.

Olsen, his father's valet, seldom spoke to anyone except the duke, but as they walked together into his father's dressing room, the older man cleared his throat and said, "Aye, he waited for you, your grace, and that's the truth."

The man's Scottish burr was even more evident in his grief. "He was a right stubborn man, your father, but he loved his three girls and he loved his son—even when the two of you argued like fishwives. Don't mourn him too long, lad. He's with your blessed mother now, and that's where he's wanted to be for years."

Avery nodded. Tears choked his words. He patted the older man on the shoulder and left him to lay out the clothes in which the eighth Duke of Easton would be buried.

And then he'd come here. Down to the first floor where the door to his father's study stood open as if trying to coax him in.

It was a room full of ghosts, but it was the right place for him to be tonight. He poured a shot of the single-malt scotch whiskey his father had taught him to favor and drank it straight down. He poured another but set it down, untouched, and then sat down at the desk under which he played as a child and in front of which he was so often reprimanded as a young man. He remembered the last time he'd seen his father sitting where he sat now. As usual, they were arguing. This time about modernizations Avery wanted to make—a constant source of friction between them.

Avery repositioned the glass tumbler on the desk and sat back in the chair.

And then there was the ghost of his mother, who always sat with a book or her embroidery while keeping her husband company. Avery could almost smell the nutmeg fragrance of gardenias she favored—an olfactory reminder of happier times, when the Furies were babies and he and Hill would burst into the castle with the unbridled enthusiasm of youth on holiday.

As a testament to their love—or to his father's lack of control—his parents had produced the three girls in the space of three years. Avery had been delighted to have siblings, although they were significantly younger than he, and, as he pointed out numerous times to his mother, they were *girls*. His mother loved playing with her trio of femininity, but was never too busy to make time for him. Avery's smile faded. Another child had proved too much. Both mother and baby died in childbirth and, to put it simply, his father never recovered.

Looking now at his mother's favorite chair—the one she instructed be brought in from her parlor in spite of much grumbling from her husband—Avery wasn't sure he had either.

He downed the contents of the glass and reached for the decanter again. Olsen was right. At least now they were together again.

"Your grace?"

Avery came to his feet automatically as a young lady with red, swollen eyes approached the desk and curtsied.

"Your grace, I just wanted to say how sorry I am for your loss. Your father and I spent quite a bit of time together over the last few weeks, and I…well, I know this sounds odd, but in a small way, I came to think of him as my father too. I will miss him greatly."

Avery nodded mutely. With another curtsy, the young woman turned to leave. She was almost to the door before he found his words. "I'm sorry. And you are…?"

The girl turned back quickly. "Oh, I do beg your pardon, your grace. I am Lady Genevieve. My mother is Lady Tangier."

"And Lady Tangier is…?"

"The Countess Tangier. We are…were…visiting your father and have been for several weeks. My mother said your father insisted we stay. Personally, I thought it would be a great inconvenience to the staff, but no one seemed to mind. I will say now that I'm glad we stayed. Our extended visit allowed me to get to know the duke. He was such a dear man."

"*My* father? The Duke of Easton? Dear?"

Lady Genevieve giggled. "Well, not all the time. He could be quite gruff as well. We often broke our fast together. He was an early riser—as am I. My mother keeps town hours and is usually in bed until noon, so most days I had your father all to myself. He showed me all around the castle and the grounds and told me about the improvements he was having done here and in the village. He said most of them were your ideas— he was very proud of you. He confessed to having given you a rather difficult time about some of them. He said he tried to argue every point with you to help you think things through. He seemed to take great pleasure in that, although I did scold him for not telling you." Almost as an afterthought, she said, " He loved you and your sisters very much."

"Have we met before, Lady Genevieve? You seem familiar to me."

"We have met, so I'm told, but I doubt you would remember—I didn't at first. It was quite some time ago. I was three years old, and you must have been eight or nine. My mother and father and I were going down to London, and there was a huge snowstorm. Our carriage got stuck on the roads, and your parents welcomed us into their home here at Terra Bella for several days. I remember I called you 'Av-wee'—I had trouble with my Rs until I was about six. I followed you and your friends all around the castle. They were twins, weren't they? The boy was Hill. I remember because I adored his name and thought him to be the most fascinating person I'd ever met—at the age of three, mind you. I don't remember his sister's name, though."

"Henriannta."

"Yes, that's right, but the two of you called her something else."

"Hen."

"Yes, that's it. You were the perfect host—always telling the others to wait for me—but your friend Hill was rather impatient. He told his sister to take me up to the nursery and play dolls with me, but you said I could stay."

"I remember now...everyone called you Eve, and you had curly red hair—still do, I see. I'd never seen anyone with red hair before, and I was fascinated. Hill was too. He talked about you long after you left and kept saying how pretty Eve was. I teased him mercilessly about it and got myself a black eye for my trouble."

"Oh, dear—I'm sorry. Do you still see your friends often?"

"No. Unfortunately, we no longer correspond." Avery's answer was curt, and a heavy curtain fell on any further reminiscing.

After just a moment of silence, Eve said, "Well anyway, my mother said she corresponded with your mother after that and continued writing to your father after the duchess died. When we started this trip to London, Mother said she planned to stop and see the duke on our way. I didn't realize we'd be staying quite this long, but I'm glad we did. It gave me a chance to get to know your father."

Eve's smile faded as she remembered her original reason for coming into the room. "I just wanted to tell you how sorry I am. I thought it might be of some comfort for you tonight to know your father loved you very much and thought of you often. Good night, your grace." Eve curtsied again and left as quietly as she had come.

Avery sighed and sat back down in his father's chair. Eve's way of talking reminded him a little of Linney and had the same warming effect. If only Linney were here with him now.

Putting his elbows on the desk, he rested his head in his hands. For a few moments he sat there, breathing slowly and—just for a while—letting go of all his sadness and responsibilities...and regrets. He breathed in, trying to smell the rose fragrance that Linney always wore and missing her with all his heart. In that moment, he understood his father's grief at the loss of his wife and his inability to really live without her. And he understood how lucky he was to still have his love.

Opening the top drawer of his father's desk—the duke's desk...*his* desk, Avery found ink and a dull quill. He scribbled a short note:

I love you. I miss you.
Easton

Finding a stick of black sealing wax in the very back of a drawer, he dripped hot wax to seal the letter, and then pressed the Easton crest into the molten black blob. The wax cooled and a familiar dragon peered up at him—black instead of its usual fiery red, for it too was in mourning.

So there it was. His first act as the Duke of Easton was writing to his beloved. The thought made him smile. His father would have approved. He kissed the seal and wrote Linney's direction on the front. Then he raised his glass in a silent toast to his mother and father, together now and for always, and quaffed the fiery contents.

Taking a deep breath, Avery stood and walked out into the hallway, closing the door to his father's study behind him. He placed his missive to Linney on the silver tray to go out with the morning post and watched for a moment as the maids covered mirrors and hung black crepe.

It was a house of mourning now, and he was the duke.

****

Agnes slipped out of the shadows and paused at the table holding letters for the post. The earl—no, the duke—had gone upstairs to his rooms, and the other servants were back downstairs. Glancing around, she quickly slipped the letter with the black ducal seal into her pocket and hurried to the servants' staircase. At the top of the stairs, she turned right and proceeded to the most well-appointed suite at Terra Bella—the Duchess of Easton's rooms—and scratched at the door.

"Come in."

Inside the room, Agnes curtsied to the countess.

"Yes, Agnes? What is it?"

"Just as you said, my lady. It's directed to a Miss Braddock in London."

"Give it to me."

Agnes handed over the folded note sealed with the Easton coat of arms embossed in black wax.

Lady Tangier broke the seal and quickly scanned the contents. "Oh, how sweet. We must see what we can do to help the new duke with his loneliness."

She put the letter in the carved wooden box on her

table. "That will be all, Agnes."

****

The folded piece of paper the messenger handed to the Frenchman bore Lord Hammond's crest. "Lord Hammond and his man should arrive at Terra Bella this evening. Here's the note his lordship wrote last night to 'is bit o' fluff."

"I've always heard Lord Hammond was a dedicated correspondent," observed Jones, scanning the contents of the new page before tossing it to the table to join another message with the same seal. "He sent another one by post just last evening."

"Sounds like a lovesick calf to me."

"Don't be fooled by his soft words," snapped Jones, his eyes flashing with anger. "Lord Hammond is one of the most dangerous men in England. That 'lovesick calf' was the man who engineered the emperor's downfall. It was he, with a few others, who paved the way for Wellington to prevail at the battle of Waterloo."

The Frenchman took a breath and continued in a more measured tone. The smile on his lips belied the hatred in his eyes. "It occurs to me that the best way to punish such men is to take away the ones they hold most dear. And for Lord Hammond, that now seems to include Miss Braddock. We must make sure he understands that she is in danger only because of her association with him, although the happy fact that Hammond's lady love is cousin to the codemaker will make my revenge even sweeter."

"Have you had word on the duke's condition?" asked the messenger.

"Nothing yet, but the fact that Lord Hammond is so

quickly on his way to Terra Bella tells me the plan is proceeding."

"You trust Lady Tangier has everything well in hand, then?"

"I trust no one, but she and I do have…a history between us. And in this particular instance, we have the same goal, so I do trust she will put all her skills toward that end. She is best when working to her own advantage."

"Shall I deliver this to London now you've seen it?"

"I think not. I will keep it—perhaps we will have use for it later. But for now, let us see if absence does in truth make the heart grow fonder. Proceed to London and make certain no correspondence between Lord Hammond and Miss Braddock is delivered."

"That's a right easy job, I'd say. The lady won't write without first hearing from him, so all's I need do is watch the incoming post."

"And special messengers. And visitors. And don't be so certain about Miss Braddock's observing society's rules. She's no shrinking violet. I've seen her flaunt the norms on more than one occasion, so keep a close eye on everyone."

Chapter 12

Linney played the first few bars of Beethoven's *Moonlight Sonata* and then stood abruptly. She was a competent pianist and—as a rule—enjoyed playing, but this afternoon even the prospect of learning a new piece by Mr. Beethoven did not spark her interest.

"I'm going to go mad if I don't figure out something to do," she muttered to herself.

She was too distracted to draw or paint or even play the piano right now. Perhaps another pastime—something that didn't require complete mental participation. Embroidery? Her mind flew to the multiple unfinished handkerchiefs that sat at the bottom of her sewing basket. No. Reading? No, that also required an engaged mind. She could go riding, but she knew from experience she was prone to periods of distraction that left her lost and far from home, so that wasn't a good choice.

She wandered into the family parlor where her mother was busy with correspondence.

"There you are, darling. Lady Priester is hosting a musicale on Thursday evening. Would you like to attend?"

"I don't think so, Mother. I don't seem to have any interest in music right now."

"Very well, I'll send our regrets. Here, then. Lady Shandy is inviting us to a dinner in honor of her youngest sister. You know the sister, don't you? She is just out this season as well. I think we were introduced at the Richardson's ball."

"Yes, I remember. Her name is Prudence...or maybe Patience—some virtue. You and Papa should go without me. I'm not really in the mood for socializing."

Lady Braddock looked up from her note. "I haven't seen Maribel here of late. Why don't you call on her? Weren't she and her mother at Vivian's wedding?"

"Maribel hates me, and frankly, I don't care for her anymore either. I don't have any friends now that Vivian is gone."

"That's a bit dramatic, don't you think, dear?"

"No, it's the truth."

Lady Thea narrowed her eyes as she watched her only child pluck at the curtains and peer out the window. She put down her quill pen and turned in her chair to give Linney her full attention.

"Linea, all the moping about in the world will not make a message from Lord Hammond come any sooner. You need to take your mind off him, my dear, and getting out and being with other people will help you do that."

"I don't *want* to take my mind off him. I'm worried. I haven't heard anything from him since he left."

Linea's stubborn tone sounded all too familiar to Lady Thea's ear. It was true the apple didn't fall far from the tree. She tried a different tack. "Darling, we cannot even imagine all the things demanding his time now with his father unwell. It must be utterly overwhelming."

"So overwhelmed he hasn't time to send me a

single word?"

"Be kind, Linney. It must be very difficult for him, don't you think?"

"I suppose so."

Lady Thea sighed. "My dear, I would be remiss if I did not point out that you and Lord Hammond are not betrothed, nor do you have any special understanding, as far as I'm aware. You have enjoyed a lovely few months of having a handsome gentleman—an earl and ducal heir—pay you his attentions. But, Linney, you are very young, and this is your first season out in society. You must remember that Lord Hammond's choice of a bride must be, at least in part, determined by his place in society and his duty to his family."

"Would not his choice also be determined by his feelings toward the lady he wished to marry?"

"Of course, and there is no doubt that Lord Hammond has shown affection for you. All I'm saying is you shouldn't count on that affection being anything more than that. We do not live in a fairy tale where the handsome prince rides up on a white horse to marry the beautiful princess and live happily ever after. Here in the real world, love is more often than not tempered by circumstances that have nothing to do with any feelings the parties may have for one another."

"He told me he loved me, Mama. More than once."

Lady Thea sighed again as she crossed the room to put a comforting hand on her daughter's shoulder. She needed to choose her words carefully.

"Linney, I'm sure the earl is an honorable man, but you must understand that men will often say things simply because they think it's what a young lady wants to hear. Scoundrels will say things because they want to steal a kiss or…well, never mind. I don't think that's necessarily the case with Lord Hammond, but he does have a bit of a past and a reputation as a rake. My point is you must not wear your heart on your sleeve. Things may be changing for him—things over which he has no control. Things that have nothing to do with you."

"But—"

Lady Thea held up her hand to stop Linney's protest. "Before you say anything, Linea, let me be clear. This has nothing to do with how pretty you are or how much Lord Hammond enjoys your company. For someone as high in society as he is, marriage is a business transaction, not a personal decision. He has not spoken to your father or declared his intentions, and I don't think you should count on him doing so. Am I wrong? Has he asked you to wait for him?"

"No, Mother…you are not wrong. But he didn't have the chance. He was—we were—interrupted. But I know what he was going to say."

"Darling, I know you want to believe that, and I do believe he cares for you in his own way and has even said he loves you, but it may not mean the same to him as it does to you. You cannot put your life on hold and wait for him to return when he has not asked you to do so. If—God forbid—his father dies, he may not be back in London until next spring. You must go about your activities and carry on with your life. You have many suitors who would like nothing more than to escort you to the park or the shops. I don't want to see you hurt should Lord Hammond decide that now is not the time for him to have a wife. Or, if he decides to pay his suit to another."

Linney's eyes were full as she looked up at her

mother. "I think it's too late for me not to be hurt if that happens," she whispered. A tear rolled down her cheek.

"Oh, sweetheart..." Lady Thea gathered her daughter into her arms and pulled her to sit with her on the loveseat, murmuring comforting words just as she had done when Linney was a small child.

"Oh, Mama, I miss him so much, and I'm so worried."

"I know, darling. I know. I know." She stroked Linney's hair until her daughter's sobs were no more than stutter breaths.

"I know it hurts, dearest, but the best thing you can do right now is keep yourself occupied. I know it's not what you want to do, but sometimes you have to do things you don't want to do. It's part of growing up, and I think it's time you grew up a bit. What about the drawings you were doing for your father? Have you finished them?"

"No," said Linney into her mother's shoulder, then she sat back, brushing at her tears with the back of her hand. "Did Papa say anything to you about finding a draftsman for the Society?"

"No, why should he?"

"Never mind. I'll let him explain it to you."

"What about the painting you were planning for Vivian? Have you started on that?"

"No. But the baby isn't due until spring."

Lady Thea looked Linney in the eye and smiled. "I think we both know that baby will be early."

Linney smiled.

"There. That's the beautiful smile I want to see."

"I'm sorry, Mama. It's just that I have... Oh, never mind. It sounds so silly."

"What sounds silly?"

"This feeling I have about Avery...Lord Hammond. I know it sounds odd—especially because there is no *official* connection between us—but I have this overwhelming feeling he needs me."

"What do you mean 'overwhelming feeling'?"

"It's rather difficult to describe and it doesn't really make sense. It's not coming from my head...it's like a worried feeling that's in the air, and then when I take a breath it's all inside of me, here." Linney touched the lace over her heart. "It's such an odd feeling, and I can't get rid of it. Have you ever had a feeling like that, Mama? Was there ever a time when you felt Papa needed you and you couldn't get to him?"

Lady Thea gave Linney a hug, and then, in a complete imitation of her daughter, rose and looked out the window.

"You may find it hard to believe," she said, "but I *have* had a feeling exactly like that. It was when your father and I were first married and I was expecting you. He had gone to see the brother of one of his clients and was due back that evening. Your Aunt Catherine and Uncle Stephen had brought little Vivian up for a visit, but right after luncheon, I had the most awful feeling that your father needed me. I knew something was wrong. Of course, everyone kept saying it was due to my delicate condition—everyone except Catherine. She could tell how upset I was, so she sent Stephen to find your father. As it turns out, the client's brother had decided to use my Will to send a message. He hired his friends to attack your father and steal his horse. They left him by the side of the road. Who knows what would have happened if Stephen had not found him when he did? So, to answer your questions, my love, yes, I have had such a feeling."

Lady Thea turned to look at Linney. "But, my dear, this is very different. You are not married or betrothed to Lord Hammond. It would be most improper for you to send him a letter without first receiving one from him."

Linney's downfallen countenance broke her mother's heart. Lady Thea said a quick prayer that this man whom her daughter loved so much would be worthy of such devotion.

"However…such a feeling should not be ignored."

She picked up her pen and held it out to Linney. "Do you need paper? If we hurry, Thomson can put it in the post this evening."

Chapter 13

A good night's rest can work miracles for the body, mind, and soul, but Avery knew that a large part of his peace of mind was because he was back at Terra Bella.

It was a little odd to feel so invigorated and so appreciative of the beautiful day when he was supposed to be in the throes of mourning his father. Maybe it was the comforting words of the bishop yesterday at Sunday services or Lady Genevieve's revelations on the night of his father's death. Perhaps it was the relief he felt in having had the opportunity, however briefly, to say goodbye to his father, or Olsen's certainty that his father was now happily reunited with the duchess he loved more than life itself. Tomorrow's funeral would be the duke's last duty on this terrestrial ball.

Avery almost envied him. Right now, his own love seemed very far away, and he missed her terribly.

In some ways Avery felt he understood his father now more than he ever had before, and he appreciated the duke's desire to pave the way for his offspring. It was not by chance that his father had sent the Furies to stay with Aunt Charlotte. It was the best possible place for them to be at this point in their lives and it provided them with something his father had been unable to provide at Terra Bella. In the same way, the duke had made sure that Avery understood the importance of history and tradition and deliberateness when he questioned Avery's every idea to renovate and change the age-old landscape of Terra Bella.

When Avery rode out two hours ago, the sun was not yet peeping over the hills, but now he paused to take in the vivid panorama before him—the bright green pastures dotted with sheep, the darker green of the forests that bordered Terra Bella lands on two sides, the golden fields of wheat outlined by hedgerows, and the great stone edifice that was Castle Terra Bella, all arranged against a rich blue sky streaked with the mare's tails that predicted fair weather for at least another day. Avery wanted Linney to paint this vista for him. He knew she would be able to capture the magic and majesty and perfectly reflect the light so everyone could see what he saw on this gorgeous morning. He couldn't wait to bring her here.

Avery urged his horse down the road that led to the small village of Eastland. He'd decided to go home this way to see what repairs his father had begun. Eve's disclosure the other night, that the duke had indeed been following some of his son's suggestions to modernize the castle and the tenant holdings, had surprised him but had warmed his heart. He was thankful to her for giving him that window into his father's actions.

Slowing the mare to a walk, he rode down the main street of the village, nodding to familiar faces. The signs of official mourning were apparent throughout the village. Black flags flew from the two public buildings and white calla lily wreaths adorned many doors. At present, the duke's draped coffin lay in state in the nave of the ancient church for those wishing to pay their private respects. Tomorrow all shops would be closed and the church bell would toll as townsfolk and tenants donned mourning attire and gathered along the processional route to bid a final farewell to their longtime patron and protector. Mourners would follow the long, slow cortege to transport the eighth Duke of Easton on the four-mile journey from the church to the family mausoleum on the hill behind Terra Bella, there to be laid to rest beside his duchess.

On the other side of the village, Avery recognized the figure walking before him on the road to the castle. "Lady Genevieve, good morning! I see you are true to your word about being an early riser."

"Good morning, your grace." Eve offered a brief curtsy with her smile. "It's a beautiful morning, is it not? I went for a walk just after sunup and detoured through town to purchase some black crepe. I brought no mourning clothes with me, and the seamstress that mother hired has been working her fingers to the bone just to get one gown finished before tomorrow. I hope you won't see it as a sign of disrespect that I am not in full mourning."

"Not at all, my lady. I appreciate all efforts on your part as I'm certain my father would. Are you bound for Terra Bella? Might I offer you a ride? This mare is sturdy enough to take the both of us the last few miles."

"My thanks, your grace, but I think I'll continue my walk. I've been slow to get over a fall I took from an ill-tempered mount when I was at school, so I'm still a bit hesitant to ride. I wasn't badly hurt—frightened mostly—but it did put me off riding."

"I assume you know what they say about getting back up on the horse?"

Eve laughed. "Yes, I do. And I do intend to do it,

but the time is never quite right. I think I've convinced myself that the horses know I don't quite trust them, so they don't trust me."

"Well, you know you are more than welcome to any mount in the Terra Bella stables any time you want," said Avery.

"Thank you for that. Your father offered several times. I used to love riding, and I'm sure I will again, but I must admit, at least at present, I am quite enjoying the morning and the time alone with my thoughts."

"Then I will leave you to them. I envy you your time to think. I'm afraid my day is not my own and will be filled to the brim with every manner of thing. In fact, on my return, I'm sure to be scolded by Jeffries for being late, though I started out early enough."

Eve laughed again. She had a lovely laugh. "Surely you can best him if you try—after all, you *are* the duke."

Her remark brought Avery back to the reality of the moment, and his eyes reflected his sudden pain. Eve looked horrified.

"Your grace, I'm so sorry. I didn't mean to…to be flippant about your loss. I was only attempting to make you smile. I didn't think. Please forgive me."

"There's nothing to forgive," said Avery. "You were not being malicious. And to be honest, I appreciate your attempts at levity. Good day, Lady Genevieve." He touched his hat with his crop and signaled the mare to ride on.

****

It was no wonder his father had enjoyed spending time with Eve, thought Avery as he approached the stables. She was easy to talk to and really quite lovely—exactly the kind of woman his father had often held up as an example of whom he should marry after Avery's ill-considered choice of bride so many years ago.

After the fiasco with Olivia, Avery had refused to speak to his father or visit Terra Bella for several years, preferring to blame everyone other than himself for the sordid outcome. During those dark days, he followed his anger down a long path of self-destruction that involved large quantities of scotch and many high-stakes games of Faro. He focused his attentions on two things—winning every game he played and perfecting his skills in the bedroom—all while drinking heavily. His title and prospects—not to mention his golden good looks—kept him on all the first-tier guest lists in spite of the mean wit he cultivated and liberally bandied about. He sharpened his penchant for sarcasm to a fine art that both titillated and terrified the *ton*. Only in bed was he still the consummate gentleman.

It was again the Duke of Whitley who intervened, jolting Avery out of a ruinous freefall by asking for his help as part of the Crown's network of spies in the fight against Napoleon. Accepting the challenge, Avery quickly became one of Whit's most important operatives and was, in fact, the architect of many successful battle strategies. His daring exploits and bravery saved many lives, but to aid his cover, Avery continued to play the role of spoiled aristocrat estranged from his family.

It was about that time that he met Miss Linea Braddock.

Avery grinned as he remembered the very thorough dressing down he had received upon his first encounter with Linney. Not since he was ten years old had anyone dared speak to him the way she did. He—handsome, wealthy, sophisticated, and one of the *ton's* most eligible bachelors—was taken to task by the young, untitled daughter of a solicitor in her first season, and totally smitten.

Their first meeting took place as he was escorting two young ladies in Hyde Park during the fashionable hour, and entertaining them with snide observations about their fellow strollers. He remembered commenting rather loudly on the back view of one of the two young ladies in front of his party when all of a sudden the lady's companion stopped and turned to face him with a forced smile and flashing green eyes.

"My lord," she said in a seemingly pleasant voice, "is it that you are *incapable* of polite conversation, or are you simply *ignorant* of how it is accomplished? With all of your commentary on the fashions of the day, I admit some surprise to find that we are not being trailed by Beau Brummel himself. Although, to be fair, Mr. Brummel is known for *clever* repartee, whereas your remarks fall with the thud of horse droppings."

Stunned and speechless, Avery managed only to gape at the young lady, to which she responded, "Your pardon, sir, if I am in fact speaking to a man with only half his wits, although I dare say that any halfwit would be more courteous to my friend than you have been this day."

To his credit, when he finally found his voice, Avery immediately apologized for his rude remarks and begged the pardon of the lady whom he had insulted. But, while the lady in question forgave him immediately, Miss Braddock was not so easily persuaded. In order to avoid further contact with him, she pulled her companion to cross to the other side of the street.

From that point on, Avery's every thought was spent trying to obtain forgiveness from the sharp-tongued and beautiful Miss Braddock. Wagers for and against his success were entered in the books at White's as well as at less respectable gambling establishments, but Avery paid them no attention. He never lost focus in his relentless attempt to acquire Miss Braddock's forgiveness, and he absolutely refused to give up.

One stormy afternoon, a little more than a week after the incident in the park, Avery arrived at the Braddock home with a bouquet of blue hyacinths, the flower of forgiveness. To accompany the bouquet, he had penned a verse about the divine nature of forgiveness which was not half bad. He was determined to deliver both the posies and the poem to the elusive Miss Braddock in person.

Alas, while Lord Hammond was more than ready to do battle in the cause of love, he was totally unprepared for the drenching cloudburst he encountered on his way to the Braddock residence. Noting his dripping overcoat and hat, the butler bid him wait in the parlor and took up Lord Hammond's card to his mistress. He returned almost immediately and dutifully informed his lordship that Miss Braddock was not at home.

"Very well," Avery told the servant, "I shall wait." If love required him to become a permanent fixture in the Braddock household, then so be it.

The butler took pity and relieved Avery of his damp outer garments after calling for a small fire to be lit. For almost an hour Avery waited, pacing the perimeter of the room, reading the titles of all the books on the shelves and admiring the knick-knacks on the mantel. He wound his watch and examined the damp front of his frock coat. He sniffed the flowers on the table in the center of the room, and noted that his hyacinths were holding up quite well. He then decided to take a pinch of snuff a friend had given him to try. Being unused to the habit, he snorted rather than sniffed the pulverized tobacco, the result of which was a rather explosive sneeze. There being no one present to beg their pardon, Avery applied his handkerchief, shrugged his shoulders, and proceeded to track the progress of several raindrops on a street-facing window pane.

Only moments later, Miss Braddock herself burst in, and in no time at all, Avery's frock coat and boots were spirited off to dry before another fire, leaving him in his shirtsleeves and stocking feet, which Miss Braddock bade him warm at the hearth. A tea tray appeared, complete with warm scones, clotted cream, and strawberry preserves. Miss Braddock poured him a steaming cup of tea with extra sugar, all while chattering a mile a minute about everything under the sun, including, but not limited to, how all manner of people died from chills they received while wandering about in the rain, the health benefits of black tea, and how hyacinths were her very favorite of all flowers. Somewhere in the midst of all those words, Miss Braddock forgave him, and Avery fell completely and irrevocably in love.

Someday he might tell his beloved Linney about his one and only experience with taking snuff—but it was his opinion that such a disclosure should best wait until after the wedding.

It was these thoughts that accompanied Avery back to the stables at Terra Bella. He quickly dismounted, tossed the reins to the stable boy, and walked purposefully toward the castle. There was much to attend to today, but at the very top of his list was finding that blasted engagement ring so he could put it on Linney's finger just as soon as humanly possible.

And he must check the post. He'd sent three letters to Linney, but as yet had received no response from her.

****

Agnes scratched discreetly on the door to the duchess's chambers and let herself in.

"This was in the morning post, my lady."

"Who is it from?"

"Miss Braddock, my lady, to the duke."

"How very forward of her, since I am almost certain she has not received any correspondence from him. Are you sure no one saw you take it?"

"No one, my lady."

"Very well. Put it with the other one." The countess waved her maid toward the carved box on her dresser, and then dramatically leaned back on the chaise lounge. "Was there anything of interest in her letter, or was it just drivel?"

"My lady, I would never think to—"

"Agnes, do show some respect. I don't doubt that you've read the letter. I expect you've read all of the duke's letters to Miss Braddock, as well as everything that comes to me and everything I send out. So please tell me, Agnes, is there anything remotely interesting in this letter from Miss Braddock?"

"Only that she worries about his grace and wonders

how he is. She asks when he will write, and after that it is mostly…"

"Drivel."

"Yes, my lady."

"Very well, Agnes. That will be all."

Chapter 14

Men were very different from women, thought Linney as she made her way to the home of her dear friend, Lady Allyce Wolcott, daughter of the Marquess of Nance. If a woman said she would write as soon as possible, one would expect a note—if not that very day—then certainly the next. Obviously it was different for men.

It had been four days since she and Avery had strolled in the rose garden at Haversham House. Four days. And not a word from Avery, the man who claimed he wanted to marry her and purported to love her above all others. Not a single word. Nothing. Linney's pace accelerated with her growing indignation.

Obviously he thought himself too busy or too important to waste time writing letters to the likes of her. Even after she threw convention to the wind and wrote to him first...although...perhaps that was the problem. Perhaps Avery thought her too forward, too unladylike—certainly her actions would be frowned upon by most of polite society. Well, if that's how he felt, then it was best they part ways now. She certainly didn't need the aggravation. Oh, the man was insufferable! She should have known the kind of man he was from their first meeting in the park a mere three months ago.

Linney smiled in spite of herself. *Met* probably wasn't the correct word to use. After all, it wasn't as if they had been politely introduced by a third party at a social event. Their introduction was more aptly characterized as introduction by banshee.

****

Lord Hammond's reputation proceeded him.

Although generally acknowledged to be the *ton's* most eligible bachelor, he was also known to be pompous, arrogant, and—to those who dared cross him—dangerous. His skill with the rapier was legend, and his deadly aim with a pistol was an important consideration for those who felt slighted by the heir to the Easton title and fortune. Lord Hammond's prowess in the boudoirs of some of London's most infamous ladies made him a constant topic of gossip. As a result, even though he did not keep a mistress, he never lacked for female companionship.

But if Linney ever thought of Lord Hammond at all, it was only in terms of taking care to ensure that their paths never crossed. And she had been quite successful in that until one beautiful afternoon in the middle of April, just as spring was returning to London, when Linney, like many others, was making the most of the welcome weather with a stroll in Hyde Park during the fashionable hour, accompanied by her friend Lady Allyce.

From the very start of her friendship with Allyce, Linney had been fascinated by the lady's utter lack of color sense. Perhaps because Linney herself was an artist, it was inconceivable to her that anyone could continue to create such calamitous color combinations—especially a person as genuinely kind

107

and selfless as Allyce and with the limitless resources available to her as the only child of the very wealthy Marquess of Nance. That anyone could so consistently choose such expensive fabrics in such unbecoming shades and then finish them with the most unsuitable of trims was, in Linney's estimation, one of the great fashion mysteries of life—second only to the question of why fabrics in such colors existed in the first place.

But exist they did, and Allyce had…well, a *talent* for finding them and insisting they be made up in the very latest style. On this particular afternoon, for example, Allyce was wearing a quite stylish walking dress in a particularly egregious shade of purple-brown puce and trimmed with a lemon-yellow ball fringe. Only that morning, Linney had vowed to herself to use the opportunity of their walk to speak to her friend about her color choices and offer to accompany Allyce on her next trip to the dressmaker. It would be so easy—and such fun—to select colors and fabrics that would complement her friend's trim figure and truly lovely complexion.

"Allyce, when is your next appointment with Madame Claudine?" began Linney, as the two walked beside Rotten Row on their way back from visiting the swans in the serpentine. But her attention was quickly diverted by a man's voice behind them quite loudly expressing some of the same sentiments that were on the tip of Linney's own tongue.

"…colors not found in nature. Any creature sporting those colors should already have been hunted to extinction by anyone with taste."

Titters of laughter from the gentleman's companions punctuated his pronouncements, and

Linney glanced over at Allyce to see if her friend had heard the man's callous words. She saw tears in Allyce's lovely gray eyes, but, thinking it best to avoid an embarrassing scene, she simply squeezed Allyce's arm and said nothing. The gentleman, however, continued, his voice loud and clear.

"...dressmaker undoubtedly works under a cover of smoked glass, and seamstresses must needs demand hazard pay. Hopefully they take turns with their basting so no eyes sustain permanent damage."

This time, Linney stopped. She willed herself to speak in a pleasant manner, but her whole being vibrated with indignation as she turned to the trio on the path behind them.

"My lord, is it that you are incapable of polite conversation, or are you simply ignorant of how it is done?"

The gentleman raised both eyebrows in surprise as the ladies in his escort instinctively took steps backward. But Linney had also taken a step—forward—and was now right under the gentleman's nose so there might be no mistaking to whom she addressed her tirade.

"Sir, your words condemn my friend for her harmless selection of unfortunate colors for her ensemble. Her faults are easily remedied with a pleasant afternoon and a color wheel. Your own sins, however, could not be exorcised from your cold heart even though twenty bishops gave it their all. You are a contemptible example of manhood—a coward who strikes at those less fortunate who are unable to respond or defend themselves. Your family's high rank is supposedly indicative of intellectual and social superiority, but you shame them all with your base behavior."

A crowd gathered quietly as Linney continued her barrage of stinging rebukes and indictments.

"Indeed, it does not surprise me that you choose to prey on those without anyone to defend them. Were I Lady Allyce, I would slap your cheek. Were I her brother, I would call you out. As it is, she has only me to tell you that you are a horrible ogre of a man, and for lack of better options I can only refuse to walk on the same side of the street as you. Come, Allyce."

Shaking, Linney pulled her friend to the other side of the road as several in the gathered crowd applauded her diatribe. Already regretting her outburst, she hurried Allyce along the opposite path, but they were almost immediately blocked by the tall and devastatingly handsome Earl of Hammond himself. Holding his beaver top hat in his hands, he spoke to Allyce clearly so that everyone could hear.

"My lady, your friend is correct on all counts. I am a scourge upon this earth and I have no right to even breathe in your presence. In my desire to impress my companions, I have wronged you greatly, for which I am profoundly sorry. I know you are, in fact, a generous soul with a kind heart who has done much to better the circumstances of many children in London's less fortunate districts. I wish I could retrieve the toads and frogs that sprang from my lips and caused you such pain, but I cannot. I can only humbly beg your pardon, Lady Allyce, and strive to emulate a fraction of your goodness in the hope you might one day forgive me."

Truer words were never spoken about Allyce. Linney knew, although few others were aware, of her good works with the children of London's poor. That Lord Hammond was somehow privy to this information was curious, and it was in that moment Linney realized there was much more to the man than was evident in the face he showed society. She studied that face as he spoke to Allyce. His dark-blond hair was slightly longer than the current fashion and included strands of gold that glowed in the afternoon sun. With his hat in his hands, wayward curls were free to blow onto his forehead, and he carelessly brushed them aside. His clipped sideburns in the style of Mr. Brummel were of a darker shade than his hair, as were the long lashes that framed his piercing dark-brown eyes.

Linney was secretly envying those lashes when he turned to address her.

"And, Miss Braddock, is it? I owe you many thanks for removing the scales from my eyes and calling out my reprehensible behavior. I am in your debt and will continue to be until the end of my life. I do not deserve your forgiveness, but, humbly, I ask for it."

Of course, true to form, Allyce immediately assured Lord Hammond no harm was done and forgave him on the spot. And so, with a deep bow to both ladies, Lord Hammond took his leave. Linney was gratified to see her friend smiling again, her hurt a thing of the past. In fact, Allyce chattered on and on about Lord Hammond's "lovely apology" and courtly manner for the remainder of their outing, while Linney, for an interesting change, said nothing at all.

The next day, Allyce's mother's parlor was filled with all manner of fragrant flowers, along with a note from Lord Hammond renewing his abject apology.

Linney also received a delivery—a single, red rose delivered with the earl's calling card and signed with his given name, *Avery*.

For the next two weeks, the earl continued an unflagging campaign to win over an unimpressed Miss Braddock. The turning point came on a rainy day when Lord Hammond, drenched to the skin from a sudden cloudburst, called at the Braddock house bearing blue hyacinths. As she had done on the occasions of his previous visits, Linney returned his card and told Thomson she was not at home. But this time Thomson returned and informed Linney that Lord Hammond had decided to wait until a time when she might receive him.

Whether Thomson *meant* to bring Lord Hammond's dripping overcoat with him when he told Linney of the earl's decision to wait is a mystery that might never be solved. However, three quarters of an hour later, when Linney slipped silently down the stairs to spy on her visitor, she was dismayed to hear an enormous sneeze emanate from the front parlor. She immediately instructed Thomson to build up the fire in the room and send in a tea tray. She then proceeded to burst into the room in a rather unladylike manner and practically drag the poor earl's damp frock coat and wet boots from his person. Somewhere during this sequence of events, Lord Hammond again begged for her forgiveness, and this time Linney responded, "Of course."

For how could she possibly refuse to forgive the man with whom she had fallen so completely and overwhelmingly in love?

Someday Linney might tell Avery about finding

the snuff box in his frock coat pocket and how she was quite aware that his sneeze signaled a questionable habit rather than a case of pneumonia, but in the meantime, there was no harm in letting him think she'd been won over by his earnest charms and a fabricated case of sniffles.

Besides, she did so love hyacinths.

So let everyone smile and whisper and think whatever they wanted about her feelings toward Lord Hammond, but she was not some silly young thing with stars in her eyes and her heart on her sleeve. She was in love with Avery, Lord Hammond, now the Duke of Easton, and he was in love with her. She knew it and Avery knew it, and the only thing that was the least bit unclear was why she'd received no word from him.

Linney stopped suddenly as a brand-new thought entered the fray. What if Avery was ill? Or had taken a fall from his horse? She started walking again, gaining speed as her thoughts flew. Avery liked to ride fast. What if his horse had missed a jump and he was even now lying in bed, injured or…or worse? Who would bring her the news? How would she know, and—

"Linney? Oh, it *is* you! Where are you going? I thought you were coming to go with me to the archives. Did you change your mind?"

Linney turned and blinked at the figure standing just behind her. "Oh, Allyce, good morning. I do apologize. I was so caught up in my thoughts that I walked right by your house. It's a good thing I didn't have to cross a street to get here—who knows where I might have ended up."

"I told John to bring around the carriage—oh, good. Here he is now. I can't thank you enough for going with me to look at the drawings. I'm hoping Grove House will be the perfect place for my girls' school. Thank you, Farley." Allyce settled into the plush seats as the footman handed Linney up into the carriage. "What were you thinking about so intently that you didn't see me waving?"

Linney sighed and sat back beside her friend. Allyce was the one person besides Vivian in whom she could confide. "Do you remember the day we met Lord Hammond?"

"I do. He was making very unkind comments about my walking dress, and you defended me. And, in the process, you cut him to shreds. It was the most remarkable thing and, I must admit, quite horrifying to watch."

Allyce wrinkled her forehead. "But I thought you said the two of you made up. I thought you said... Oh, Linney, don't cry." Allyce reached into her reticule for a handkerchief. "Tell me what's happened. When I saw you at Vivian's wedding, you and Lord Hammond looked so happy."

"Oh, Allyce, I don't know what to think. Avery was called away from the wedding because his father was in an accident. He was in such a hurry that he didn't have time to tell me goodbye. He asked his brother to tell me he would write as soon as he could, but I haven't heard anything. And then Father read in Monday's paper that the duke had died."

"Oh, that's right. The Duke of Easton was Lord Hammond's father. My father is actually attending the funeral today."

Linney's tears started again. "I haven't received any word from him, Allyce. Nothing. Mother even allowed me to send a letter to him at Terra Bella because I was so worried. Allyce, what if he's changed his mind? What if all his words were just in the heat of the moment and he has decided he must marry a titled lady? What if he loves someone else? I just don't think I could bear it."

Allyce was a good friend to Linney and as any good friend knows, there is a time for wise counsel and a time to simply offer company to that friend's misery. Allyce patted Linney's shoulder and listened quietly as her friend poured out her soul.

"You know I never dreamed of beautiful dresses, or fancy balls, or marrying a prince like some little girls. All I ever wanted to do was travel to places all over the world so I could draw all the magnificent buildings and monuments—the pyramids in Egypt, the canals in Venice, the cathedrals in Paris, the Taj Mahal in India, and of course—"

"The Parthenon in Greece. Yes, I know, dear. You're quite consistent, Linney. I think it's possible I know more about the Parthenon than the Greeks themselves."

Linney sniffed and gave Allyce a small smile. "I do want to travel to Athens and draw the Parthenon. It's always been my dream. And then, after I met Avery, we talked about traveling together, and I knew he was what I'd been missing from my dreams. He was so excited about taking me to places he'd already visited and about us exploring new places together, so my dreams changed to include him. We would travel and see wonderful sights, and then, someday, we would have a home and family together. We talked about it all the time. Was I so foolish, to believe what he told me?"

Allyce was very much a no-nonsense lady. Even if she had been raised as the only child of adoring, wealthy parents, she was known for getting straight to the point of any conversation, and now she did nothing less with her distraught friend.

"Do you think Lord Hammond has changed his mind and no longer loves you?"

Linney's face puckered up again as she nodded. "He's the Duke of Easton now. I think he knows he should find someone more suitable to be his duchess, and he is trying to tell me that he does not want to marry me."

"And if that were the case? If he did think to bow to the norms of society and seek a blue-blooded daughter of a marquess whose lineage goes back to the Magna Carta, would you meekly stand aside with no objection?"

Linney's nod was half-hearted at best, and, as Allyce watched, it slowly changed itself into a denial.

"No, I wouldn't," said Linney in a low voice, as if trying out the response.

"Why not?"

Linney's voice grew stronger and more sure. "Because he belongs to me. Because I love him and because he deserves to have a wife who loves him as much as I do. If he could look me in the eye and tell me he no longer loves me or that he loves another, then yes, I would stand aside, but until then... Allyce, he's the only person I know who is genuinely interested in what I say. He's the only one who listens to my opinions and my observations and never seems to mind that I talk on and on. Oh, I know you listen to me and so does Vivian, but you only listen with your ears.

Avery listens to me with his heart. I know I am the wife he needs, and if he doesn't know that by now, then I just need to make it unmistakably clear to him."

"Well, then," said Allyce, smiling broadly, "you must take your own advice." She handed Linney a fresh handkerchief. "I'm glad we have that all cleared up. Now you can pay attention to me."

Linney smiled and sniffed a final sniff. "Thank you, Allyce."

"You'll thank me even more once you take a look at the drawings. I'm almost certain I've found a hidden passageway in the family wing, but I can't quite figure out where it starts. I can't wait for you to take a look and see if I'm right."

Chapter 15

Considering how isolated the eighth Duke of Easton had been in his later life, his funeral procession was longer than Avery had anticipated. But tradition and status will out, and the assemblage, which included all but two of the sitting dukes, was quite respectable and provided a postscript worthy of his father's life. Even the Prince Regent had managed to send a representative from London to bid farewell to the late duke and offer condolences to his heir. But Avery was especially touched by the number of people from the village standing solemnly along the side of the road as the procession passed by on its way from the church to the gravesite.

"...earth to earth, ashes to ashes, dust to dust..."

The bishop sounded truly sad to have lost his weekly chess partner. As they left the cemetery, Avery spoke briefly with the other mourners. At the end of the queue was Whit, who, casting away all formality, embraced his half-brother.

"I'm so sorry, Avery. I know how much you loved your father—even though the two of you fought like cats and dogs. Vivian sends her love, by the way. I won't be staying, but I wanted to see if there was anything I could do."

"I'll let you know, Whit. Something is not right, and the pieces don't add up. I haven't had time to find out too many details, but I'll know more soon. I'll keep you apprised. By the way, has Vivian heard from Linney?"

Whit looked surprised. "I know she has received at least two letters." He frowned. "Haven't you?"

"No. I've written to her several times, but I've heard nothing back. I'm not sure what to make of it."

"I'll ask Vivian and see what I can find out. She's been horribly sick every morning and sometimes on into the day. I don't know how women do this, Avery— there's nothing I can do to help. It's not a position I enjoy."

The worry on Whit's face made Avery want to comfort *him*. "She'll be fine, Whit. She has you, and it is my experience that the ladies are much stronger than they—and society—would have us believe. Please give her my best."

All in all, everything had gone well. The time of year had necessitated haste in all the rites of mourning, and this morning's heat wave only served to confirm the wisdom of Avery's decision to proceed with yesterday's services even though some mourners were unable to make the journey in time. Avery had spent every minute of the past few days making arrangements and tending to the most pressing business matters, of which there were many. The castle had been full of guests to entertain, the last of whom were just now taking their leave.

The one oddity of the day was the almost complete absence of Lady Tangier. Eve was present in a non-obtrusive way, but the only sign of the woman who claimed to be the duke's spouse was the black-clad figure in one of the family coaches. Luckily, word about *that* particular aspect of his father's death had not reached London, so Avery did not have to dodge questions for which he had no answers.

Avery opened the doors to his study and went to stand behind the desk. Today was the first day he was able to spend any time at all thinking about anything other than his father's funeral. He was tired to the bone, but the time had come for some answers. Merton hustled in behind him, followed by a footman carrying a tea tray. Avery smiled his gratitude at the older man. Merton had a long history of service at Terra Bella and, after Avery's mother died, he and Mrs. Chapman had smoothly taken over the day-to-day running of the castle.

"Thank you, Merton. That is exactly what I need. That and an hour or two of solitude."

"I will make sure you are not disturbed, your grace," said the butler, nodding to dismiss the footman. "Will there be anything else?"

Avery scowled at the darkness. The heavy damask draperies were closed as a sign of mourning that he didn't want to feel. "Please open the drapes. I've no wish to go blind while I try to understand what has been going on around here."

As the older man went to each of the floor-to-ceiling windows, Avery sat down at the desk. "Merton, how long have Lady Tangier and Lady Genevieve been in residence here?"

"They arrived in the middle of May, your grace."

"Did my father invite them?"

"I do not believe he did. The countess and Lady Eve appeared late one evening in the middle of an unusually fierce storm. According to Lady Tangier, they were on their way to London, but took a wrong turn and were lost. They were traveling with only the one maid, a footman, and their driver."

"This isn't the dark ages. Was there no one in town who could direct them? Why didn't they stay at the inn there? Why come here?"

"Lady Tangier explained that she was a friend of the family. She said she knew your father when she was a debutante. Her maid told Mrs. Chapman that the duke planned to offer for Lady Tangier until your mother appeared late in the season. Of course, this is all second- or third-hand information, your grace. Lady Tangier has not taken me into her confidence, but this is the story she has put about. Evidently, she, Lady Eve, and her late husband also stopped here some years ago when your mother was still alive. Lady Tangier claims to have corresponded with both your mother and your father over the years."

"Did my father seem happy to have them here?"

Merton hesitated. "As you know, the late duke had grown quite solitary in his habits, your grace. He certainly did not begrudge them shelter from the storm. On the night they arrived, he had already retired for the evening, but he instructed Mrs. Chapman to make rooms ready for them. At breakfast the next morning, Lady Eve joined his grace and he seemed to enjoy her company. In what I thought to be an unguarded moment at dinner that evening, he invited the ladies to extend their stay as long as they wished. I believe he immediately regretted his invitation, because when Lady Tangier thanked him profusely for his hospitality, he looked…"

Avery looked up from the papers at the sudden

silence from the family servant. "He looked what? Excited? Happy? Annoyed? What?"

"Pained, your grace. Your father looked pained. He did not say anything, however, and the lady took that as confirmation of the invitation. We all assumed they would be here a week—two at most—and yet, more than three months later, they remain."

"Where is their home?"

"It is my understanding that the late earl's country estate is in Sheffield. His heir was a cousin who evidently dislikes Lady Tangier as much as Lady Tangier dislikes both her dowager house and the new earl's countess."

"What do you know about her journey to Scotland with my father?"

"Very little, your grace. It all happened rather quickly. Your father and Lady Tangier were quite secretive about it—it was very unlike him. None of the house staff knew anything about the trip until after they left, and then, of course, when they returned, the duke was injured and unconscious. I sent immediately for the doctor."

"I understand it was Lady Tangier's coachman who was killed, but what of the footmen who accompanied them on the trip? Am I right to understand they didn't return with Lady Tangier and my father?"

"They did not, your grace. One was the footman who had initially accompanied Lady Tangier and Lady Eve on their travels here, and, as I understand it, he was sent back to Sheffield. The other man, our own Nathan Foote, was too injured to travel—or so I was told."

"Do we know Mr. Foote's condition?"

"We do not, your grace. I sent a message to see

what could be done to bring Mr. Foote back to Terra Bella, but I have not yet received an answer."

"Let's send someone to interview Foote and bring him back if he's able to travel. I need to understand what happened."

"Yes, your grace. I'll see to it immediately."

"One other thing, Merton. Did my father have a place where he kept valuables in the castle?"

"The silver plate and other valuable items of that nature are kept locked in the butler's pantry, your grace. I do not know where the duke kept his personal valuables. Perhaps Mr. Olsen could assist you?"

"I've already spoken with Olsen. He pointed me to a locked drawer in the dresser full of stick pins and buttons, and also to a secret cupboard in the dressing room that contained the ducal coronet. I'm specifically looking for the Easton engagement ring. Father was to have it brought up from London, but I don't know if it arrived or where it is now."

"It did arrive here, your grace. A special courier brought it from the bank in London just a few days after your father received your letter saying you planned to marry. The duke and Lady Tangier were at dinner, but the bank's courier insisted I interrupt them to have the duke receive the ring personally. Lady Tangier was curious and begged to see the ring, which your father showed to her—rather reluctantly, I thought. He explained its history, and she insisted on trying it on, which he allowed her to do even though it clearly upset him. I remember her asking how he could keep something as valuable as the ring out here in the country, and he replied that Terra Bella had many places to keep secrets."

"Did you know that the note the countess sent to me was signed 'the Duchess of Easton' and sealed with my father's signet ring?"

"No, your grace. I was most certainly not aware of that. I handled much of the duke's correspondence—including most of the letters he sent to you, but I knew nothing of that one. It must have been when the doctor insisted she inform you of your father's condition. As to why she signed it as she did, I do not know."

"Do you know whether my father offered to marry Lady Tangier?"

"I do not know whether the duke made any such offer or whether they were actually married in Scotland, your grace. The first I heard of any such plans was from Lady Tangier upon their return. However..." Merton hesitated.

Avery, at the desk, looked up at his very proper butler. "Please speak freely, Merton."

"The duke was often...lonely, your grace. It was my understanding from Lady Tangier's maid that the duke and Lady Tangier engaged in...relations."

Avery returned his attention to shuffling papers. "I have no trouble believing the duke engaged in...relations if the countess was willing, but I do have trouble believing he asked her to be his wife. I have been attending to his duties in London and helping Lady Charlotte take care of my sisters because I was—we all were—under the impression he still grieved for my mother and could not bear to leave Terra Bella."

"And that is not incorrect, your grace. In my estimation, your father was still in mourning for her grace." Merton cleared his throat uncomfortably. "From what I observed, it was Lady Tangier who pursued your father. She arranged many late dinners alone with him while Lady Eve took a tray in her room. She always dressed…rather provocatively, I thought…and I believe your father was not unaffected by her assets in that regard. In fact, a few nights before they left on their trip, the countess went directly to Mrs. Dartmore and asked her to prepare an intimate dinner to be served in his grace's rooms. Of course Mrs. Dartmore went to Mrs. Chapman, who asked me before preparing the meal, but the footman who cleared away the dishes mentioned there was evidence of…"

"…relations?"

"Just so, your grace."

"Yes, well. Was there anything else unusual that I should know about?"

"Olsen did mention that your father had taken to locking his door at night."

Avery looked up at the older man in surprise. "Truly? That adds a bit of a mystery to the whole situation, doesn't it?"

Avery poured himself a cup of tea, adding a lump of sugar to the strong brew. He stirred the cup twice and then picked up the cup and saucer. "Just as a matter of information, Merton, which rooms does the Lady Tangier currently occupy?"

"She has moved into the rooms formerly occupied by your mother, your grace."

"Did my father put her in those rooms?"

"No, your grace. When the ladies first arrived, Mrs. Chapman put them in the guest wing. Lady Tangier had the blue room and Lady Eve the canary corner room."

"Then why is Lady Tangier now in the duchess's apartments?"

"When she and your father returned from their trip, her ladyship insisted that the maids move her to the duchess's rooms—ostensibly so she could be closer to the duke and assist with his care."

"And did she do that? Assist with his care?"

"Not to my knowledge, your grace. Mr. Olson was there most of the time, and Lady Eve spent a great deal of time by your father's bedside, but as far as I know, Lady Tangier never sat with him. She did, however, seem to think she should direct the efforts of the doctor and everyone else."

Avery choked on his tea. "Lady Tangier tried to direct Olsen in his care of my father?"

"I don't believe it was a very *successful* endeavor, your grace." Merton allowed himself a small smile. "As you well know, Mr. Olsen was quite protective of your father. And a Scot. He was quite beside himself when Lady Tangier and the duke went off on their journey without him—without any of the duke's regular attendants."

"And where is Lady Tangier now, Merton?"

"She remains in her rooms, your grace."

He still had not met the woman—he refused to think of her as the Duchess of Easton. One would have expected her to present herself upon his arrival, or at least the next morning after his father's death. Or at dinner that evening or at Sunday services. Certainly at the funeral. He'd spoken with Lady Eve a number of times, but never with her mother. He found it hard to believe anyone could be that "prostrate with grief," and yet her maid insisted that to be the case. With a house full of distinguished guests, Avery had not wanted to make a scene, but now that the guests had departed, the time had come.

"Merton, please tell Lady Tangier I wish to speak with her in my study at her earliest convenience."

"Yes, your grace, although…"

"Yes?"

"The lady has—up to this time—not been receiving and, according to her maid, is—"

"Prostrate with grief. Yes, so I've been informed. Numerous times. Let me rephrase my request."

"Your grace?"

"Please tell Lady Tangier that I wish to speak with her in my study today at half-past one. If she is unable to make it to my study at that time, then I will call on her in her rooms."

"Very good, your grace."

Avery looked up at the gray-haired butler and met his eyes. "Is there anything else I should know about the countess, Merton?"

"Not at the moment, your grace, not about the countess. But you should know your father had grown quite fond of Lady Eve. They spent a great deal of time together, and he seemed to be happier than he had been since your mother died. She is very well liked below stairs, and we have all done our best to make her feel welcome. The same cannot be said about her mother."

Merton paused for a second or two and then said, "I feel that I—that we all—let your father down by allowing Lady Tangier to take him on that trip and then assume control of the situation when they returned."

Avery shook his head. "Thank you for your candor, Merton, but it was not your fault. If there is any blame to be had, it is mine. I was too long in London. I should have come down to tell him in person that I wished to marry. If I had, then I would have met Lady Tangier and at least been able to talk with my father about her. As it is now, I'll have to ask my questions of the countess herself. I mean to get to the bottom of this."

"Very good, your grace. Will there be anything else?"

"Please have the morning post sent in."

"Yes, your grace." The faithful retainer closed the door on his way out.

Avery leaned back in his chair and turned his thoughts to the other mystery that plagued him. It had been six days now, and he'd heard not had a single word from Linney.

Six days.

He'd sent almost that many letters to her, including a quick note that first night from the inn in Farnham. He craved her company—her comfort and sympathy on the death of his father, her keen observations about his would-be stepmother, and her gentle touch that both soothed and aroused him. He was desperate to hold her in his arms and hear her sigh when he caressed her curves and kissed the nape of her neck. He grew hard every time he remembered how she tasted when he covered her lips and tangled his tongue with hers, the faint scent of roses all around them. He imagined her saying his name and confessing her undying love for him as he took her to his bed, kissing her all over and showing her all the pleasurable things a man can do for a woman before finally claiming her for his own.

Damn it! Why the devil hadn't she written? And where the hell was that damn ring? Hearing nothing from Linney made him wonder if she was developing an interest in someone else. He should have demanded she see no one else while he was away. Better yet, he should have gotten a special license and brought her to Terra Bella with him so they could marry. The jealousy he felt when he thought of her with another man was so strong that it physically hurt.

A scratch on the door pulled him back to his current world. "Come in."

He was grateful that the bold evidence of his longing and frustration was hidden by his desk.

"The post, your grace," said the footman, bowing as he placed a tray of letters on the blotter in front of him.

Avery scanned the pile of correspondence for Linney's familiar scrawl. He sighed.

Seven days.

Chapter 16

"It's so good of you to call, Lady Charlotte." Lady Thea and her daughter stood to welcome their late-morning caller. "Won't you come in?"

"I am so happy you are receiving, my dears. I thought to send a note, but since I was out, I decided it would be easier just to drop by."

"I'm so glad," said Lady Thea, gesturing to the settee. "Please have a seat. Would you care for—"

Lady Thea never finished her sentence.

"We didn't get a chance to chat at your niece's wedding," said Lady Charlotte, settling herself beside Linney. "And then with the terrible news about the Duke of Easton...well! Who would have thought the duke would be the first of his generation to go? We all thought his younger brother, George, would go before him. George was quite ill for a while, you know. In fact, he was unable to attend the wedding between the duke and my sister. At the time, George was the duke's heir, but, of course, all that changed when Avery was born. What a dear boy. He wrote that the duke's funeral was very well attended. I just received his note this morning. He said Whit was there, but couldn't stay long because Vivian wasn't feeling well. So like a man...of course she's not feeling well in the mornings."

Lady Charlotte pursed her lips and drew off her gloves, setting them down beside her. "Weak, please,

130

Lady Thea, and two sugars. Vivian was *such* a lovely bride, wasn't she? It's really all anyone wanted to talk about. Her dress was exquisite, although I thought you favored Madame Augustine's shop for couture."

"Well, yes, we…"

"And then I realized that Vivian's gown *was* a Madame Augustine creation—because who else would have put those seed pearls on that luscious dusky brown instead of on ecru or light blue? Those rich colors are her hallmark. I am such a devotee of fashion, you know. I have been in despair these past few years because that wretched Corsican had the whole continent in such a stir and Paris fashions were—well, politically *unfashionable*. But now, with him safely locked away on Saint Helena, I am looking forward to celebrating with a whole new wardrobe—after a suitable period of mourning, of course. I realized that it was the *fit* of Vivian's gown that had thrown me off a bit. I said to myself, 'Madame A. would *never* have allowed a gown that pulled across the bust like that.' And then I remembered the look in Whit's eye when he told me the date of the wedding, and I put two and two together and came to the conclusion that he and Vivian must be in anticipation of a happy event, which I gather is also why she is feeling unwell in the mornings."

Linney's eyebrows shot up, and Lady Thea smiled.

"Oh, I *am* right, aren't I? How very delightful. I adore babies, and Whit will be the most devoted father. Not that Vivian won't be a devoted mother. I didn't mean to imply that at all."

Lady Charlotte accepted a cup and saucer from Lady Thea. "Thank you, my dear. My friend Lady Islington was also at the wedding. She and Lady

Haversham are related through their husbands, and she is often present at some of the more important events at the house. She can be a terrible gossip, though, so when she asked if the hasty nuptials were because Lady Rowden and my nephew had anticipated their vows, I told her even if they had, it was none of her business. But all it would take is for someone to see how Whit looks at Vivian. I don't think I've ever seen my nephew look at anyone the way he looks at her. My nephew, the duke, I mean. Oh, dear, I forgot that Avery is also a duke now. I suppose I will have to say, 'I've never seen the elder of my ducal nephews look at anyone the way he looks at Vivian' because, of course, I *have* seen Avery look at you in much the same way, Linney dear. Everyone has. How does he say he is bearing up?"

Lady Charlotte took a sip of tea, pausing long enough for Linney to inhale and start a sentence.

"I—"

"I'm sure he must pour out his soul to you. He was ever a good correspondent. You must keep all of his letters, my dear. I have all the notes that my dear Charlie wrote to me all tied up in a pale blue ribbon. Charlie always says that he fell in love with me when I was wearing one very special pale blue gown."

Lady Charlotte leaned forward to whisper to her hostesses. "I've always believed it had very little to do with the color of the gown and everything to do with amount of *décolletage* I was showing when I wore it." Lady Charlotte sat back, smiling a knowing smile, and took another sip of her tea.

"Would you care for some cake, Lady Charlotte?" Linney finally managed to say an entire sentence as she offered a plate of iced plum cake slices.

"Thank you, dear. It looks delicious. Plum cake is one of Avery's favorites—but then you must already know that. He has such a sweet tooth. You must make sure to have a very large wedding cake. I was at Mathilda Everett's daughter's wedding to Sir Reginald last week, and they ran out of wedding cake before everyone was served a piece. Of course, there were so many other sweets and savories that no one went hungry, but it was a bit of embarrassment, all the same."

Lady Charlotte took a dainty bite of plum cake, and then continued her monologue.

"Have you thought about where you want to have the wedding, my dear? Avery's first letter said they had a dreadful storm the night of their trip, but his next letter went on and on about how lovely Terra Bella looked. Evidently Easton was having quite a bit of work done inside and out. Avery said the grounds were perfect. In today's post, he sent each of the little girls a pressed flower from the garden. He writes to them—separately, mind you—every day when he's away. He is such a wonderful big brother. I think it's because there is such an age difference—they are almost like daughters to him. Now, talk about someone making a good father…"

Lady Charlotte smiled slyly at Linney, who inwardly cringed. As if sensing her daughter's embarrassment, Lady Thea again held out the cake plate to Avery's aunt.

"Just one more slice, Lady Thea, if you please. It is very delicious." Setting the Spode cup and saucer daintily on the low table in front of her, Lady Charlotte selected a slice of the plummy cake.

How was it possible for the lady to talk as much as she did, sip her cup of tea, and daintily consume two slices of plum cake? Linney was fascinated—and furious! How was it that Avery was able to send his aunt three letters of significant length—along with daily notes to each of his three sisters—but had not sent her a single word? She focused her attention back on the conversation, because Lady Charlotte was talking again.

"Lady Genevieve sounds lovely, don't you think, Linney? Oh, I'm sure there's more to that story, what with them arriving under such a flimsy pretext. But Lady Eve—that's what Avery said he calls her—sounds perfectly delightful. The Standish men always did have an eye for beauty. Avery says it's no wonder that his father enjoyed Lady Eve's company. I think she has been quite good for Avery, too. Of course, I'm reading between the lines, but Avery says she's quite clever and has been very helpful with receiving guests and making all the arrangements that needed to be made. He says the staff at Terra Bella simply adore her and listen more to her than they do to him. I'm sure he exaggerates, but I do get the feeling they approve of Lady Eve a great deal. I dare say not the same can be said for Eve's mother, don't you agree, my dear?"

Lady Charlotte turned slightly to aim her follow-up explanation to Lady Thea and paused slightly to take a breath.

She's like one of those pearl divers, thought Linney out of nowhere. The ones that dive a hundred feet in a single breath to collect the oysters.

"Evidently when Lady Tangier first arrived, she wasted no time getting close to the duke. There were even rumors that Edward asked her to marry him, which is utterly absurd. The Standish men appreciate beautiful women, but once they find the one they want, they don't take another even after death has parted them. Edward has been in mourning for my sister for eight years, and now, God rest his soul, he is finally united with her. He never had any intention of marrying again, I don't care what this countess person says. That's why he sent the little girls to live with me. Lady Tangier does remind me of Avery's first fiancée, Lady Layton. Now *she* was a piece of work—even Edward saw through her, which is why I'm surprised he didn't send the countess packing after a day or two. Most likely it was because he wanted Lady Eve to stay on. Oh, my goodness, is that the time?"

Lady Charlotte put down her cup and stood up gracefully, pulling on her gloves. Linney and Lady Thea stood as well.

"I'm afraid I must go," she explained. "I told Lady Islington I would stop by this afternoon on my rounds. Thank you for the lovely tea, Lady Thea. I have so enjoyed our little *tête-à-tête*. And Linney, dear, please let me know just as soon as you decide on a color for the girls' dresses. I thought using those green sashes with the white muslin dresses for Whit and Vivian's ceremony was inspired. I know we should observe a year of mourning, but that's really only required for the widow these days, isn't it? Certainly six months would do for Avery and the girls. Especially if we make the wedding a small event, just for family and close friends, you know. We could limit it to only a hundred guests or so."

Lady Charlotte clasped her hands together. "Oh,

wouldn't a Christmas wedding be lovely? Lady Thea, would you mind if I have my cook ask your cook for her plum cake receipt? I do believe it is the best I have ever tasted. Good day to you both!"

Thomson showed Lady Charlotte out, and the door to the parlor closed softly in the quiet. Linney looked at her mother and dropped onto the brocade covered seat recently vacated by their guest.

"I don't know what to say," said Lady Thea, slowly sitting back in her own chair. "I don't think I have ever witnessed anything like that before in my life."

"I wonder if it would have been the same had there been several ladies here. Would we all just sit, slack-jawed, listening to Lady Charlotte?"

"The thing is, she is quite entertaining and obviously full of gossip and news and…well, everything, but I am quite exhausted. Would you like another cup of tea, dear?"

"No, thank you, Mama. I was planning to do some drawing this afternoon."

"Very well, but I am quite exhausted. Perhaps I'll go for a bit of a lie-down. Please ring the bell for Nancy on your way out."

Linney tugged the bell pull before making her way out the door and up the stairs to her room. Once there, she closed her door and leaned back against it as she replayed Lady Charlotte's chatter about all the letters she'd received from Avery. Even the little girls were receiving regular notes from their brother. Linney couldn't decide whether she loved Avery even more for caring so about his sisters or hated him with every fiber of her being for ignoring her. The one thing she did know was that right now she wanted to think of something—anything—else.

****

The drawing Linney was doing for her father was almost complete, but where had she put it?

Crossing her room, Linney got down on her hands and knees to retrieve a wooden box of sketches from beneath her bed. The box scraped noisily on the bare floor as she pulled it out and sorted through its contents. The drawing wasn't there.

"Where *is* it?" she muttered to herself, abandoning the first box for another box even farther underneath the bed. After rifling through the contents of the second box, she sat back on her heels and looked around the room. Where else could it be? And why was nothing ever where she put it?

Spying a smaller box on the floor of her armoire, Linney pulled it out into the center of the room with a bang and a thump and more scraping. She perched on the edge of her bed to look inside, forgetting about the large art history books she'd borrowed from her father's library and left on the other side of her bed. Three of the books slid to the floor in a series of loud thuds. She scowled at the scattered volumes, and then returned to her search.

One small drawing. Had she imagined doing it? No—she could see the sketch in her mind's eye. "I've tucked it somewhere," she sighed to herself. "I'll never find it."

It was the curse for her talent. An absentmindedness that bordered on complete forgetfulness when she worked on a project. But she wasn't working on a project right now, was she? At least she wouldn't be until she located that sketch.

Even as she continued to look around her room for potential hiding places, Linney knew the real problem was not the disappearance of the sketch. Counting today, it had been six days—almost a week—since Vivian and Whit were married at Haversham House, and six days since Avery had been summoned home to Terra Bella, leaving Whit to relay the message that he would write "as soon as possible."

Granted, "as soon as possible" was an indefinite length of time, but surely it was sooner than six days. Linney remembered the gossip she'd overheard at Haversham House. *Had* Avery simply been amusing himself with no intentions of marrying her? Is *that* what he was trying to tell her with his silence?

The last of the art history books fell from her bed with a loud thump.

Vivian said perhaps she wasn't ready to be in love with Avery if she didn't trust him. Her father said to turn her attention to other gentlemen. Her mother warned her not to wear her heart on her sleeve. Allyce…dear Allyce…told Linney to listen to her own heart.

Linney angrily wiped away the tears that tried to escape from her eyes. Avery was hers and she was his. If he didn't want her anymore, then he was going to have to say so to her face because he *had* wanted her before. She was not that naïve. She knew when a man was attracted to her, and on those few occasions where there had been more than a few stolen moments between Avery and herself, she was not the only one left breathless with passion and aching with desire. She'd heard it in his groan when she pressed against him and felt the hard ridge of his arousal. She'd seen it in his eyes, and she'd felt it in the thundering beat of his heart when he held her close.

"I've a mind to go to Terra Bella and confront him outright," she muttered. And not for the first time did the distinctly unladylike urge to punch her beloved in the stomach present itself.

More distracted than ever, Linney continued going through the motions of searching for her sketch, opening and closing drawers and closets with one satisfying bang after another. Every item in her wardrobe, every drawing in her portfolio, and every piece of correspondence was fair game as she ripped through her room. A scratch at her door made her pause, but before she could call "Come in," her maid entered.

"Ah...Miss Linney? Your mother would like to speak to you."

Chapter 17

"The duke has asked that you join him in his study, at half past one of the clock, my lady." Agnes set the tea tray down on the table in front of the fireplace.

"Did you inform his grace that I was indisposed and prostrate with grief?" asked Lady Tangier.

"I did, but Mr. Merton said the duke wanted to express his condolences to you personally and said if you do not come to his study, then he will attend you here in your rooms."

Lady Tangier glared at her maid. "Such impertinence! Very well. I suppose I shall have to see him at some point. Are there any other demands from our host?"

"No, my lady, but there was another letter from the duke to Miss Braddock in the morning post."

"Goodness, but he is a prolific writer. Does he say anything interesting?"

"He asks how she spends her day and if she might be interested in traveling to Terra Bella with her mother and father."

"So, no. Nothing interesting."

"Well he does seem rather impatient. He points out that he has written to her several times and still has not received any word from her. Then he asks if there is something amiss. He seems a little put out."

Suddenly Lady Tangier sat up. "Perhaps I am

going about this the wrong way. If the new duke thinks his sweetheart is tiring of him or being wooed by another, then maybe he will lose interest and look closer to home for a bride."

Agnes' face showed her disbelief. "My lady, surely, you don't think *you*—"

"Why not," snapped the countess. She stood and walked away from Agnes to sit at her dressing table. "I am... Oh, don't be absurd. It would be unseemly to have the duke marry his late father's fiancée. I am referring to Eve, of course. She is only just out this season and the perfect age for the duke. She is, in fact, exactly what dear Edward wanted for his son."

Lady Tangier caught the eye of her maid in the looking glass. "Remember my telling you it was the duke's most fervent wish to have our families united, first with our wedding, but then—realizing our union was not meant to be—with his son marrying my daughter?"

"No, my lady. I don't remember you telling me that at all."

"Then you should *start* remembering right now. It was just before my darling Edward gave me this." Lady Tangier reached into the box containing the purloined letters and took out the small, enameled box. Opening it, she took out the Easton engagement ring and put it on her finger, holding out her hand for Agnes to see.

"Oh, my lady," said Agnes, drawing in a sharp breath. "It's lovely. Look how it reflects the light, like a hundred candles. That's the ring that's missing, then, isn't it? The one the old duke's haughty valet is searching everywhere to find. It's all the talk below stairs."

"I told you. We were betrothed. He gave it to me."

"But Cook told me the ring is given only to the heir to give to *his* bride."

Lady Tangier narrowed her eyes at her maid. "Very well. Perhaps I misunderstood the duke's intentions. Perhaps he gave it to me because he knew he was dying and he wanted me to keep it for his son to give to Eve. Yes, now that I think on it, that is what he said. Of course, as the mother of the Duchess of Easton, I would have a place in society and a very generous allowance."

"When did the duke give you the ring, my lady?"

"It was when we were in his chambers after…well, you know." Lady Tangier's sly look spoke volumes. "He went into his dressing room, and I saw him open a door in the wall between the two rooms. Later, as I was gathering my things, I looked more closely and realized there was a small cupboard cleverly hidden in the wall between the rooms. He had left it unlocked."

Agnes raised a doubtful eyebrow.

"When I looked into the cupboard, I saw this box. I opened it and saw the ring. I had seen it before when it arrived from London. He said it was for his son to give to his intended, but I think it will look better on my own dear Eve's finger, don't you?"

"Will Lady Genevieve go along with your plan?"

"Not unless she thinks it's what Edward wanted, and even then she'll probably need some persuasion."

A knock at the door made Lady Tangier jump. She hid the hand with the ring behind her skirts just as Eve opened the door.

"Mama, I hope I'm not disturbing you. Merton asked me to tell you that his grace requests your presence in his study at half past one. He said he asked

Agnes to tell you, but—oh, there you are, Agnes. Did you give my mother the message from the duke?"

"She did, Eve. I would like you to accompany me to the duke's inquisition. I am still faint with grief, but if the duke insists, I will obey. You need to change, dear. Agnes will help you into your ruby silk."

"But that's an evening gown, Mother. I am happy to go with you, but I don't need to change."

"Must everything be an altercation with you, Genevieve?" Lady Tangier threw herself back down on the chaise, the back of her right hand placed dramatically across her forehead while her left hand stayed out of sight. "I simply do not have the strength to argue with you about every little thing. You will change into the ruby silk gown and have Agnes do your hair— your maid doesn't know how to do all the curls properly. You may stop for me at ten minutes past the hour—I will need time to make my way down to the duke's study."

"But, Mother…"

"That will be *all*, Eve."

As the door closed after Eve, Agnes said, "My lady, you know the ruby silk has yet to be altered. The neckline was too low and showed Lady Eve's—"

"Must *everyone* argue with me? I simply cannot bear it. I am far too fragile for this incessant questioning. As to Eve's gown, as far as I am concerned, necklines can never be too low when one is interested in attracting the attentions of a gentleman. Now, lay out my new gown before you go. It's fortunate that black has ever been my best color. Oh, and, Agnes?"

"Yes, my lady?"

"Until I determine the proper time to tell the duke about his father's last wishes and about the ring, it will be our secret. Do you understand?"

"Yes, my lady."

"You are a treasure, Agnes. It *is* comforting to know that you are privy to my deepest secrets."

Once Agnes had closed the door behind her, Lady Tangier arose from the chaise lounge, followed her maid to the door, and turned the lock. She retrieved the small enameled box from her dressing table and placed the ring back inside. She then proceeded to the wall sconce to the right of the windows that overlooked the formal garden and pushed slightly on the side of its base. A latch clicked, and beside the armoire an almost invisible panel opened to show a dark passageway beyond.

Lady Tangier stepped over the threshold into the passage and felt along the left wall for the small alcove with two shelves. She placed the enameled box on the top shelf, pushing it to the back, then stepped back into her room. Sliding the panel back into place, she heard a quiet click and smiled. She unlocked the door to the hallway and then took her place again at the dressing table in front of the looking glass.

"But not *all* my secrets, Agnes," she whispered to her reflection.

Chapter 18

The new duke signed "Easton" with a flourish, dropped a blob of black wax upon the folded missive, and sat back with a sigh of relief. That was the last of the correspondence needing his personal attention. Jeffries could deal with the rest. He added a letter to Linney to the top of the pile for the post and sighed. He couldn't decide if he was worried or annoyed with his intended and her lack of response.

Avery stood up and opened the French doors to look out across the gardens and the park to the hills beyond. This was what he missed when he was in London—the deep blue sky and that feeling that you could see all the way to the ocean. The storm that had moved in last night as a grand finale to his father's funeral had moved on and given way to a beautiful day—a day in juxtaposition to a house in mourning.

He took a deep breath, letting the clean, fresh air fill his lungs. There were many things he must do here, and the sooner they were accomplished, the sooner he could return to London and to Linney, starting with—"

"Your grace, Lady Tangier is here to see you."

"Send her in."

Seconds later, Merton returned. "Lady Tangier and Lady Genevieve, your grace."

Avery inclined his head as his guests approached. Genevieve curtsied, her ruby gown clashed pleasantly with her red curls, but its inordinately low neckline surprised him with a not unpleasant view of her full and almost totally exposed breasts. Her face flamed as if she could read his thoughts, and she immediately fell into the background as her mother gushed forward.

Lady Tangier's deep curtsy also revealed a rather improper expanse of creamy white skin against her jet-black gown. Considering the purported intensity of her grief, her eyes were amazingly clear, with no evidence of weeping.

"Your grace," said the countess, extending her hand so he could raise her from her bow. "Dear, *dear* Avery. Let me express my very *deepest* sympathies on the passing of your father. Such a great man. Those of us closest to him must cling together in this, our time of great sorrow."

Avery concealed his surprise at how lovely the older woman was—but of course, his father would never be attracted to a plain woman. The black gown she wore was in the very latest style, putting the rather intriguing thought in his head that she'd had it made in advance by a very talented modiste, and not—as she'd told Eve—by the village seamstress.

"Lady Tangier. Lady Genevieve. I thank you for your condolences. Will you sit?"

Eve took a seat near the door while Lady Tangier settled herself in one of the two large, red damask chairs. Avery propped himself against the front of the massive desk that had belonged to many dukes before him and folded his arms across his chest.

Sighing deeply, Lady Tangier touched a finger wrapped in a handkerchief sporting the Easton monogram to one eye. She sniffed and looked up at

Avery from beneath blackened eyelashes. "I apologize for my unseemly show of emotion, your grace, but your father and I were so in love. Of course, as his fiancée, I was constantly at his side since the accident."

"And yet no one was with him when I arrived," observed Avery to no one in particular. "Pardon my curiosity, Lady Tangier, but I had no idea the duke was entertaining guests here at the castle, much less traveling or proposing marriage. I hope you will fill me in on the details. When did you and Lady Genevieve arrive at Terra Bella?"

"We were rescued by your father's hospitality in the third week of May, your grace. My husband, the earl, died a year ago, right after Eastertide—he was much, *much* older than I. When darling Eve and I came out of mourning, I decided to take her to London."

"And what made you stop at Terra Bella on your way?"

"A terrible storm came up just as we were passing though Eastland, and we sought shelter here. Eve said you remembered the time your family gave us refuge once before at Terra Bella, in a snowstorm. You can't imagine how surprised your father was when Eve and I found ourselves again at his mercy."

"I think I have some idea," commented Avery dryly.

"This must all look very odd to you, Avery, dear, but I assure you, it was fate. Your father and I were immediately attracted to each other again—almost as if no time at all had passed since Edward was paying court to me. Of course we had known each other previously. In fact, before he was introduced to your mother, we were quite the item. Marriage was dear

Edward's idea, as was the trip to Scotland. He said he simply couldn't wait for the banns to be called, so he convinced me to elope with him to Gretna Green. He said all we had to do was cross the border into Scotland and say our vows, and then we would be husband and wife till death parted us." Lady Tangier's voice trembled, but she bravely continued.

"We had just crossed the border when my dear Edward suffered an attack of some sort. I wanted to find a doctor to attend him there, but he insisted we turn around and come back to Terra Bella. Before we crossed back into England, we whispered our vows to each other in the carriage. Unfortunately, in his haste to get the duke back to Terra Bella, my driver broke an axle, which caused the carriage to turn over. My driver was killed and your father was seriously injured trying to save me. He gallantly cushioned my fall, and n-now he's gone."

The lady dissolved into tears right before Avery's eyes. As he waited for her to regain some semblance of control, he glanced over and caught a confused look on Eve's face. Was this her first time hearing this explanation as well?

"If it hadn't been for me," Lady Tangier pronounced dramatically, "the duke would still be alive today."

"Well, that does stand to reason," agreed Avery pleasantly. "I doubt he would have taken himself off to Scotland by himself."

"When we returned to Terra Bella, I told the doctor I was sending for you at once. He said it wasn't necessary, but I insisted. I'm so glad I didn't listen to him. You must know, Avery dear, when I sent you that note I truly believed Edward and I were married. Which is why I signed it as I did. In my heart I had pledged to be with your father as his duchess, in sickness and in health, until death—" The lady was simply too emotional to continue.

"Until death parted you, yes, of course. Tell me, Lady Tangier, what made you realize you were not, in fact, the Duchess of Easton?"

"A solicitor I consulted pointed out that the words we vowed to each other were not legally binding, and that I had no marriage lines nor any witnesses."

"A solicitor?" said Avery. "That certainly was an expeditious and rather timely consultation, was it not? And quite prudent of you to accept his opinion. I'm gratified to know that protracted legal proceedings won't be necessary."

The countess narrowed her eyes at Avery. "How dare you speak to me that way! Your father asked me to marry him."

"With all due respect, Lady Tangier, I have only your word on that. Was anyone else privy to that information? Your daughter perhaps?" Avery glanced over at Eve, who made not a sound.

"No," said Lady Tangier quickly. "I never told her. Your father wanted to keep it all a secret. I told my maid, of course, so she could help me pack, but no one else knew."

"I will speak to your maid, but first, explain to me why a man who hasn't left his home in years and who, from all appearances, still mourns his first wife, why he would suddenly decide to marry a woman whom he last saw more than seventeen years ago?" Avery's tone was still pleasant, but unyielding in his quest for information.

Lady Tangier looked away for a minute, and then, with a huge sigh, bravely smiled up at him. "As you are most likely aware, your grace, your father was a man of great…appetites. We had anticipated our vows more than once, and there was some speculation that I might be…" The countess valiantly choked back a sob. "…that I might be carrying his child."

Avery raised both eyebrows to previously unknown heights and smothered a guffaw in a cough as he quickly retreated behind his desk. Was it his imagination or had he heard a similar sound from the direction of Lady Eve? The countess was not ancient and certainly attractive enough, but Avery was fairly sure her childbearing years were behind her. He managed not to smile as he saw Eve hastily bring a handkerchief to her face.

"I trust you have been spared that, uh…inconvenience, my lady?"

"Eve, dear, would you excuse us? I must speak to the duke alone."

"Certainly, Mother." Eve scurried out before anyone could object.

Coward, thought Avery with envy as she closed the door behind her.

Lady Tangier continued her narrative. "It is too early to say with all certainty, your grace, but it certainly would have been no inconvenience—especially if we had been married as your father promised me. Perhaps you would have had a younger brother as handsome as you and your father." The countess began to sob loudly into her handkerchief.

After a moment, Avery pressed on. "Lady Tangier,

I have just one more question for you. Merton says you were present the night the courier from London delivered the Easton engagement ring to my father. I wonder if you have any knowledge of its whereabouts."

"Yes, I *was* there. We were having one of our intimate dinners that Edward so loved when Merton interrupted us because the courier was insisting that your father must sign for receipt of the ring himself. At first I thought he meant to give the ring to me, but then he explained it was actually for you to give to *your* bride. That's when he told me it was his dearest wish to see you put the Easton engagement ring on my darling Eve's finger. I didn't want to tell you this in front of Eve because I know she would be embarrassed, but she and your father had grown quite close over the time of our visit, and he told me more than once that she was like a daughter to him. His very last words to me were, 'Tell Avery I want him to marry Eve.' "

Only years of good manners drilled deeply into his subconscious kept Avery's jaw from dropping open. He tried to comprehend what Lady Tangier was saying. His father wanted him to marry Eve? Avery had told his father of his plans to marry Linney. Was his father afraid his choice of a bride might be as unwise as it was five years ago? Eve was lovely, and Avery certainly enjoyed her company. And, as a titled lady, she was more than a suitable match for him, but she—why was he even entertaining this line of thought?

He was in love with Linney. He loved her and she loved him—at least, he thought she loved him. And he had asked her—well, he had almost asked her—to wait for him so they could be married. All of these thoughts flashed through his head in the seconds that he searched for a response to Lady Tangier.

"I am flattered, my lady. Eve will certainly make someone a wonderful wife, but as my father well knew, I am engaged to marry another."

"I wonder why he never told me of your previous commitment," said Lady Tangier, cocking her head. "When was the official announcement of your betrothal?"

"We have not made an announcement as yet."

"Oh, I see. When did you offer for the young lady?"

"I have not yet made her an offer. I plan to present her with the Easton engagement ring when I ask her to become my wife."

"Oh, so you have spoken only to her father?"

"As I said, I wanted to wait until I had the ring and my father's blessing before presenting my case."

"Oh, dear. And now I've mussed that up, haven't I? Telling you that your father wanted you to marry Eve and not some girl you met in London. Is she very well connected? Perhaps I know of her family."

"With all due respect, Lady Tangier, my choice of fiancée is none of your concern."

"Oh, but it is, your grace. As I am the only one to whom your poor, dearly departed father made his last wishes known, I feel obliged to do all I can to make sure they are carried out." She rose from her chair, and Avery instinctively came to his feet.

"I won't take any more of your time now, your grace. I know how overwhelming all this has been for you and how difficult it must be for you to try and fill your father's shoes."

Smiling, and after only the very briefest of curtsies,

Lady Tangier turned and gracefully departed, leaving Avery stunned and—he admitted it—more than a little impressed with how smoothly she'd turned the tables and maneuvered her way into his father's affairs...and his own. He inclined his head in mock salute to the departing countess. He'd do well not to underestimate her again.

Chapter 19

"Mary said you wanted to see me, Mother?"

"What in the world is all that ruckus, Linney? I can hear you banging around up there from everywhere in the house. What are you doing?"

"I was just drawing," said Linney.

Lady Thea raised both eyebrows. "Drawing makes all that noise?"

"I was going to draw, but I couldn't find the sketch I'd been working on. I thought I'd see if it was in with my other sketches in those boxes under my bed—that may have been the dragging noises you heard."

"And the banging that sounded like you were slamming doors and drawers in every room in the house?"

"Well, when I was looking for the drawing, I remembered I needed the measurements that were in the pocket of a dress I wore last week. I couldn't remember which dress, so I had to look through my entire wardrobe."

"Did you at least find what you were looking for?"

"No, because about half way through I remembered I'd shown the numbers to Papa in his study, and he wanted to double-check them with his client because he thought a few of them were off."

"Your father isn't home."

Linney sighed. "Yes, I know. So then I thought I'd

154

look at some of the art books I borrowed from Papa's study. Vivian wants me to do a mural, you see, and I've never done one before, so I had taken several up to my room to read, and they fell off my bed when I was looking for my sketch, and—"

"That's enough, Linea. You're going to put us all in Bedlam. You must have patience, child. If Lord Hammond—pardon me—if the Duke of Easton is going to write, then he will write when he can. And if he doesn't write…well, then you must accept the fact that he sees this as a friendship between the two of you and nothing more than a casual flirtation. Nonetheless, this behavior of yours is not helping anything."

"But, Mother, I—"

"No 'buts,' Linea. Here. I want you to deliver this to Madame Augustine for me."

"Can't you send Edie?"

"I could, but Edie isn't the one disrupting the entire household. You need to get out. Take Mary with you and come back home through the park. It's a lovely day and the fresh air will do you good. No. Don't say anything, just go."

With an annoyed look at her mother and an exaggerated sigh, Linney took the note for Madame Augustine and slowly walked out of the room. She was only mildly surprised to see Thomson in the front hall already holding her pelisse and Mary beside him holding Linney's gloves and bonnet, her own cape already about her shoulders.

"Fine. I'm going," muttered Linney, donning the outerwear and heading out into the sunshine. "See that you keep up with me, Mary. I'll not spend all day doing this, and I'm not waiting for you."

Setting a pace that would tax most ladies and not a few gentlemen, Linney proceeded up Sudbury Street toward the center of town and Madame Augustine's fashionable business establishment. She was mildly surprised when, with Mary panting several feet behind her, she entered the shop and found it completely empty.

"Good morning," she called toward the muted conversations coming from behind the curtains at the back of the store. "Madame Augustine?"

An elegantly coiffed head appeared, quickly followed by the rest of London's most popular dressmaker. "Mademoiselle Braddock, *bienvenue!* Welcome! I was unaware we had an appointment today, but I am always happy to see you in my shop. How may I be of service?"

"You're right, Madame. I don't have an appointment. My mother asked me to deliver this message to you about her gown. I believe it says she has decided on the straw-colored jacquard."

"*Très bonne!* That color suits your mother beautifully. Would you care to look at some swatches for a new gown for yourself while you are here, mademoiselle? There are several new patterned silks that just came in. The colors are quite lovely. There is an exquisite ice blue that would be *très chic* on you."

"I believe I will, Madame Augustine. Thank you."

Linney wandered to the big picture window where Madame Augustine's fashion dolls sported the latest French designs in a rainbow of colors and a variety of luxurious fabrics. One of the dolls was dressed as a young boy in a bright blue taffeta suit with dark blue buttons and a white, lace-trimmed collar.

"Oh, this is darling," cried Linney. "I never realized you also made clothes for children, Madame. My cousin is in anticipation of a happy event, so I seem to be far more aware of things for babies and children than I ever was before. The poor things, though. How are they to play without spoiling such splendid outfits?"

"This ensemble would be for a special occasion where the young gentleman would be expected to be on his best behavior." Mme. Augustine smiled broadly and gestured toward the back of the shop behind the curtains where a display of small shirts and trousers could be seen. "The suits for daily wear, I keep in the back. Boys need plain, sturdy clothes if they are to make noise and get dirty."

Linney smiled at the woman. "That sounds like advice from an older sister."

"*Mais, oui!* A sister who was in charge of the laundry as well. I have one sister who is older and six younger brothers who made a great deal of noise and were always making messes and getting in trouble."

"Six? My goodness! You must have had a glorious time. I was an only child. I was quite lonely until my cousin Vivian came to live with us. Even so, I always longed for brothers—although six might have been too many. Might I have a sample of this silk to take back and show Mama? The design in the weave is unlike anything I've seen before."

"It would make an elegant ball gown for you, mademoiselle, and would be lovely with your coloring." Mme. Augustine snipped a sample of the clear, ice-blue fabric and handed it to Linney.

After chatting for a few more moments and setting a time with Mme. Augustine for her mother's first fitting, Linney stepped outside. She smiled at Mary's still-red face and began a more leisurely return through the park per her mother's suggestion. It *was* a beautiful day—a rarity in London—and her mother was right, the fresh air would do her good. But her mother *wasn't* right about Avery.

If only there was a way for her to see Avery, talk to him. If she could only—

"Linney? It *is* you! I told you I was right, Gordon."

"Miss Braddock. You are looking quite lovely this afternoon."

He always said it with such surprise, thought Linney. Only Gordon could deliver a compliment that felt like a slight. She pasted on the requisite smile.

"Good afternoon, Nadine. Mr. Bateman-Jones." Linney curtseyed and smiled to Gordon and his sister.

"I did not see you at Lady Fitzrobin's ball on Saturday night, Linney, dear," said Nadine. "Have you been unwell? You do look a little peaked."

Normally, Linney would engage and counter Nadine's snide remark with a spirited retort. But today she was feeling quite vulnerable. "We just arrived back from celebrating my cousin's wedding at Haversham House, so I was unable to attend."

Linney was not herself, but she was also not so fatigued that she couldn't make the point that neither Nadine nor her brother had been invited to the Duke of Whitley's nuptials.

"Oh, that's right. I remember now. Maribel told me all about it. She said Lord Hammond left the gathering rather early. Did you see him there?"

"He's the Duke of Easton now, Nadine," corrected Gordon.

"*I* know that, silly! I thought perhaps *Linney* might not understand, what with her father being just a solicitor and all."

Nadine turned to Linney and spoke slowly as if to a small child. "You see, dear, when his father died, Lord Hammond became the Duke of Easton."

"Yes, thank you, Nadine. I am aware." Linney's words were equally slow and very frosty. "Absence of a title doesn't mean ignorance, just as the presence of a title is no guarantee of intelligence, as I'm sure you are well aware. Are you out shopping?"

Although momentarily distracted trying to parse Linney's pointed response, Nadine quickly regrouped.

"We are. Gordon insisted I go with him to his tailor to see the fabric he selected for his new waistcoat, and, of course, I needed some black trim for my handkerchiefs."

"Black trim?"

Nadine simpered and traded secret smiles with her brother.

"I wanted to show my respect for the late duke, of course. Our families have known each other for *years*, and Lord Hammond—pardon me, the *duke*—and I have always been quite close. Now that he is responsible for the succession, he is certain to marry as soon as the official mourning period is over, and he will need a real lady to be his duchess."

"Perhaps the daughter of an earl and sister of a viscount?" chimed in Gordon with a smug smile.

"Oh, you!" protested Nadine with a high-pitched giggle, but she smiled as she resumed her conversation with Linney.

"Of course, there is nothing official, but the duke's

fiancée would be expected to express her sympathy in some way—like trimming her handkerchiefs in black. Don't you agree?"

Later, Linney would wonder what on earth had come over her. Perhaps it was all the frustrations of the day coming together to form some kind of cosmic burr under her saddle. Perhaps it wasn't earthly at all and simply the result of the devil at work. Whatever it was, it proceeded to take over her mouth and dispel her good sense.

Leaning in, and whispering so only Nadine and Gordon could hear, she said, "I have it on very good authority that the new duke will be wed next month. He is secretly betrothed even at this very moment. My cousin recently married his brother, you know."

It was worth all the flames of potential damnation to see Nadine's jaw go slack and to watch her grab her brother's arm in a sort of wounded hissy-fit.

"Well! I *never* pay attention to gossip, Miss Braddock, and I would counsel you to do the same. Good day."

Unfortunately, Linney's moment of triumph was fleeting.

What had she done now? Nadine was right. Avery needed a real lady to be his duchess. He would never marry such an immature, spiteful child as herself even if he had told her he loved her. And there she was, back at the beginning of her circle of thoughts and going absolutely nowhere. She waited to cross the street while two hackney cabs and a mail coach rumbled down the street in front of her.

"That's it!" Linney stopped so suddenly that Mary almost ran into her. "I need to stop going *nowhere*, which means I must start going *somewhere*."

"I beg your pardon, miss?"

A vision of the boys' clothes in Madame Augustine's shop popped into her head—along with the beginnings of a plan. If Avery was unable to write to her, it only proved that he needed her now more than ever. She would go to Terra Bella and find him and ask him in person why he had not written. It was a brilliant idea, and as it grew in her mind, Linney watched the details fill in just as they did in her drawings—brick by brick, wall by wall, tree by tree.

Putting her chin up as she did when she was about to do something she probably shouldn't, Linney started walking again, this time her head full of logistics for her new plan. A lady could not go off unescorted to call on a gentleman at his country home, but a lad carrying a message to that gentleman would raise no eyebrows at all. Nothing could be easier. She would take the mail coach to Terra Bella—the post must get delivered there somehow—and it was only a two-day journey from London. All she had to do was stay in disguise until then. She could deliver her message and, at the end of it all—in only two days—she would explain everything to Avery as he held her in his arms.

And this time, whether there was an engagement ring or not, she would insist that he ask her to marry him. She was very tired of waiting.

Chapter 20

"Has the duke retired to his rooms yet, Agnes?"

"No, my lady. I saw a footman leave the library with several dishes not a half hour ago. I believe his grace is reading and enjoying a brandy before retiring."

"Excellent. Please tell Lady Genevieve I must speak with her."

"Lady Eve has already retired for the evening, my lady."

"Then you'll need to wake her up."

"Of course, my lady."

Several minutes later, a sleepy Eve in a hastily donned flowered wrapper and matching slippers stumbled into the room. "Agnes said you needed me, Mama. Are you ill?"

"No, darling, I'm fine, but I cannot sleep, and I would like you to go to the duke's library and select a book for me to read."

A sleepy silence filled the room until Lady Tangier wondered if her daughter had fallen asleep on her feet. "Eve? Did you hear what I said?"

"Yes, Mother, I heard you. I'm just having a difficult time understanding why you told Agnes to wake me."

"I told you, dear. I seem to have a bit of insomnia and cannot sleep. I thought I would try reading for a while."

"Yes, I *heard* you, Mother. I just don't understand. Why don't you go down to the library yourself? Or send Agnes? I am in my night clothes, and I was asleep."

"Yes, I know. That's why I told Agnes to wake you up. I certainly cannot go traipsing around the castle while I am prostrate with grief, and Agnes doesn't know what I like to read."

"Do you really expect me to get dressed, go down to the library, and—"

"There's no need for you to change, Eve, don't be silly. You have on your wrapper. Just go."

"Do you even *like* to read, Mother? I don't know what books you like to read any more than Agnes. I can't—"

"Eve, stop arguing with me and just go! Fetch me a book that *you* would enjoy. Anything that will let me stop thinking about my dear, departed Edward. Agnes is busy preparing a tisane for my headache."

Eve sighed. Shaking her head, she turned and closed the door behind her.

"If the duke has inherited any of the same urges that drove his father, seeing Eve practically naked in that filmy nightgown should arouse those desires," said the countess after Eve left. "Watch the clock, Agnes, and in twenty-five minutes go down to the library so you can bear witness to the scandal of my virginal, unmarried daughter in her night clothes, in the library, alone, late at night, in the company of a man who has the reputation of a rake."

****

"Oh, your grace, I do beg your pardon. I did not know anyone was in here."

Avery rose as Eve blurted out her greeting. "I'm so sorry to disturb you, your grace. My mother sent me down for a book."

"You're not disturbing me, Eve. Please come in."

Avery removed the spectacles he used for reading and motioned Eve to a chair before the fire as he resumed his own seat. "Please sit down. A fire would not seem to be needed in the middle of the summer, but I forget how damp these old rooms can be. Might I offer you refreshment? I can ring for tea, if you like."

"Oh, no, your grace, thank you. I'll only be a moment."

"I thought you had agreed to call me Avery—with the r's pronounced correctly, of course." He smiled, remembering Eve's confession about her early speech impediment.

Eve returned his smile. "Yes, that's right, I did. Is Avery a family name?"

"Word is that it belonged to a pirate—at least that's what my mother told me when I objected to the name at a rather young age."

"It seems so long ago when we were all playing here together. This is your mother's favorite chair, isn't it? I remember your father pretending to be dismayed when she had it brought in. He said it was too—"

" '—too feminine for my library,' " finished Avery in an exaggerated voice. He chuckled. "Mother just laughed and told him the library belonged to both of them, and then she had the footman bring in a side table as well. I think my father was often struck dumb when she made her pronouncements. I used to think it was because he was angry at her, but now I understand it was because he was so in love with her. I feel the same about the woman I plan to marry."

"Oh, that's right, your father mentioned you were seeing a young lady in London, but I didn't realize you were actually betrothed. That's lovely! May I offer my congratulations? What is her name?"

"Miss Linea Braddock. We're not officially betrothed as of yet, but thank you. You remind me a little bit of her."

Eve smiled. "Another redhead?"

Avery laughed. "Actually, she doesn't look anything at all like you, even though you are both quite beautiful. She has white-blonde hair and hazel eyes that change with her mood. She is an extremely talented artist. She is also loquacious and very opinionated—a characteristic that I suspect the two of you share. Am I correct?"

"I will not deny that," said Eve, kicking off her slippers and tucking her toes up under the satin wrapper. "Tell me how you met."

"I insulted her friend, and she took me to task for it in the middle of Hyde Park during the social hour. It was quite the item of gossip for some time. I eventually convinced her that I was not the horrible person I first appeared to be, and she forgave me—out of pity, I suspect, but I gladly accepted it."

"That's very romantic," sighed Eve.

"It was blackmail, plain and simple, on my part," said Avery. "I vowed to remain in her mother's parlor until she accepted my apology."

"But she did forgive you, and that's all that matters, is it not? It sounds as if you love her very much. May I ask why you are not officially engaged to marry? Does she still have doubts? Or is it you?"

Avery laughed. "I like that about you, Eve. You don't stand on ceremony or spend time on small talk. My Linney is like that. She wastes no time getting right to the heart of things. No, I don't have any doubts nor does she—at least none that I'm aware of. It's my own stubbornness that's preventing me from formally asking her to be my wife. I wanted to give her the family engagement ring when I proposed, but since it was here with my father, I couldn't ask her to marry me until I came to Terra Bella and procured the ring and…well, you know the rest."

"Oh, Avery, I'm sorry. This was supposed to be a happy journey for you and instead it has turned into a nightmare."

"Thank you. It is not the trip I'd imagined, I agree."

"Is Miss Braddock a good correspondent? I should think the letters between the two of you would be of great comfort."

Avery paused for a long minute. "She hasn't written."

"Oh, of course. A lady would never write to you first. She is waiting to reply to a letter from you. You should write to her at once. I'm sure she is longing to hear from you."

Avery looked down at the book he still held in his hand, the book he had chosen to help him take his mind off the fact that Linney had not replied to any of his letters or messages of love.

"I've written her five times," he said abruptly, "and she hasn't written back."

"Nothing?" asked Eve, doing a poor job of hiding her disbelief.

"Nothing."

"Is she traveling? Could the posts have been delayed or lost?"

"No, and my brother was here for the funeral and told me that his wife, Linea's cousin, had received several communications from her this past week."

"Well, I'm sure there is some explanation. What did she say when you told her you were leaving to come here?"

"Well, there's the thing." Avery put his book on the table beside him and rubbed his eyes. He leaned forward, resting his forearms on his knees. "You see, we'd had a bit of a quarrel because she said she'd received no actual offer of marriage from me..."

"Which is true, is it not?"

"Yes, but we did have an understanding—at least I thought we did."

"Is it possible that you might have had more of an understanding than she?"

Eve was silent as Avery frantically thought back over the most recent conversations he'd shared with Linney. Every time he reran their last encounter, he became more and more unsure. *Had* he correctly interpreted Linney's words and feelings?

After a few moments of silence, Eve gently asked, "Were there other marriage proposals she was considering?"

"I'm sure there were. Everyone wanted to be with her. She could have her pick from a number of eligible suitors." There was despair in his voice as he put his head in his hands. "Oh, my God, Eve, what if she falls in love with someone else while I'm away? What if she is trying to send me a signal by not writing? What if she no longer loves me?"

Eve didn't respond but immediately crossed the room to comfort her friend. Kneeling before Avery, she leaned forward to pat his shoulder.

"What is your heart telling you? Does that sound like something Linney would do? You said she was direct and forthcoming. Do you think she would be anything else in her dealings with you? From what you've just told me, I rather suspect that if she were no longer interested in marrying you, she would have no qualms about letting you know."

The door to the library opened on the tableau of Eve in her nightgown kneeling in the vee of Avery's spread legs. "Oh, pardon me, your grace," said Agnes, "I did not mean to interrupt. I... Lady Eve! Your mother was afraid you had come to some harm. Shall I... What shall I tell her, my lady?"

"Leave us," commanded Avery, coming to his feet and too late realizing what this moment of comfort might suggest to an onlooker. The door closed, and he looked down at Eve's innocent face as she sat back on her heels. "Eve, I'm sorry. I should not have allowed you to be here alone with me. It's not proper."

Light dawned in Eve's eyes, and she quickly got to her feet, pulling her wrapper tightly around her. Stepping into her discarded slippers, she said, "Don't be silly, Avery. I'm the one who should apologize. I invaded your privacy. No one could possibly think anything else. Please don't worry. I will explain everything to my mother. And now, I have imposed on you too long. Let me get a book, and I'll leave you to your brandy."

"Thank you, Eve. Thank you for your kind words

and for your understanding. Do you need me to light you to your room?"

"No. No, thank you. I can find my way." Flustered, Eve pulled out a book and smiled at the lengthy title of the tome. "This should do the job of putting my mother to sleep. Good night, your grace…Avery."

She headed toward the library door but stopped after opening it and turned back to face the duke.

"Keep writing to her, Avery. Keep writing to your Linney. Find out what's going on and why she hasn't answered your letters. You should have the woman you love by your side as you mourn your father."

Avery watched the door close. He understood why his father had played host for so long. Eve was so easy to talk to and—even though he'd been foolish to entertain her alone in the library—she made him feel better. Her husband would be a very lucky man. Just for a moment, Avery flashed on how it would feel to be that lucky man instead of being racked with uncertainty about the woman he loved.

He sighed and determinedly turned back to his book.

Chapter 21

Linney's first mistake was leaving by the front door instead of using the servant's entrance.

Really…she had to focus. She couldn't afford to make more errors like that. Her very reputation depended on it. She breathed a great deal easier when she attained street level without notice from Thomson or any of the other servants.

Patting the pocket that held the sheathed knife Vivian always insisted she carry whenever they were out on an adventure, Linney called on her best efforts to imitate the slump of a fourteen-year-old youth—even scuffing her shoes on the cobblestones in front of the house for good measure. Four blocks farther and she could hail a hackney cab to take her to the inn at the edge of town where the Birmingham-bound mail coach started its route.

Oh, how she missed Vivian! This was exactly the kind of exploit her cousin would adore. Nowadays, whenever she went out, she was forced to take Mary with her—Mary, whose idea of a grand adventure was a new tea cozy. Just last week, when Linney wanted to see the exhibit of the classical Greek marbles donated by Lord Elgin to the British Museum, the whole outing turned into an enormous undertaking, with her mother insisting she take the carriage—and her maid—even though the museum was only eight blocks away.

Linney grinned in spite of her qualms. The next few days would be like heaven. Mary's younger brother was just the right size, and after many threats, much cajoling, and the promise of several days off, Mary produced not one but two suits of clothes, as well as strips of cloth to bind Linney's full breasts. Mary's older brother provided directions detailing where the mail coaches stopped and the best place to spend the night. She had plenty of money for tickets and for the inn, and had given Mary a message to send to Vivian that explained everything.

That last bit—leaving it to Vivian to pass on the explanation of her absence to her parents—was actually one of her more brilliant ideas.

Freedom and adventure beckoned. With a skip of excitement, she turned the corner, whistling like Avery had taught her—scandalous behavior for Miss Linea Braddock, but all very aboveboard for Linden, the fourteen-year-old under-footman from the Braddock household on his way to visit his sister in Eastland.

****

Linney's second mistake was riding *inside* the coach.

She should have taken into consideration that the advice to procure an inside seat came from a woman with the soul of a tea cozy. She would have vastly preferred the rushing wind, fresh air, and breathtaking views to be had from the top of the carriage. Unfortunately, with window seats at a premium, Linney was stuck between a rather plump elderly man in an ill-fitting suit and a grim, angular woman who was either on her way to be tortured or about to take a position as second chambermaid to Napoleon himself.

As a result of Mary's advice, Linney's first-ever view of the environs north of London—from the Blackbird Inn where she boarded the coach on the outskirts of London to the first stop—looked a great deal like the floor of a mail coach.

Against all odds, she napped. The day had started early that morning, and Linney had slept little the night before, so it was understandable that when the excitement of the journey waned a bit, the stuffy interior and constant motion of the coach would have her dozing, with only a few reflexes awake enough to keep her from sliding off the worn seat.

Four hours later, the driver stopped to change horses, and Linney followed the slow progress of the elderly man beside her as he painstakingly fumbled his way down the steps of the coach, only to realize he'd forgotten his hat and then a worn Bible on the seat inside. Linney retrieved first one and then the other for him, for which he thanked her profusely, vigorously shaking her hand and clapping her on the back. She bid the man good day at last and found her way to the necessary. Upon her return, she took the opportunity to claim an up-top seat and pulled out the bundle of bread and cheese Mary had procured from the kitchen.

As the coach departed on its next leg, Linney watched the people and scenery around her. Just before the carriage rounded a curve, she saw the elderly man from the coach walking quite sprightly into the local ale house. Chuckling at his obvious ruse, she proceeded to tuck herself between two relatively soft bundles and fall fast asleep.

****

"You there! Throw down those bags."

Linney awoke with a start—stiff and confused until her morning adventures came rushing back to her. She crawled to the edge of the coach and saw an irate coachman gesturing at her makeshift bed. She obediently picked up the first bundle and dropped it over the side. Standing, she grabbed the second bundle and hefted it over the side as well, belatedly hoping the driver was paying attention.

"Now you."

"I beg your pardon?"

The coachman was waving toward the building behind him. "Aye, this is where you get off. Your ticket won't take you no farther with me."

Mary's brother's directions said the mail coach stopped at the Dog and Pony Inn, which was where she was to catch the morning coach north to Eastland. Linney glanced around and saw a sign over the door of the building showing a small horse with a dog on its back.

Climbing down the side of the coach, she marveled again at the freedom afforded young men in breeches. No wonder ladies were prohibited from doing all manner of things—imagine climbing to the top of a coach in two petticoats, a corset, and an overskirt. Just for good measure, she jumped the last four feet to the ground—and landed on her bottom.

"Here now, don't be hurting yourself on my watch," said the driver as he pulled her to her feet and dusted off her bottom.

Startled by the informal gesture, Linney blinked and blurted out, "Thank you," in a voice that was entirely too feminine. The man gave her an odd look, glanced at the cap that covered less of her hair than it should have and then stared at her chest.

Linney pulled her coat more tightly around her and thrust her hands in her pockets. She turned her back on the driver and started whistling as she made her way to the front door of the Dog and Pony Inn. She was looking forward to a hot meal and a pleasant night's rest before catching the morning mail coach. Maybe she would even request a soaking bath.

****

The third mistake was not really her fault at all.

Everything had gone exactly to plan—except the part where the little purse containing her money for a room and hot meal at the Dog and Pony Inn disappeared.

Or was taken.

Linney remembered her nap beside the seemingly elderly man in the coach with the Bible. She remembered the forgotten items that had her running up and down the coach steps as the old man disembarked, and the way he shook her hand and patted her on the back. Her shoulders slumped as she remembered watching the man trot briskly into the ale house.

How naïve she was…how gullible. Now she was at the inn with no money, no ticket, and no way to get to Avery. With no other choice in sight, Linney walked through the doorway and into the front room of the inn. A cheerful but tired-looking woman looked up from a ledger.

"May I help you?"

Suddenly all of Linney's bravado was gone. It took every bit of her determination just to keep her tears at bay.

"Someone stole my money," she blurted out. "And

174

now I can't buy my ticket for the rest of my journey or pay for a room to spend the night."

"Let me guess," said the woman coming to stand behind the reception desk. "There was a heavy-set old man on the coach who got off at the stop right before this one. He forgot his hat and his cane in the carriage and you retrieved it for him. He was very grateful, and he shook your hand and patted your shoulder as he thanked you."

Linney was astonished. "Yes! Except it was a Bible instead of a cane. How did you know?"

The woman—the innkeeper's wife, judging by the way she called orders in the general direction of the kitchen—laughed not unkindly and shook her head.

"That's Arvid." She crossed her arms over her chest and leaned against the counter. "Every week or so he finds his way onto a mail coach and picks the pockets of unsuspecting travelers, like you. He's like smoke—he vanishes into thin air. Nobody knows exactly where he lives, and he never gets caught."

The innkeeper's wife looked Linney over from tip to toe. "I suppose you can sleep in the barn. It's not too cold at night. Two nights and meals in exchange for two days of chores. My eldest boy is hurt, and my husband could use the help."

"That would be wonderful. I can…well, I'm sure you'll tell me what needs to be done. Thank you, Mrs…?"

"I'm Mrs. Pearson. Go and put your things in the barn, and I'll tell Mr. Pearson you're here."

"Thank you, Mrs. Pearson. I am truly grateful."

"Go on with you now."

Mrs. Pearson turned back to her work as Linney

exited the inn and walked toward the barn. A man came up quietly behind Mrs. Pearson and placed a kiss on the back of her neck. She looked up and him and smiled.

"Another one, my dear? Are you running a home for runaways?"

"That one ran across Arvid on the coach, poor thing," said Mrs. Pearson shaking her head.

"Maybe it would be easier for us to hire Arvid. Then he and his brothers wouldn't keep pickpocketing the travelers."

"You tried that once, remember?"

The man sighed. "Yes, I do, and you were right. He prefers to pick pockets."

Mr. Pearson kissed his wife again. "I'm off, then, putting your charity cases to work. If you do decide to open that home, you might also consider opening a school for them. Your first lesson should be 'How to act when dressed as a boy.' "

Mrs. Pearson chuckled as she waved her husband away and went back to her books.

Chapter 22

Avery hadn't slept well, and the morning ride that usually put him in high spirits was more of an ordeal than a pleasure.

He'd dreamed about Linney. Again. And he'd awakened with a fierce erection and an overwhelming sense of loss. He'd tended to the former as best he could, but the feeling that he had lost his true love lingered.

Thus this punishing ride across Easton lands in an unseasonably chilly mist.

Linney had not responded to any of his letters, and he was past being worried—Whit confirmed she was well, and just yesterday he'd received a note from Charlotte saying she planned to call on Linney and her mother for tea. Now he was just confused. And angry. If silence was her way of telling him she wanted to end their relationship, then, by God, he wouldn't stand in her way. He urged his horse forward at an even faster speed.

His aunt would most likely spend the entire visit with Linney and her mother talking about wedding preparations and whom to invite. He wondered what Linney's response would be. Would she be embarrassed because his aunt still assumed they planned to marry? He hoped so, damn it. He hoped she was horribly embarrassed. It served her right. Let *her* be the one to tell Charlotte there would be no wedding. Let *her* explain what he could not.

Avery pulled up atop the rise that flanked the village to give his mount a chance to rest. Looking back across the valley, he took a deep breath of the fresh air, willing his own heart to stop racing.

He hated the uncertainty. Eve had encouraged him to keep writing to Linney, but was there any point to that? She was simply trying to be supportive as she had since his father died. Eve provided him with comfort even if Linney did not. His own intended was probably too busy entertaining other suitors who were more conveniently available.

Frustrated all over again, Avery turned his horse and started down the road toward the castle. He would cut over to the bridle path that led to the open fields and have one more hard gallop before returning. But as he rounded the curve, he saw a familiar figure on the road before him. What in the world was Eve doing out in this weather?

"Hullo," he called, waving his arm. "This isn't walking weather, Eve. Give me your hand and I'll take you up."

"Thank you, your grace. I would appreciate the ride."

Avery easily pulled her up in front of him, catching a whiff of citrus as she clutched at his neck for a moment to keep her balance. His arm circled her waist to steady her.

"The morning started out fine," she said, "but you're correct—it's no longer weather for walking. I only hope your dignity allows you to be seen in the company of such a harridan as myself. I was playing

Drop Handkerchief with the Greenleigh children after their lessons, and they teamed up against me. I'm sure I look a sight. Promise me you won't tell anyone how disheveled you found me. You can just say that you gave a ride to a daft woman out in the weather without a wrap."

Eve's laugh was contagious and made everyone— even him—want to join in. He'd be lying if he denied being attracted to her on some level.

"Being a gentleman, I wasn't going to say anything," he demurred, "but you do look as if you were on the losing side of the skirmish."

"If not for you, I expect I would also soon be soaked to the skin."

"It's rather a long walk on the road, but fortunately it's a quick ride across the fields. Are you settled?" asked Avery, bending his head to hear her answer.

Eve turned her head to reply just as he leaned down, and for a second his lips were a mere hair's breadth from hers.

"Yes—oh, I do beg your pardon, your grace," she said, laughing and quickly turning to face the front. "I'm surprised Mrs. Greenleigh didn't send you home in their pony cart."

"She did offer, but I've never driven one by myself, and I knew she didn't have time to take me, so I insisted I wanted to walk. Which I did—at least at first. I have to say I'm very glad you came along when you did."

"We'll cut through at the next cottage and be home before the rain starts in earnest." Avery hesitated for a scant second. "Actually, let's cut through at the cottage after that. This next one belongs to Widow Daley, who holds the title of town gossip. I try to avoid her and her front window whenever possible."

"Oh, yes, your father mentioned her to me, although I didn't know where she lived. The duke told me if there was ever anything I wanted the entire town to know, I should tell the Widow Daley and then pledge her to secrecy."

Avery laughed. "That sounds about right."

Eve chatted for the remainder of the ride back to Terra Bella, and more than once Avery thought about the good fortune that awaited the man who claimed her for his own. It was only after he and Eve parted ways that he realized the thing that attracted him most to Eve was how very much she reminded him of Linney.

He scowled as he handed off his reins to the stable boy and stalked toward the house. Eve deserved to have a man who loved her, but he was not that man. All of a sudden he remembered his conversation with Linney in Lady Haversham's rose garden, when he'd told her he wanted the kind of love and marriage that Whit and Vivian had. The kind his father and mother had. Was that no longer true? Was he simply giving up on that dream?

Avery nodded at the footman who opened the door for him, and stopped to check the incoming mail on the table in the great hall. Nothing from Linney.

So be it, but he wasn't giving up without a fight. He needed a plan, but first he needed to find that damn ring.

****

"You're right, Mrs. Daley. That *is* Lady Eve with his grace. What is she doing out so early, I wonder?"

"She often visits the Greenleigh children,"

confirmed Mrs. Daley to her guest. "I heard Lady Eve was teaching them to read. A waste of time, if you ask me—especially for the youngest. Not the sharpest knife in the drawer, if you know what I mean. Would you care for tea, Miss Horton?"

"Perhaps just a quick cup, and do call me Agnes. Lady Tangier will be abed for several hours yet, so I'm not needed back until then."

"Thank you for bringing me that sewing, Miss...uh, Agnes. I'll send it up to the castle just as soon as I finish. Most likely the end of the week, but maybe sooner. Now that Mr. Daley is gone, I have more time to myself. I like to sit here by the window to do my sewing—especially the fancywork. The light is good, and I can keep up with the comings and goings about town."

"There aren't many other people about at this time—and in this weather. I was surprised to see his grace."

"His grace always rides early, and Lady Eve seems to favor early mornings as well. Lady Eve doesn't ride, does she?"

"No. She knows how, of course, but she had an accident a few years ago and no longer enjoys it as she did before." Agnes took a sip of her tea. "You don't suppose the new duke and Lady Eve are...meeting, do you?"

Widow Daley's eyes lit up. "Now that you mention it, she did look quite cozy up there on his horse—him holding her close and all. But I thought you said his grace had a young lady in London. Do you think he's changed his mind and has set his sights on Lady Eve?"

"I don't know, but I certainly hope his intentions

are honorable." Agnes leaned closer to her hostess. "Last night when I went down to get Lady Tangier a book from the library, the two of them were in there all alone, and her wearing only a thin nightgown. His legs were spread wide and she was kneeling between them. I think we both know what was happening there. I trust you can keep a secret, Mrs. Daley. If it got out that Eve and the duke were... Well, her reputation would be beyond repair—unless, of course, his grace did the honorable thing and offered for her."

"It's certainly a good thing it was you who saw them and not one of the other servants who might not be so discreet." Mrs. Daley sniffed. "Men are so predictable, aren't they? And it's always the woman who suffers—never the man. Both his grace and his father had well-deserved reputations for... Well, let's just say between the two of them, they've sowed plenty of wild oats."

"You must promise not to breathe a word of this to a single soul," implored Agnes. "I'll let Lady Tangier know what's going on with her daughter before it's too late."

Mrs. Daley's eyes glowed. "I understand, Miss Horton—Agnes. Mum's the word. Poor Lady Eve."

Chapter 23

"You wished to speak with me, Avery?"

Lady Tangier used the informal address without his permission and didn't even pretend to curtsy. He frowned. He was growing weary of her games.

"You may refer to me as Your Grace, Lady Tangier. I have summoned you here because I believe you are in possession of a family heirloom. As you are not and will never be a part of this family, I must insist you return the Easton engagement ring to me at once."

"Avery, dear—your grace—you wound me," said Lady Tangier, one hand dramatically covering her heart. "If I were holding such a valuable item, surely I would have returned it to you upon your father's death. Yes, your father and I were engaged, but he did not give me the ring. He merely showed it to me when it arrived from London, and expressed his hope that you would put it on my darling Eve's finger and take her for your duchess."

The countess dropped her voice to an intimate whisper that implied shared confidences. "He told me he was very concerned about your choice of a bride, Avery—your grace. A young lady without a title and only a small dowry? He worried this might be another one of your bad decisions, like Lady Layton."

Ignoring the flash of betrayal he felt upon hearing his father had shared family matters with this woman,

Avery spoke evenly. "With all due respect, Lady Tangier, neither my current nor my former affairs are any concern of yours. Do you or do you not have the Easton engagement ring in your possession?"

"I told you the ring is not in my possession…your grace."

The lady bowed her head slightly, breaking eye contact. Avery knew she was lying.

"I don't know who told you otherwise," she said silkily, "but it was obviously a mistake or said with the intention of slandering me."

Avery spoke in the same ducal tone he'd heard his father use on so many occasions. "Lady Tangier, the Easton engagement ring is missing, and it is my opinion that you know its whereabouts. Olsen said the ring was in the cupboard in my father's dressing room on the night that you and he…that he…had relations with you. The ring is now missing. No one else, other than Olsen, had access to it. If the ring is brought to me within twenty-four hours, I will not pursue charges. However, if it is not in my possession by this time tomorrow, I will be forced to call in the magistrate and turn the entire matter over to him. Do you understand?"

Lady Tangier glared up at him, her fury barely contained. He had no idea how she would respond to his decree. Would she burst into tears? Fly at him like a mad woman? Throw the closest *objects d'art*? Maybe she would pack her bags and leave.

"Will that be all, your grace?" Ice was not colder than the lady's response.

"That will be all, Lady Tangier."

After making the very slightest of curtsies, Lady Tangier turned and walked quickly out of the room, slamming the door behind her.

Avery expelled the breath he had not realized he was holding, and took another. The clock in the hall chimed eleven o'clock. Bloody hell! He was late for a meeting with his steward, and it was too damn early for a whiskey.

Chapter 24

"*Marry* him? Whatever are you talking about, Mother? Avery—the duke—is all but engaged to Miss Braddock in London."

"According to Agnes, it is all over town that you and the duke are involved in an affair, Eve. Your reputation is ruined, so don't tell me you want no part of this plan. He owes you this. He has compromised your virtue—no other man will marry you. He must do the honorable thing."

"I don't know what you're talking about. Avery and I are friends—nothing more. He gave me a ride back to the castle this morning before it started raining. There is nothing nefarious about that—in fact it was rather gallant, if you ask me."

"The gossip flying about the village is that the two of you had an early morning tryst. Perhaps because your assignation last night was interrupted."

"What?"

"Do you deny that you were in the library alone with the duke wearing only your night rail?"

"Yes. I had on my quilted robe as well. You should know. You are the one who told me to fetch you a book in my night clothes."

"I didn't know the duke would be lying in wait for you. You are the innocent in all of this, Eve, darling. You don't understand about men and their insatiable appetites. All you have to do is say the duke kissed you and took liberties with your person."

Eve's stunned silence filled the room. When she finally found her voice, she spoke slowly to make her position clear. "Mother, he was in *his* library reading. I interrupted him to find a book for you to read. We talked for a few minutes. He was sad about not hearing from Miss Braddock, and I walked over to pat him on the shoulder. He did not kiss me."

"Do you deny that he made you kneel in front of him with his legs spread apart and insisted you perform—oh, I don't know what immoral acts that reprobate had in mind."

Eve flushed at her mother's insinuation. "Yes, I do deny it. I was simply comforting a friend."

"Well, innocent young girls who comfort men in that way don't remain innocent for long. Did he force himself on you? Did he make you touch him? You are so naïve, dear. I don't hold you responsible. His reputation is quite lurid, but I never thought he would be so depraved as to take advantage of an innocent child under his own roof. I'm so sorry, darling. I should have kept you safe from him."

"Mother, that's not—"

"The only thing to do now is for him to marry you. I have already sent for the magistrate."

"You *what*?"

"The duke must do the honorable thing and marry you, Eve. It won't be all that bad. You will be a duchess and I will be the mother of a duchess—the dowager duchess, of sorts. I will live here and help you—"

"No! No. I am not going to marry the duke," said Eve, "and neither you nor I is going to live here. Agnes is the only one who saw the duke and me in the library last night. All that's necessary is for Agnes to keep silent."

"The gossip is already all over town, my lady," put in Agnes. "I don't know how they heard, but everyone's tongue is wagging about it."

"This is ridiculous," said Eve. "I refuse to—"

"Enough, Eve," said Lady Tangier, her voice getting softer and softer in her anger. "I'll tell you what is ridiculous. Ridiculous is your husband and his heir making no accommodations for you and your daughter. Ridiculous is not being able to buy clothes or entertain in society because you don't have enough money to maintain a respectable house or pay servants."

Fury simmered just below the surface as she continued. "Don't be stupid, Eve. I am doing this for you...for us. When the magistrate comes, you will tell him that the duke made improper advances and forced himself on you, and then, at the end of the day, you will marry the duke, just like his father wanted."

"Mother, please listen to me. The duke has no romantic interest in me, nor I in him. This is not going to happen, and I shall tell the duke all about it myself when I next see him. Right now, I am going to my room to rest. I'm tired of all this arguing. I am not going to marry the duke, and we will speak no more about it."

Rubbing her temples, Eve turned and walked quickly out of the room, closing the door behind her.

"Do you think she will do it?" asked Agnes after a minute.

"I don't know," snapped Lady Tangier. "Go and find some more laudanum. If she won't accuse the duke, then at least she won't be able to refute my claims."

Both women jumped at the sudden knock. Agnes opened the door to find the first footman.

"The magistrate is here to see Lady Tangier. He says she sent for him. Mr. Merton put him in the front parlor."

"Tell the magistrate the countess will be right down."

****

"Mother?"

Receiving no answer to her knock, Eve slowly opened the door to her mother's chambers. "Mother? I want to talk to you. I understand your concerns about our future, I do, but there's another way to…"

Eve stopped talking as she realized the room was unoccupied. Walking toward the dressing room, she called out again. "Mother? Agnes?"

"Fine. I'll wait," she muttered. Surely her mother would be back soon.

Eve sat down in front of her mother's dressing table. Peering in the looking glass at her red-rimmed eyes, she sighed and then looked around for the small bottle of Warren and Rosser's Milk of Roses potion her mother swore by. She opened the carved box on top of the table. There were no bottles, but there were several letters. The direction on the topmost letter caught her eye—*Miss Linea Braddock, Sudbury Street, London.* Why would her mother be writing Miss Braddock? Eve picked up the letters and examined them more closely. Her mother was not writing to Miss Braddock, these letters were from Avery. One was actually addressed to Avery from Miss Braddock. No wonder he'd not heard from her. His letters were never posted and he never received the letter she sent to him. What on earth was her mother up to?

Taking the letters from the box, Eve made an instant decision. *She* would send the letters to London. She started at the sound of the door opening and Agnes' voice calling into the room. She quickly closed the lid to the box and stood up, concealing the letters in her skirts.

"Lady Eve? You mother is not here, my lady. She is downstairs with the magistrate. Will you join her?"

"No. I…uh…I have a headache," stuttered Eve. Agnes was certain to be complicit in everything. "I was looking for some rose water." She started toward the door but then turned as she thought of something else. She narrowed her eyes at Agnes. "You are the only person who saw the duke and me last night, Agnes. Are you the one who spread the rumor?"

"I'm sure I don't know what you mean, my lady."

"I know it was you. What is that you have in your hand?"

"It's laudanum, Lady Eve. Shall I fix you a draught for your headache?"

"No. Thank you. I think I will just go and lie down. Tell my mother I will take a tray in my room for dinner this evening."

Hurrying back to her room, Eve closed her door and locked it behind her. She couldn't believe it. Her mother—undoubtedly using Agnes—had taken the letters Avery had written to Miss Braddock. And now her mother wanted Eve to claim Avery took advantage of her so he would be pressured to marry her. She didn't want to believe such horrible things of her own mother, but the evidence was there in her hand.

Eve had to make things right. Perhaps *she* could send the letters to Miss Braddock—it was the very least she could do after all the kindnesses the late duke and his son had shown her family. But what about the magistrate? And what about the falsehoods her mother and Agnes were spreading? By the time the letters reached London, Avery might be forced to marry Eve to save her reputation!

Unless... What if she wasn't here for Avery to marry?

Eve smiled her first smile since her mother had proposed her outrageous plan to trap the duke into an unwanted marriage. She would take the letters to London herself.

If she hurried, she could catch the afternoon mail coach from Eastland. It stopped in Alysbury—the duke had mentioned the inn where it stopped when he talked about his family going down to London. From there she could catch the night coach to London. She could be in London the following day and deliver the letters to Miss Braddock.

Olsen would know about the coaching schedules and the inn and could give her directions. Perhaps he could also help her with some clothes from the stable lads. Traveling disguised as a boy would be easier than traveling alone as a young lady without a chaperone. And after that? Well, perhaps Miss Braddock would have some idea of what to do from there. But the best part was that when her mother insisted she be wed to the Duke of Easton, Eve would not be present to participate in the farce.

Chapter 25

"Your grace, the magistrate is here."

"Did we call him already, Merton?"

"*I* called him," announced Lady Tangier, standing in the doorway of his study, triumph shining in her eyes.

Avery stood slowly behind his desk. "Have you decided not to return my family's ring, then, Lady Tangier? Is that why you have summoned local law enforcement?"

"On the contrary, your grace. Since I have no male relatives to look out for my daughter, I have asked the magistrate to see that the honorable thing is done. You, sir, have compromised Lady Genevieve. She is ruined—unfit for any other man—all because of you."

Avery furrowed his forehead in confusion. "I'm not sure I understand. Has someone dishonored Eve? If so, they will answer to me. I will not countenance any slight to her."

"Oh, that *is* rich, coming from you. The whole town is talking about it. Even your own servants talk of nothing else."

"I'm sure they talk of *some* other things," said Avery pleasantly, refusing to take the lady's wild accusations seriously. "I am certain I have heard them speak of other things."

"How *dare* you mock me!"

"Merton, please show the magistrate in. Oh, good, I see he's already here. Good afternoon, Sir William. Won't you come in? I understand Lady Tangier asked you to join us here."

"Good afternoon, your grace," said Sir William, bowing to the duke. "Let me assure you that I feel certain we can resolve this whole situation as soon as possible and avoid any scandal for all the parties involved. Your father would have wanted it that way."

"I'm sure he would, Sir William, thank you. However, I expect he would first want me to know what the situation is that we are talking about. Lady Tangier, is Eve in some sort of danger?"

"The danger to my poor Eve is you. You have taken advantage of an innocent, vulnerable girl under your protection. You have forced yourself upon a lady with no father or brother to defend her honor." Lady Tangier hurled the words at him in a shrill voice. "Your father would be ashamed of your grievous behavior, especially toward my dear Eve. He always said you would bring shame and disgrace to your family and he was right. You should be horsewhipped."

The duke narrowed his eyes and raised a single eyebrow. When he spoke, his tone was cold and deliberate. "Lady Tangier, please be careful with your accusations and remember to whom you speak. I am the Duke of Easton, and you are—for the moment—a guest in my home, on my land, eating my food, and enjoying my hospitality at my pleasure."

"Lady Tangier, if you will permit me," said the magistrate, stepping forward. "Your grace, Lady Tangier asserts—and word around town confirms—that you have...well, you have been seen with Lady

Genevieve in rather compromising circumstances. According to her mother, Lady Eve's good name and reputation have been tarnished due to actions on your part. I do not know if your attentions were unwanted—"

"Of course they were unwanted," hissed Lady Tangier. "My darling child—just out of the schoolroom—is an innocent who was duped by this rogue. He took advantage of her just as he has done to countless women in London. He has ruined the reputation of an innocent girl who spent her time caring for this vulture's father."

"Lady Tangier, am I to understand you are accusing *me* of compromising Eve in some way while she is under my protection? You are aware, are you not, that I am all but betrothed to a young lady in London, and—"

"What I am aware of, your grace, is *like father, like son*. Your father took advantage of me, and you have taken advantage of Eve and done God knows what to her. She is ruined in the eyes of society, and I insist you take responsibility for your actions and marry her."

Light dawned in Avery's eyes, and he was again struck by Lady Tangier's shrewd strategy.

"Sir William, won't you have a seat so we may discuss this situation further? Lady Tangier, will you be so kind as to send your maid to fetch Eve? It would seem her presence is needed for this conversation and may help us bring a resolution to the whole matter. Certainly, if she confirms I have been in any way ungentlemanly or taken advantage of her, I am honor bound to make amends. The best way to get to the bottom of this is to ask Eve herself."

The magistrate stopped halfway down to his seat as

Lady Tangier snarled, "I will do no such thing! Lady Genevieve is in her room, mortified and prostrate with embarrassment and humiliation because of you. She is so frightened she will not come down. She says she never wants to see you again, but she is a foolish girl and doesn't realize that marrying you is the only way she will ever be able to hold up her head in polite society."

"Very well, then I shall go up to her." The duke stepped around his desk and started toward the door. He saw a flicker of fear in Lady Tangier's eyes.

"No! Not you. She would never say a word against such a powerful man as you. She knows you will be angry with her if she says anything. She said you told her not to tell a soul what you did to her."

"Then we seem to be at an impasse, do we not? I hardly think I can do the honorable thing if the lady in question refuses to see me."

"Your grace, if I may?" The magistrate had stayed silent throughout the conversation, watching the interaction between the two parties with great interest.

"Please, Sir William. I welcome your counsel on this."

"Perhaps the young lady would be willing to speak to me? I could wait on her—in the company of her mother, of course—in her chambers, and I'm sure we could put this whole misunderstanding to rights with just a word or two."

"An excellent idea, Sir William. Lady Tangier, please let Eve know the magistrate will attend her in her chambers in half an hour. Would you care for a whiskey while you wait, Sir William?"

"Thank you, your grace. I would indeed—

especially if it's the single malt scotch your father preferred."

As the two gentlemen continued their conversation, Lady Tangier hurried from the room.

****

"What do you mean she's gone?" Lady Tangier stood just inside her daughter's room.

"She's gone. I can't find her anywhere," said Agnes.

"Well, she can't be gone. The magistrate will be here in just a few minutes to question her."

"I can go look in the stables. That's the only other place I can think to look, but she's never gone there before."

"There's no time. You will have to pretend to be Eve."

"I, my lady? But—"

"Don't argue! Just put on Eve's night rail and night cap and get into her bed. Pull the covers over your head and when the magistrate comes, simply keep your head covered and answer his questions between sobs."

"But, my lady—"

"Do it now! There's no time. Just do as I say."

****

"Your grace?"

"Yes, Merton, what is it?"

The mandated half hour had passed, and the magistrate had just left to question Eve in her chambers. Avery was pouring himself another scotch.

"Mr. Olsen has a message for you, your grace. He asked that you meet him in the hallway outside Lady Eve's room so he can deliver it to you."

"Would it be too inconvenient for Mr. Olsen to

deliver the message to me here, Merton?"

"Mr. Olsen insists you will want to hear it in the hallway, your grace."

Avery sighed. He tossed back the amber liquid in his glass and got up from his desk. As he walked to the door he looked sideways at the butler. "Does anyone ever disobey Mr. Olsen, Merton?"

"Not to my knowledge, your grace. I know your father never did. The man doesn't speak often, but when he does, I've found it's usually something worth hearing."

"Just so," said Avery. "Please accompany me up to the hallway outside Lady Eve's room, Merton."

"I have every intention of doing so, your grace."

Murmured voices punctuated with loud sobs drew Avery closer to Eve's chambers. Mr. Olsen stood waiting in the hallway, and as Avery approached, the valet opened the door to Eve's room and waved the duke inside.

Following Avery into the room, Olsen then announced in the loudest voice that Avery or anyone else had ever heard from him, "I have a message for you from Lady Eve, your grace. She asked me to inform you that she has left for London to deliver some letters to your intended, Miss Braddock."

Avery's curiosity turned to surprise which turned to laughter as he realized the impact of the message Olsen had just delivered so theatrically. He surveyed the panorama of Lady Tangier with her mouth open like a fish out of water as she tried to hide her aging maid, who lay on Eve's bed with her hair stuffed up under a mop cap, sobbing with great gusto while the magistrate respectfully averted his eyes and tried to conduct his interview.

Smiling as he took it all in, Avery said, "Thank you, Olsen. I believe I shall do the same. Merton, please send Mr. Jeffries to me in my study. I'll be departing for London first thing in the morning. Sir William, I leave you to deal with Lady Tangier and her...er...grievances. Good day."

And with that, Avery exited the scene, leaving the tableau to play out behind him.

Chapter 26

There had been no choice but to confide her mission to Olsen and beg for his help.

Agreeing with Eve that traveling incognito would be safest, Olsen facilitated her plans by producing a set of boy's clothes—trousers, boots, stockings, shirt, waistcoat, cravat, frock coat, and hat. Eve found several old chemises she could use to constrain her breasts. Fortunately, she had not inherited her mother's voluptuous figure, so, for the most part, the tight undergarments sufficed to create a relatively flat surface beneath the neck scarf, waistcoat, and soft cambric shirt. Dressed as the son of a country squire and with her hat pulled low, she would be able to travel without any special notice.

Avery's letters to Miss Braddock were in her coat pocket, and she carried a small bundle containing bread and cheese from the kitchen. Olsen had commandeered one of the stable boys to drive her to the Lion and Compass, the inn at the edge of town where the southbound mail coach stopped each afternoon. Olsen had also given her directions and told her to change to the London-bound coach at the Dog and Pony Inn in Aylesbury. The lad from the stable assured her that the Dog and Pony was quite respectable and suggested if she were quick, she might have time for a hot meal there before catching the evening coach to London.

Once in the city, Eve planned to hire a cab to take her to the Braddock residence. She tucked the little purse containing all of her money more securely in the pocket of her trousers. It would never do to become a victim of the talented pickpockets who frequented the coaching routes.

They arrived at the Lion and Compass just as the southbound coach pulled in to change horses. Eve hurried to purchase her ticket, dispatching the stable boy back to Terra Bella with a guinea in his pocket and a pledge of silence. Ten minutes later she was on her way.

****

The interior of the southbound mail coach was crowded and stuffy in the late afternoon heat. Squeezed from one side by a mother with two very wiggly children and from the other side by a tall thin gentleman whose ancient suit had a distinctly musty smell, Eve wrinkled her nose discreetly and settled back on the seat. Perhaps at the next stop she would see if one of the lads up on top wanted to ride inside. The fresh air and views would be a pleasant change, and, as long as the rain held off, she would enjoy the ride under the summer evening sky.

The events of the day had exhausted her, so it was really not surprising that the rhythmic motion of the coach soon lulled Eve to sleep. She awoke, not when the coachman stopped to change horses, but just as they were leaving the yard, giving her no opportunity to trade places with anyone. Sighing, she accepted her fate and opened the packet of bread and cheese Mrs. Chapman had sent along.

"Would you like to trade seats for a while?"

The gentleman beside her had just finished his own meal and now waved vaguely toward the window. "I always take a nap after eating. Seems like a waste of a view."

"Thank you, yes," said Eve, smiling. She stood up at the same time as the man, causing them to bump into each other. After several more bumbling tries, Eve ended up scooting on the seat under the man's arms while he hung on for dear life, and then settling herself into the corner. The window was closed and covered with dust, but it did provide a view of sorts and a way to pass the time in the long twilight.

For the first time since she'd made her decision to go to London, Eve considered her role as a cupid in disguise. It was funny, she thought as she watched the fields and hedgerows fly by, but in all the times the duke talked to her about Avery, she never once sensed he was trying to foster a romance between his son and herself. She simply didn't think of Avery in romantic terms. He was more like a brother—most likely because all of the conversations with his father seemed to fall under the category of "information a sister would know," like the duke's first impression of his son as a "a round, red, squalling bundle" or his frustration with Avery's "reckless choices" as a youth or even his pride in Avery's more recent accomplishments. Eve sighed. She missed the old duke. She hoped he would be pleased with her efforts in the quest to help his son find happiness.

Even though Eve had no romantic inclinations toward Avery, she did envy Miss Braddock—especially when she saw how Avery looked when he talked about her. Eve saw the faint smile he wore when he remembered some interaction he'd shared with Miss Braddock, and she heard the pride in his voice when he talked about her talent. She also saw the pain in his eyes as he tried to understand why she had not responded to his letters.

That's what I want, thought Eve wistfully—a man who loves me the way Avery loves Miss Braddock. A good man who cherishes me and respects me. A man who holds my hand when we're in public and then holds me in his arms when we're alone. I don't want a rich duke that everybody flatters and fawns over, nor some handsome flirt who has women falling at his feet. I want someone who loves me for who I am—not my title or my position in society. I want to fall in love with someone who enjoys a quiet life, maybe a farmer or a professor or even a vicar. Someone who wants dozens of children and who would adore and delight in each one of them. Someone with golden hair and lovely blue eyes. Someone who was not too tall to dance with and who moved around on the dance floor with the grace of a gazelle—Eve loved to dance. Smiling as she thought about her dream man, Eve dozed off again.

"Didn't you say you were getting off here, dearie?"

Someone was shaking Eve's shoulder. Sitting up, she saw the sign for the Dog and Pony Inn outside. "Oh, my goodness, yes," she said, standing up quickly.

"They're almost ready to leave," said the woman with the two children.

"Thank you." Eve grabbed her bundle and climbed down the steps, turning and waving to the woman and her children as the coach started on its way. What a narrowly averted disaster. If the woman had not woken her, she would have missed her stop entirely.

Thoroughly awake now, she made her way inside the inn.

"Excuse me," she said to the pleasant-looking woman behind the counter. "Can you tell me when the next London-bound coach will be here?"

"Half-past nine," the woman replied.

Excellent. She had plenty of time to eat.

"Tomorrow night."

"Tomorrow? What about tonight? It's only just nine of the clock, and the schedule says the mail coach leaves at half-past," said Eve, her voice rising with her dismay.

"Most days it does," the woman agreed. "But today it left early. Got here early and left early. Full to the brim. The driver had all the mail sacks he was supposed to have and there wasn't any need for him to wait around for passengers he couldn't take."

"But I needed to catch that coach to London. What am I supposed to do now?"

"Well, I suppose that depends on how fast you need to get to London and how much money you have. Are you traveling all by yourself?"

Eve bit her lip. She was reluctant to give too many details about her travel plans. Dressing as a youth had many advantages, but it also had several disadvantages—such as the fact that she was unfamiliar with what a boy would do in certain situations.

"My...uh...tutor is meeting me in London. Now he won't know what's become of me."

"Well, I expect if you're not on today's coach, then he'll look for you tomorrow."

Eve sighed. The innkeeper's wife cocked her head and said, "We have rooms if you need a place to stay the night."

"That's very kind of you," said Eve.

"It's not kind," said the woman. "It's our business. One room, one night is five shillings. That includes a hot breakfast in the morning."

"I suppose that's what I need to do, then. Thank you." Eve reached into her trouser pocket for the little purse. It wasn't there. Her heart beat faster as she tried the other trouser pockets and then searched her waistcoat and coat.

"I...I...I don't seem to have my money," she stuttered, patting herself all over as her forehead wrinkled with worry. "Or my ticket," she added in alarm.

All of a sudden, she remembered the dance she'd done with the gentleman in the musty suit with whom she had switched places. In the fast-moving coach, there had been quite a bit of bumping into each other and many opportunities for picking an unwatched pocket. Full-blown panic showed on her face.

"Let me guess. Someone picked your pocket?" Looking at Eve's stricken face, the woman sighed. "What kind of chores can you do?" she asked gently.

"I can cook and sew and—" Eve stopped abruptly, remembering she was a *boy*. What chores would a boy be expected to do? "And I can help with the...serving...or the horses." She realized she had no idea what chores needed to be done at an inn.

The woman considered Eve for a moment and then said, "You can sleep in the barn. Two nights and meals in exchange for two days of chores. My boy, Robbie, broke his arm last week, so we can use some extra help. Two coaches come in around half-past seven in the morning and they'll be wanting fresh horses. The passengers want a clean necessary and a bite to eat. Put your things in the barn and then come back here. There's some apple pie left from supper, and my husband will tell you what needs to be done in the morning. If he has all the help he needs, then come find me in the kitchen. There's always something to be done there. And no dawdling. The drivers expect everything to be ready when they come through."

"Oh, thank you," said Eve, breathing again. "I'm very quick. Thank you."

"Off you go, then," said the innkeeper's wife brusquely, but not unkindly. She watched as Eve, with a backward wave, left through the front door.

The innkeeper's wife shook her head. "Now where do you suppose a little bird like that came from?"

****

Eve walked into the barn and saw a boy about her age piling up straw for a makeshift mattress. "Hello," she said. "Are you sleeping here too?"

"What do you mean?" said the boy, a frown creasing his forehead. "Are you sleeping here?"

"The innkeeper's wife said I could sleep here tonight and tomorrow night," said Eve.

"Well, I'm already here," said the boy standing up and crossing his arms defiantly over his chest.

"I'm not trying to push you out," said Eve, pulling a horse blanket from a pile in the corner and moving as far away as she could from the boy. "I'm just trying to find a place to put my things."

"Fine," said the boy, sitting back down, but watching Eve like a hawk.

"Fine," said Eve. She spread out her blanket and

sat down on it to open her bundle, glancing up every now and then to check on the only other human occupant of the barn. Out of the corner of her eye, she saw him scowl. Human, maybe, she thought to herself, but definitely not a boy.

****

Linney scowled as she watched the other boy put down his small bundle and spread out a blanket on the straw. The last thing she needed was someone else who knew her business. It was enough to be constantly on her guard to make sure her disguise was holding up, but by now it was quite likely her parents knew she was missing and had people out looking for her. She was almost certain the innkeeper and his wife knew her secret, but she couldn't afford to let anyone or anything else stand in the way of getting to Avery.

"You don't have to watch my every move," the boy said over his shoulder. "I'm just going to put this blanket down, and then I'm going to sleep."

"I'm not watching you and I don't care what you do," replied Linney.

"Fine."

"Fine."

How could she sleep in the same place as a stranger—a *male* stranger? This was *not* how her plan was supposed to go. Through half-closed eyes Linney watched the other boy carefully tuck his blanket around the bed of straw he'd prepared. As he sat down to pull off his boots, Linney abruptly realized what was bothering her about her bunkmate.

He was no more a boy than she was.

Chapter 27

"You in there! The coach is coming. You boys get out here."

Shouts from Mr. Pearson and the noise of a coach-and-four arriving in front of the inn woke Linney and Eve and brought them frantically to their feet. They emerged sleepily from the barn just as the innkeeper and another man came out to unharness the heaving team. Mr. Pearson held the reins of the first horse and gestured toward the barn.

"One of you fill up the feed bags with oats—they're in the barn. The other one walk this fella down and around that tree. Let him go into the paddock and then come back and get the next one."

"I'll get the oats," called Eve, heading back to the barn before Linney could say a word.

Taking the reins of the lead horse, Linney stroked his nose and led him down the road. Who would have guessed, she thought to herself, with all of her many accomplishments, it was leading a horse to water that paid for room and board. She pulled gently on the reins of the tired beast, coaxing him to cool down properly from his exertions. Maybe later, when the equine and his friends were eating their oats, she could record her first day of work with a drawing of her four-legged clients.

"What, ho! Who are you?"

Linney froze. Surely no one here recognized her, but what else could the boy—actually, he was almost a man—want with her?

"You there! I asked you a question. You got cotton in your ears?"

"No," Linney replied carefully.

"You must be new around here."

Linney shrugged. "Uh…I guess you could say that."

"I just did, didn't I?"

She shrugged again and turned back to walking the horse, but the boy came up behind her and gave her a punch on the shoulder.

"Turn it over," he said, holding out a dirty palm.

"Turn what over?"

"Don't play dumb with me, grub. Turn it over."

"I don't know what you're talking about. Now move. I need to walk this horse."

"Don't you be holdin' back on me," said the boy, "or I'll make you eat mud. Walking the horses for this coach is *my* job. The driver always gives me tuppence when he comes through."

Linney pointed back at the innkeeper who was busy directing two new guests. "Mr. Pearson told me to walk the horse, so I'm walking the horse. I don't know anything about any pence from any driver, so get out of the way and leave me alone."

The boy crossed his arms over his puffed-out chest. "I'm not going anywhere until I get my coin."

Linney rolled her eyes at the bigger boy, and then guided the horse off the path and around him. Her companion's tail switched the boy's arm as they passed by, and that was all it took.

"Watch out!" cried Eve from the barnyard where she'd been scooping oats into the feeding buckets and watching Linney's every move.

Linney turned just in time to see the bully winding up to hit her from behind. She ducked, dodging the blow and dropping the reins. When she stood up, she brought a knee up with her—and jammed it right into the bully's private parts. He fell to the ground, clutching himself in pain.

"I told you to leave me alone," said Linney, picking up the reins and leading the horse to the part of the yard where Eve was grinning from ear to ear."

"That was brilliant," said Eve, rubbing her own shoulder. "He deserved every bit of it."

"Did he hit you?"

"Yes. He wanted to know who you were, but I wouldn't tell him. He ran away when he heard Mr. Pearson coming."

"You should learn how to defend yourself," said Linney.

"I should," agreed Eve. "Where did you learn how to do that?"

"My cousin taught me. It's come in handy a couple of times. Gentlemen are not always gentlemen—if you know what I mean. Men think we don't—" Linney stopped abruptly, realizing she had just completely given away her cover.

Eve smiled. "I do know what you mean. Can you teach me? It's all right," she added. "I already figured it out—just like I think you did. You'd best tuck your hair back under your cap before you go for the next horse."

That afternoon in the barn, after helping the scullery maids with the pots and carrying water for the

209

guests' baths, Linney showed Eve the simple movement of applying one's knee to an ungentlemanly groin.

"You can also grab onto their forearms and step on this soft spot on their foot, if they're wearing court shoes. It's even more effective if you're wearing heels, but it doesn't work very well if they're wearing boots. No matter what you do, just remember to let go and run afterwards because the gentleman will not be happy."

"Is that why you're traveling disguised as a boy? Are you running away?" asked Eve.

"Actually, I'm not. I did run away once when I was younger, but this time I'm going to find someone. How about you? Are *you* running away?"

"Not exactly," said Eve cautiously. "I'm on my way to London to deliver some letters to someone."

"Have you ever been to London before? It's a pretty big place. You'd best be careful."

"I will be. And if anyone bothers me...well, they'll sure wish they hadn't." She grinned at Linney. "Thanks for teaching me that trick."

"You're welcome. I hope you don't need it, but you never know." Linney giggled. "Being a boy is harder than I thought it would be. I hope we can get through today without any other mishaps."

Chapter 28

Everyone took this shortcut to the Dog and Pony. It wouldn't surprise him if there were more people taking this shortcut than taking the main road with its extra mile. Of course, the coaches had no choice but to stay on the main road, so it was kept in good repair. This shorter route—even though it was more popular with riders—had more than the usual number of ruts and loose stones. And even though it did prove that the shortest distance between two points is a straight line, it also reminded Avery of the kinds of roads he sought out when he was undercover for Whit's web of spies—it was the perfect place for an ambush.

Up ahead, for example, the road narrowed so that only a single horse and rider could pass at a time. The tall trees shut out the bright sunlight, causing shadows that could cover any number of men lying in wait. But the real problem was the road itself. Consistently interrupted with ambitious roots and draped with persistent vines, it demanded your attention—and could exact a stiff penalty if your thoughts wandered.

In hindsight, it was probably foolish of him to have traveled without Jeffries, but the man was needed to sort things out at Terra Bella. "I know, I know," he muttered to the specter of Whit's warnings. "It's stupid to ride alone with Napoleon's own revenge-minded spymaster on the loose."

But truly, what were the odds that Monsieur Jones would be privy to his plans to return to London so soon after his father's death? He'd only made the arrangements late yesterday. Surely no one would—

The first bullet pierced his coat, grazed his arm, and buried itself in a giant oak to his left. The second ricocheted off his saddle, causing his horse to rear. Like any good horseman, Avery kept his seat, but when his mare bucked her answer to a third shot, Avery flew through the air, his mind uselessly registering that riding alone on a newly trained mount was the second worst decision he had made that day.

The huge trees allowed little light to enter the woods, so Avery could make out few details of the man on horseback looming at the edge of the small clearing where he lay. Oddly enough, the man looked dressed for an evening out on the town rather than riding in the country, but his first words left no question as to his identity.

"Well, well. If it isn't the Ice Duke's little brother fallen off his pretty horse."

"Half-brother, if you please," corrected Avery, struggling to sit up.

"Of course. I do beg your pardon. It's quite understandable you would not care to share more blood than absolutely necessary with that coward. How *is* the Duke of Whitley, your grace? I understand he married the codemaker and they are living happily ever after."

"I don't recall seeing you at the wedding."

"Yes, well, that's rather what I am known for, wouldn't you agree? Not being seen? However, just because you didn't see me, means nothing. Like your own spymaster, I have many faces and many associates who function as my eyes and ears—especially in situations where I might be recognized."

"I think you exaggerate your celebrity. I doubt many would know, much less care, who you are. You might have at least offered your congratulations to the woman who bested you."

Keep the enemy talking. Whit had taught him that on their very first mission together. It distracts them from shooting you, and any distraction can be turned into an opportunity to act. A silent enemy is the most deadly. At the time, Whit used Lord Edgewood as his example. "The man never talks. He is single minded, he is focused, and he can shoot a man between the eyes from a hundred paces. Rule number one: *Never* make an enemy of Edgewood."

It was amazing the things one's mind pulled out of thin air as one faced the prospect of imminent death.

Jones laughed. He actually had a very pleasant voice, realized Avery. Deep and soothing. British. Reminiscent of...something...someone familiar. Avery couldn't pin down the brief impression, and it vanished as quickly as it appeared.

"I saw no need to waste felicitations on what will be a lamentably short union. I do hope you didn't bother with a gift. And did you enjoy Lady Haversham's lovely gardens? Who was the beauty you were strolling with behind the hydrangeas, near the statue of Diana? Such a wonderful replica of the French master's work, by the way. Am I mistaken, or was that the codemaker's cousin? She is lovely...all that beautiful silken blonde hair. A man could get lost in such bounty, and such an unusual color, don't you agree? I'm half inclined to keep her for myself."

Avery's rage blinded him for a moment. If that bastard so much as touched Linney...

He commanded himself to slowly exhale the breath he was holding. He couldn't protect Linney if he was dead. He had to focus and find something—anything—to take the attention off him. He needed to keep the leader talking and then distract the two mounted men who were holding pistols behind him. How many others were there? He saw only the two behind Jones, but his peripheral vision registered a slight movement to his left.

In a deceptively pleasant voice, Avery said, "I'm afraid I can't allow that. We're to be married, you see. Also, I don't think she fancies traitors. Or short men. Speaking of which, how is your leader enjoying his stay at Saint Helena's? What a laughingstock he made of himself—of all of you. I'm sure the Crown could arrange for you to be buried on the coward's island with him."

"Shut up! How dare you speak about the emperor that way. You talk a great deal for a man with four pistols pointed at his head."

Four. So there was one more. Keep the enemy talking and, if possible, make him angry. That's when he gets careless. It was as if Whit was right there beside him. Stealthily, Avery felt the ground for a rock or even a handful of dirt to throw in the man's face. He issued a low whistle. Where was that bloody horse of his? He'd trained her to come back at that whistle—he and Hill had perfected the trick years ago. But then again, this was the poor steed's first time being shot at.

Avery continued his campaign of distraction.

"What did your little general say when he found

out you'd let the codemaker get away? When he found out the great Monsieur Jones had been outsmarted by a woman?"

"You have just sealed Miss Braddock's fate, *mon ami*. Any leniency I might have afforded her is forfeit, and all because you could not keep your bloody mouth shut. Now get up. There is a shallow cave nearby that will hide your body until the buzzards have picked your bones clean. And before you die, I promise to describe in great detail what I plan to do to your Miss Braddock before I kill her."

On the other hand, Whit always reminded him, it's important not to let the enemy get to you.

Avery took his time about coming to his feet, trying hard to ignore the fear and disgust the madman's words unleashed inside him. If he had to die, so be it, but if he did, he would take the man with him even if it was the last thing he ever did. At least then, Linney would be safe from the traitor. He pretended to stumble, covering his movements as he unsheathed his knife with his left hand. He awkwardly brushed himself off with his injured arm. Which was the better plan? A distraction that let him seek cover behind a nearby tree, or a deadly throw that would kill Jones, but would see his own demise as well? In the meantime, keep him talking...

"You're English."

"What of it? So are you."

"Yes, but unlike you, I have not betrayed my country."

"All that proves is that you are English and a fool. England cares nothing for you."

"And you think Napoleon cares about you?"

A distraction to draw their fire and then an accurate throw to take out Jones before they could reload was his only choice. Only a miracle would save him, but a well-placed knife to the heart would ensure that Jones died too. Keep talking…

"My spymaster knows you're here."

"I would hope so. I left him enough of a trail. A blind man could have followed me."

Avery heard the same low whistle he himself had just issued. He heard rather than saw his horse returning to the scene—at least he thought it was his horse. The men heard it too and for a second looked away from Avery. Now was his chance!

Avery threw his handful of dirt and rocks right at Jones' mount. The horse shied and reared, and by the time Jones had the beast under control again, Avery had vanished into the bushes.

"Do you really think to escape? You're severely outnumbered," Jones called in Avery's general direction.

All of a sudden, a shot rang out and one of Jones's men screamed and fell from his horse. Avery couldn't tell from which direction the shot had come—or for that matter, from whom. But beggars can't be choosers. He'd take any help he could get. He saw his mare, her reins tangled in the branches of a downed tree. He looked closer—not tangled, tied. Someone had tied his horse there.

As he waited for Jones to take the next step, Avery saw a movement in the trees to his right. Another shot rang out and another of the mounted men cried out in pain. This time the man stayed on his horse, but he shouted something at the third man and turned his horse. Jones bellowed out a threat to the retreating horsemen, but soon he followed the two men down the trail and out of sight.

As the dust from the retreating horses settled, Avery called out, "I don't know who you are, but I owe you my life."

"On the contrary. If memory serves, I'm the one who owes you. Now we're even."

The familiar voice was one Avery had not heard in years, but one he would never forget. "Hill Barbour! What the devil are you doing here?"

"Saving your sorry arse."

A man dropped down from the big oak tree behind Avery. A head of dark, cropped curls topped a familiar grinning face in a lanky frame that was almost a head taller than Avery. Bending over to brush at his shiny Hessians, Hill continued. "You may have to buy me a new pair of riding boots, however. They really aren't designed for climbing trees."

As he straightened up, Hill took one look at Avery still crouched on the ground and scowled. "Are you badly hurt? I didn't know the bastard got a shot off. I just saw you ready to butcher him with your knife and thought to save you messing up your cutlery." Hill knelt beside Avery and started to help him off with his coat.

Avery hissed in pain. "It's not the bullet that hurt me as much as the fall. I think I dislocated my shoulder. I can't move my arm very well."

Hill tore open Avery's shirt. "You're right. The bullet wound is just a scratch. You've had worse. I'll just tie it up to stop the bleeding." He felt along the collar bone of Avery's right shoulder.

Avery gritted his teeth at the pain from Hill's

cursory examination.

"And you're right about your shoulder. That bone is not where it should be. We'll have to put it back in the socket." Hill sat back on his heels. "So...what was the plan? Your shoulder is out of joint, so you were going to...what? Throw that knife of yours with your teeth?"

"I can throw with either hand—you know that."

"I *do* know that, but I also know that your right-handed throws are more accurate."

"He was a big target," grumbled Avery. "I would have gotten something."

"Yes, and then they would have made mincemeat of you." Hill stood up and gave a low whistle. *His* horse obediently trotted into the clearing.

If he hadn't been in such pain, Avery would have laughed. He watched Hill rummage through his saddle bags and pull out a silver flask. "Not to be ungrateful, but do you really think this is the proper time for a nip?"

"I always say there's no time like the present," said Hill cheerily, "but this is for you. If we're to set that shoulder right, you'll have to relax. Here, take a nice long swig—that's it. Now lie back on your coat and close your eyes and think about that lady of yours."

Avery immediately tensed and his eyes snapped open. "What do you know about my lady?"

Hill rolled his eyes. "Good God, Avery. I meant nothing by it. I just assumed you had one because of the way you looked at Jones when he said something about her. If looks could kill, you would have dropped the man on the spot. She must be something special."

Avery put his left forearm over his eyes and took a

deep breath, slowly letting it out. Whit's training and his own time in the trenches had taught him the value of being able to control his breathing. He took another deep breath and tried to clear his mind of everything except Linney's smile.

"Now, do what I say, but do everything very slowly," said Hill. "Take a deep breath…now let it out, slowly. Now extend your right arm straight out to your side."

Avery thrust his arm to his side and immediately recoiled in agony, an oath springing involuntarily from his lips.

"Damn it, Av! What did I just say? You've got to go a lot slower than that. Here. Relax your shoulders. Good, now try it again. Move your arm straight out—slowly…slowly. That's it. Now slowly move your arm over your head—you know, like you're leaning back on the headboard after the best sex of your life and she's tucked up beside you taking a bit of a cat nap with her head on your chest."

Avery smiled in spite of himself. Hill was right. That was about as relaxed as a man could get.

"There you go…slow down…that's right. Now turn your arm and reach like you're going to scratch the base of your neck. Slowly…slowly…keep going… good. Now this part's a bit tricky. You've got to reach back like you're trying to touch your other shoulder. That's right. Slowly…slowly…reach…a little more—here let me help it a bit…"

"Hill!" bellowed Avery, just as a resounding pop was heard.

"There it is," said Hill. "How does it feel?"

"Better," said Avery, using the sleeve of his

bleeding arm to wipe the beads of sweat from his brow. "Definitely better."

"Here. Take another swig or two of this. I've got another shirt in my bag we can use to make a sling."

Avery watched as Hill pulled a clean white silk shirt from his bag. "Silk? I wouldn't want you to rip up your only good shirt, my friend."

"Actually this is an old one, and it's a little small, so I'm happy to be rid of it." He quickly fashioned a sling to hold Avery's arm immobile and close to his chest. "That should do until the doctor has a look at it. I'll go get your mount. She seemed to be of two minds about what to do, so I tied her to that branch. Is she new?"

"Yes. She's fast and has the smoothest gait you've ever seen, but she still argues with me about who's really in charge."

"That's a woman for you."

Once Avery was back up on his horse, he and Hill started out toward the inn Hill had just recently left. And whether it was time or a common enemy or a common purpose, the two men soon settled back into the comfortable friendship they'd known since they were small boys. Over the next hour they covered four miles and five years, catching up on each other's lives since that fateful day when Avery had found Hill in bed with his then fiancée. The years had slipped by quickly, and time—even if it had not healed all the wounds entirely—had been gracious enough to leave only faint scars.

It was no great surprise to Avery to find that his friend was also a member of Whit's network of operatives working undercover for the Crown. Hill's contacts and assignments had kept him on the continent for most of the war. Even now, he, like Avery, had not officially resigned from his duties.

"I was part of the delegation that took the little general to his new home on Saint Helena," Hill explained. "He didn't deserve to live at all—much less in a place that had a roof and a bed and food and servants. If it had been up to me, I would have had the man drawn and quartered and stuck his head on a pike, so I guess it's just as well it wasn't my decision."

"I know what you mean," said Avery, taking a swig from the flask Hill continued to share. "I watched too many good men die because of that bastard's thirst for power. Working with Whit was hellish, but what was unbearable was getting intelligence too late to use it. Too late to stop a ship from getting blown up or too late to keep a regiment from marching into an ambush."

Hill nodded and took another long drink. "I thought I'd make it to Whit's wedding, but the weather refused to cooperate, so we were late getting back to England. I did see Edgewood when I was in London. He told me the Frenchman was spotted near Scotland, but the trail had gone cold. I was close to home, so I decided to stop in at Brockway House and see Mother. I took the shortcut like I always do, and there you were."

"How is your mother? How is Hen?" asked Avery. "Is she still at home, or has she married? She probably has six or seven little ones running around by now."

"Mother's well as far as I can tell. She remarried, and I'm not fond of the man she chose. As for Hen, she's...actually, she's in Paris right now. Has been for most of the war. She and her maid were stranded there when the hostilities began, and she ended up staying. I was on the continent for most of the war, but we never saw each other. We don't correspond—there wasn't much for me to say after she told me she was in love with one of Napoleon's officers."

Avery was stunned. Henrianna, in love with an enemy soldier? "Did they marry?"

Hill laughed and took a very long drink before handing the flask over to Avery. "No. The man was already married. So my baby sister is a Frenchman's whore. And not just any Frenchman, mind you, a high-ranking officer under Napoleon's command."

Hill's fine whiskey helped Avery with the pain in his shoulder, but he knew it did little to help Hill with his pain. After a few moments of silence, he said casually, "You know what you said is not true."

"Damn it, Avery. She's being kept by one of Napoleon's married officers. In my book, that's a whore."

"Some people would call her his mistress…"

Hill scoffed. "Splitting hairs."

"…but that's not what I was talking about."

"What do you know about it anyway? You didn't even know she was over there."

"I know she's not your baby sister, and she would have my head if I let you say she was."

Hill looked at Avery and then broke into a grin. He chuckled and then laughed out loud. "By God, you're right. She never, *ever* let me forget she was older— even if it's only by twenty-two minutes." His smile faded. "But I'm right about everything else."

The haunted look in Hill's eyes was anything but accepting of his sister's choices and predicament. Avery dared to press his friend further. "What is she doing now that Napoleon has been defeated? Was her protector also imprisoned?"

"I don't know. That's part of why I'm here. I'm hoping she's written to Mother and said how—and where—she is."

The two had reached the top of the rise. The Dog and Pony Inn was on the north side of the crossroads in front of them.

"We're almost there, Av. How's the shoulder?"

"Good, Mr. Barbour, thanks to you."

"Oh, hey, you don't know, do you?"

"Know what?" asked Avery as they rode toward the inn's busy courtyard.

"You'll see," grinned Hill.

The innkeeper of the Dog and Pony caught the reins Hill tossed to him and bowed slightly as he dismounted. "Back so soon, your grace? I'll take your horse."

"Thank you," said Avery and Hill together.

Avery looked down at Hill. "Your grace?" Something Whit had mentioned at his wedding suddenly made sense. "You're Camberton!"

Hill made a mock bow. "At your service, your grace." He laughed at his friend's astonished face. "My second cousin was next in line for the title, but he died in a hunting accident about three years ago. He was unmarried, so they had to roust around for a successor and they found me. I always knew I was somewhere in the queue, but there were so many names before mine that I never really gave it much thought. Isn't that a pip?"

Having turned over Hill's mount to a stable boy, the innkeeper turned to Avery. "Your grace! We

223

received no notice of your travels. Will you be needing a room for the night?"

"I do indeed, Pearson." said Avery.

Seeing the blood on Avery's shirt, Mr. Pearson let out a colorful oath as he caught the reins of the mare. "Are you bad hurt, your grace?" He led the horse to a mounting block so he and Hill could help Avery down, and he called back toward the inn, "Jemma, come quickly." Gesturing impatiently at one of the boys in the yard, he said, "You, boy—go fetch my wife."

"Pearson," said Hill, "right now his grace needs a doctor, a chair, and a pint in that order. And a hearty bowl of stew wouldn't go amiss. After that we can figure out how long he needs the room. He and I have a lot of catching up to do."

Chapter 29

The doctor pronounced him as good as could be expected and provided a slightly better bandaging of his left arm and a tighter sling for his right shoulder. Mrs. Pearson produced two bowls of hot, hearty rabbit stew and a crusty loaf of the inn's famous brown bread, and the barmaid was overly solicitous about keeping their tankards full of what was generally accepted to be the best ale around.

Avery reached for his mug with his left hand and brought it to his lips, drinking deeply.

Hill watched, intrigued. "I've always known you were ambidextrous, but I thought you favored your right hand—wait, when we played cricket, you always batted right-handed."

"Yes, but I throw and shoot with my left. I'm not surprised you noticed that. You always did notice everything. Whit's the one who encouraged me to be equally competent on both sides, and today it may have saved my life." Avery took another long drink of ale and then set the mug down carefully. "I haven't thanked you for coming around when you did, Hill." He looked thoughtfully at his friend. "How is that you're always there at the most critical points of my life?"

Hill raised his eyebrows and said, "The last time I was with you at a critical point, you almost challenged me to a duel."

Avery signaled to the barmaid to bring another round. "I've a feeling that's another time Whit saved my life. You were always the better shot, and there's no doubt in my mind you could have put a bullet right between my eyes."

"I hope there's also no doubt in your mind that I never would have." Hill traced a pattern on the table with his finger. "Avery…"

"I know," interrupted Avery. "I should have said this to you before, but I was too angry, and then I was too embarrassed, and then… Well, after that I was just too busy feeling sorry for myself. I know Olivia sent you a letter threatening to tell lies about the two of you, and I know you responded out of loyalty to me. I cannot tell you how often I've wished for this moment when we could sit down over a pint as friends again."

"To old friends." Hill raised his tankard.

Avery clanked his own against it as he answered, "Old friends."

****

"So that was the infamous Frenchman. The notorious Monsieur Jones," said Hill. "I know it's impossible, but something about him seems familiar. Like he and I have met before. I can't quite put my finger on it."

"It's his accent," mumbled Avery, his mouth full of bread. Soaked in the juices of the savory rabbit stew, it was possibly the best thing he'd ever eaten. "He sets you up to expect a Frenchman with all that 'Monsieur Jones' twaddle, and then you hear a perfectly correct British accent. It's jarring."

"He's definitely sporting the proper aristocratic inflections. I mean, he sounds like both of us.

Obviously he doesn't wear a mask, so how is it that no one knows his identity?"

"He doesn't wear a mask in the normal sense, but he does something to his face. Edgewood and I were with Whit in Selsby when Jones kidnapped Whit's duchess. Jones was there at the inn—as close to me as I am to that table there, and I didn't recognize him, but I had the same feeling you had—that I'd met him before." Avery chewed silently for a moment. "I should have been more careful. Last week, at his wedding, Whit told me they believed Jones was back in England to get revenge. He warned me to be careful, but I was in too damned much of a hurry to get to London."

Between bites washed down with copious amounts of ale, Avery brought Hill up to date on how he met and fell in love with Linea, about their abrupt separation, and how he'd heard nothing from her since his departure. He also told Hill about his current house guests and Lady Tangier's accusations.

"Do you really think your father told Lady Tangier he wanted you to marry Lady Eve?" asked Hill.

"Honestly? I think my father liked Eve. They evidently spent a lot of time together, and I think he enjoyed her company a great deal. I also think the duke would have said anything to get Lady Tangier into bed. She's a very attractive woman, and my father was…well, you knew my father."

Hill chuckled and raised his mug in a mock toast. "That I did."

"That said, I'd already told him I was coming home to get the Easton engagement ring so I could give it to Linney, and he'd already had it brought down from London to give to me. I don't think he would have hurt

Eve by setting up false expectations of a match between us."

Avery finished his bowl of stew with gusto and sat back with a sigh.

"You know," he mused to Hill, "the funny thing is, if I hadn't fallen so hard for Linney, if I didn't know without a doubt that she's the perfect woman for me, I would have been very attracted to Eve. As it is now, she's more like a sister."

"So let me see if I've got this straight. You're following Lady Eve, who is like a sister to you, to London because she is delivering some letters to the woman you love. What's in the letters?"

"I don't know for certain, but I hope they're the letters I wrote to Linney and somehow Eve found them and decided to deliver them. In person."

Hill raised his eyebrows at his friend. "That's not a lot to go on, now is it?"

"It's all I have until I find Eve and ask her a few questions."

"So did you bring the ring so you can ask Miss Braddock to marry you like any other man in his right mind would have done before he left?"

"I have to find Eve first and make sure she's safe. And then, yes, I'm going to ask Linney to marry me. But no, I still don't have the bloody ring. I'm almost certain Lady Tangier has it hidden somewhere. Merton and Mrs. Chapman searched her room, but found nothing. And then yesterday afternoon, the lady calls in the magistrate and announces to everyone that I have compromised Eve and must marry her, but she won't let me talk to Eve because she's in her room cowering from my depravity. That was about the time Olsen announced that Eve was on her way to London to see Linney. You should have seen the look on Lady Tangier's face. So I decided to follow Eve to London."

"It's a bloody mess you've got yourself in, your grace."

"Thank you for your understanding and support, your grace."

"Not at all. What are best friends for? So tell me more about this Miss Braddock you're so enamored with. Do I know her?"

"You damn well better not," said Avery, with a little more vehemence than was necessary. He took a drink and softened his response. "You'll like her, Hill. She's an extremely talented artist and not at all impressed with my title or family lineage. She's young—this is her first season out—but for all her youth, she's amazingly confident. And smart. And she's the most beautiful woman I've ever met."

"That's saying a lot," said Hill into his mug.

"It is," agreed Avery. He lowered his voice. "And, my God, she's so sensual. She teases and flirts with me, but it's not really flirting, because it turns out she's as hungry for me as I am for her." Avery paused for a scant second to regard Hill's raised eyebrows. "Well, almost." Linney's teasing smile appeared in his mind's eye. "But heaven help me, she's going to send me to an early grave."

Hill choked on his ale and came up laughing. "She *what*?"

"God's truth, Hill. Half the time I want to kiss her until we both expire and the other half of the time I want to strangle her or lock her in her room and throw away the key. She is the most ornery, irreverent,

229

disobedient, willful person I have ever met in my life, and she's stubborn as hell."

"She sounds perfect for you, then. You know you can be a bit of a stick-in-the-mud if left to your own devices, your grace. Do you truly love her?"

Was that a touch of wistfulness in Hill's words?

"More than life itself," conceded Avery. He drained his mug and set it down carefully. "When I think of the possibility of living my life without her, I can barely countenance it. I feel short of breath and I'm tempted to borrow Auntie's smelling salts, but—"

"But what? We need more ale," said Hill, signaling the barmaid. "Does she love you?"

"I don't know. I don't recall her ever saying the words, but she seems to enjoy being with me."

" 'Being with?' Never say you've already taken liberties!"

Avery waited until the barmaid set down two full mugs and moved on to her other customers. A dangerous tone edged his reply. "Be very careful, my friend. If you again make the mistake of referring to my future duchess with anything but the utmost respect, I'll call you out without fail."

Hill bowed his head in apology. "I meant no insult, Avery, but I don't understand. You have all of these wonderful feelings about the woman and she for you, so what's the problem?"

"I've heard nothing from her since I left, so I think maybe I'm more in love with her than she is with me. And then I think maybe it's unseemly for a duke—for any man, damn it—to be this bowled over about a woman. And then I can't think what to do." Avery slumped back in his chair. "I don't know, Hill. I have a bad feeling I've made a proper mess of things."

Hill rolled his eyes at his friend. "For God's sake, Avery. You've been a duke for all of...what? A week? And already you're condemning yourself for not living up to imaginary expectations set up by someone else? *You're* the duke, man. Just by definition, everything you do is ducal. You can feel any way you want." He scowled at his friend and finished off his tankard of ale.

"And that's the other thing," said Hill. "Don't try and *think* your way through this. When you first told me about Miss Braddock, you told me how you felt about her from your heart. It's when you start thinking about things you should be feeling—that's when you get into trouble, my friend. I assume you've told *her* how much you love her, right?"

The silence was deafening to Avery's ears.

"Good Lord, Avery. Any other suitor would have professed his love seven times over by now. Do you understand how lucky you are to find someone you feel this way about? Someone who feels the same way about you? I would give everything I own to be able to say that. Don't worry about being a duke, just be a man. A man in love with a woman who is in love with him. You're a lucky fellow."

An embarrassed smile spread slowly across Avery's face. "This from the man who pledged his heart and hand to the first actress he ever met."

"She was a beauty, though. Admit it."

"She was," agreed Avery, grateful for the change in subject. "All of her husbands thought so. What about you? Is there a lady who has captured the Duke of Camberton's heart?"

"No, but it's not for lack of trying. You wouldn't

believe how quickly word spread and how fast my marriage value increased once I went from being a mere mister to being a duke."

Avery laughed. "Actually, I would. A little advice? There's safety in numbers. Never be alone with any of the young ladies, and never let yourself be drawn into a private conversation or you'll be setting up your nursery before your cock can crow."

Hill guffawed at his friend's attempt at bawdy humor and leaned back in his chair. A movement out the window caught his eye and he motioned for his friend to have a look.

"You're good with mysteries, Av. I was sitting in this very spot yesterday when one of those boys arrived. The other one came about an hour later. Separate mail coaches, an hour apart, but with at least one thing in common. Take a look. It's not easy to catch them—they dart about like minnows—but look, there's one. And…there's the other one, well at least the backside. So what's wrong with this picture? Do you see what I see?"

Avery scanned the courtyard scene in front of him. No coach was currently in the yard, so there was not much activity. In fact, the only two people in the yard were two youths running back and forth at the apparent behest of someone in the barn. Both were rather slender lads and both wore ill-fitting clothes that seemed to envelop their small frames.

"I doubt I see what you see since I can't see their faces, but I do know one thing. They aren't boys."

"Exactly." Hill sat back in his chair. "So tell me, what yarn can you spin that has two…females, coming from opposite directions, meeting at an inn in the middle of England on a late summer evening?"

Avery watched the taller of the youths and felt a strange sense of familiarity come over him. He stared harder to find a clue that might confirm or deny the odd squeezing of his heart.

It couldn't be.

And then he saw it—an escaped strand of white-blonde hair, hastily tucked back into a cap, its owner casting a furtive glance about to make sure no one had seen.

Except he had.

"I'll be damned!"

Chapter 30

The knock on his door caught Avery dozing in front of the fire in his rather commodious room at the Dog and Pony Inn. He was exhausted, but sleep would have to wait.

After *several* tankards of ale and two servings each of rabbit stew, Hill decided the answer to the stiffness Avery was experiencing was a hot bath. He went to arrange things with Mrs. Pearson while Avery dragged himself up the stairs, his shoulder throbbing and the rest of his cuts and bruises also making themselves known.

"Avery!"

Only Hill would call him that. To everyone else he was Easton or your grace. "Come," he called, straightening up and trying to stretch out the aches in his back.

Hill closed the door behind him and flopped down in the opposite chair. "I talked with Mrs. Pearson. We were right. They aren't boys and they're not from around here. One is headed to London and the other seems to be headed north. Mrs. P. said they had no money, so both are doing a couple days of chores to pay for meals, a place to sleep, and then passage on the mail coach. She said she and her husband figured the girls have their own reasons for the disguises, so they leave them alone."

Hill stretched his long legs out toward the

fireplace. "I told her you wanted a bath, and she's having the one you thought you recognized bring up the hot water."

"You *what*? Are you daft? Why would you do that? I've already been accused of compromising one innocent. Do you want to add another to my tally?"

"You said you needed to see her a little closer to be sure, so I've arranged it. You're welcome."

"For God's sake, Hill. I'm in no shape to entertain."

"It's a bath, Avery. Don't overthink it." Hill rose to his feet at the noisy commotion in the hallway. He opened the door to reveal a copper tub standing in the doorway.

A muffled voice from beneath the tub spoke. "The missus said you wanted a bath, your grace. Where would you like the tub?"

"It's for my friend," said Hill, "but I expect he'd like it by the fire." He called good night to Avery and then vanished down the hallway.

Avery watched from beneath half-closed eyes as the boy set the tub on the hearth rug. "I'll be right back with the water," the lad promised without looking at Avery.

"Just let yourself back in, then," replied Avery. Even coming from a trouser-clad youth, the voice was all too familiar. Avery knew that voice. He dreamed about that voice and the young lady it belonged to. He stuck his legs out toward the fire. Stable boy, my arse. The clothes were good enough—even the boots looked authentic, but no lad kept his cap on in front of his betters.

And Avery had no doubt that underneath that cap

was the silken white-blonde hair of his beloved.

What the hell was she up to? He closed his eyes to wait.

The ale, along with the events of the day and the warm fire, conspired to lull him into a light sleep, and his ever-present dreams of Linney had him more than a little aroused when the clank of pails against the tub woke him suddenly. He opened his eyes to see the boy—who had evidently managed to carry two buckets in each hand multiple times—pouring the last of the buckets of steaming water into the tub.

The boy gathered up the buckets noisily and, still not making eye contact, headed for the door. "If that's all, your grace…"

"Actually, I need some help." The short nap had refreshed Avery, and he decided he deserved a bit of amusement before he delivered the verbal thrashing that was in order. "My man is not traveling with me."

The boy put the pails inside each other by the door and walked slowly back to behind Avery's chair. "What do you want me to do?"

"I need help with my boots." He held in the smile that quirked his lips when he heard the lad's sigh and settled back in his chair, sticking out one leg. The boy kept his head ducked and bent slightly to take hold of the first boot. Avery kept his foot angled so it would be impossible for the boot to come off. The boy tugged harder and harder and finally decided to get a better grip by turning his back on Avery and straddling the leg.

At the sight of the nicely shaped bottom in tight breeches, Avery felt himself harden, and he shifted in the chair to cover his straining erection.

Listening to the grunts coming from the boy, he didn't know whether to laugh or groan as he admired the view in front of him. Somewhat reluctantly, he finally allowed the boot to be removed, but was immediately rewarded with the same lovely bottom straddling his other leg. He again kept his foot angled until the boy changed back to his original pulling position. When he felt the boy pulling with his entire weight. Avery changed the angle of his foot. The boot came off easily and the boy sat down hard on the hearth.

Pretending not to notice anything, he waited until the boy had dropped the second boot with the first and headed toward the door before saying, "And I'll need some help getting my shirt off over these bandages."

Sighing again, the boy came back to stand behind Avery's chair and started tugging at the back of his tucked-in shirt.

Avery flinched. "Be careful, there! You have to undo the cuffs first and then pull the sleeve down a little at a time."

Avery sat motionless as the boy reached around to undo the cuff buttons that Mrs. Pearson had refastened after the doctor bandaged his shoulder. "You can just put them up on that table there."

With his eyes still half closed, Avery watched the graceful movements of his intended as she walked away from him to deposit the silver buttons on the table across the room. He couldn't help but admire the shape of her legs and the sway of her hips in the close-fitting breeches. That little idiot. How could she think anyone would ever take her for a boy? He could even smell her scent—roses, always roses. But she had gone too far this time, and it was up to him to teach her a lesson she would never forget.

She was behind him again, gently gathering the left sleeve and easing it over the bandages. Free of one sleeve, he leaned forward so she could pull the rest of his shirt from his body. Out of the corner of his eye, he saw her drape the shirt on the bed and start toward the door.

"I'm also going to need some help with these damned breeches," he called over his shoulder as he came to his feet. "Give me a hand here, boy." He glanced furtively at the figure by the door and saw her shoulders slump. He heard yet another sigh and then soft footsteps coming toward him. He turned back to the fire, grinning.

When a slender hand crept around his waist feeling for the buttons of his falls, the effect on Avery was immediate and unmistakable. The hand jerked back from the accidental contact as if burned, and the boy scurried back toward the door. Avery chuckled and delivered the final thrust of his offense.

"Wait a minute, boy. I'll give you a guinea to deliver a message to that pretty barmaid with the red hair. Tell her I've always fancied women with red curls and wondered if she might like to keep me company tonight. Can you do that?"

The answer was not what he expected. Before he knew what was happening, a bucket of very warm bath water was thrown in his face.

"Tell her yourself, you...you...you pig!" Linney's eyes blazed a bright green as she stood before the half-naked, fully aroused and dripping Duke of Easton. Her cap was on the floor and a long braid of hair the color of corn silk hung down her back.

"I cannot believe I ever thought myself in love with you or that you were ever anything other than the foul, loathsome, disgusting bully you were when I first met you. How could I think I loved you? How could I ever believe you loved me? All the time I was worrying about you and missing you, all you were doing was rutting about like some sort of vulgar pig."

Linney threw the empty bucket at his chest and started toward the door. Avery grimaced in pain as he reflexively caught it with his right hand. With his left, he grabbed Linney and pulled her around to face him.

"What in the name of all that's holy are you doing here, Linney? Is this what you do when I'm away? You enter the bedrooms of strange men and help them undress? Are you mad? Do you know what could have happened to you?" He stopped to catch his breath. "Why are you looking at me like that?"

"Oh, my God, Avery, you're really hurt."

"Of course I am. I said I was. Did you think I made it up?" Disgruntled, Avery sat down in the wet chair.

"I tried not to look," said Linney. "I mean, I *thought* it was you, but I wasn't sure, so I thought I would…"

"You thought you would what? Go alone to a man's room wearing nothing but tight breeches and a boy's shirt and hope it was me? And if it hadn't been me? Do you expect an undressed man to introduce himself before he has his way with you and slits your throat? Explain yourself, madam."

"I was coming to Terra Bella to find you. I was so worried…and angry. You said you would write to me, but you never did—even after I wrote to you. And then

Lady Charlotte said you had written to her and the Furies so many times…"

Linney lifted her chin defiantly. "I decided I didn't want to continue our relationship—romantic or otherwise—any longer, but I decided I needed to tell you to your face. So I—" She stopped and stared at Avery. "I-I…I've never seen you like this."

"You mean this angry? I have every right to—"

"No, not that. I mean this…this way…" She gestured to his bare chest. "Without a shirt. You're beautiful, Avery," she whispered.

With a groan, Avery grabbed Linney around the waist and crushed her against him. His lips hungrily covered hers as he pulled her close, his kisses expressing his anger, his fear, and his need all at once. His shoulder ached, but he could not let her go. He backed her up against the wall, his lips finding and dominating hers even as he used his good arm to touch her face, her hair, her throat, everywhere. His erection strained at his breeches as he ground himself into her and ran his hands down her sides and over the bindings that squeezed her breasts tight against her body.

"I want you, Linney," he whispered in her ear. "I want you here and now. I want all of you. Tell me I can make love to you, Linney. Let me make you mine. Please, darling. Tell me you want me as much as I want you."

"Yes."

The significance of that single word finally pierced his desire, and he froze.

"Yes, what?"

Linney blushed and whispered back so softly he could barely hear the words. "Yes, I want you too."

Panting, Avery took a step back and stared at the love of his life. Still propped against the wall, she looked back at him with brilliant green eyes full of desire. Her face was red with burn from his unshaven face, her shirt was open to the waist, and she was breathing as hard as he was.

"I'll stop if you say so, Linney—if you want me to, but darling, you must tell me now."

"I don't want you to stop. I said 'yes,' Avery, and I mean it. I can't bear the thought of being without you for even one more minute. That's why I had to come and find you. Please, Avery. Please don't stop."

She closed the space between them and wrapped her arms around his neck, pressing her bound breasts to his chest and kissing away his attempt at further words. Timidly, she teased her tongue over his lips. He opened his mouth to allow her entry and gently suckled her tongue. When she sighed, he kissed her lips again, trying to find the most perfect place for his and marveling at the many sensations that could be felt with two tongues and four lips.

He lifted her up so she could wrap her legs around his waist. Nuzzling her throat and down the vee of her shirt to the tops of her breasts, he carried her to the bed and sat on the edge with her on his lap, straddling him.

"I've never undressed a woman wearing a man's clothes before," he said as he unbuttoned the falls to her breeches and raised her to her knees. He removed the garment one leg at a time, noting with delight that she wore nothing underneath. Covering her mound with one palm, he used his other hand to spread her legs wider until she was cradling the huge bulge in his breeches between her bare thighs.

"That's probably a good thing," she replied, continuing her exploration of his lips and face. "It would cause many questions otherwise."

"I'm happy to answer any questions, but later. Not now. Right now I want this shirt and these bindings gone, and I want you in my bed."

"Let me," she said, gently pushing at his hands.

He watched, mesmerized, as she slowly pulled her shirt over her head, revealing the lengths of white muslin wrapped tightly around her to cover and restrict her luscious breasts. Dropping the shirt behind her, she bowed her head, searching for the end of the cloth strip that was tucked in to hold the strips tight. Once she found it, she slowly started unwrapping the strips of cloth, gathering them up in her hand as she went.

The material loosened gradually, allowing her breasts to swell right before his eyes. He cupped one, still covered, with his palm. After several more layers of cloth were gone, he could almost see the crests of her nipples in the center of the soft, full mounds. He brushed them with the pads of his thumbs and smiled as Linney made a small sound and paused her unwrapping to arch her back, subconsciously offering herself to him.

He took the rising tips between his thumbs and forefingers, plucking and rolling them into hardened points as she closed her eyes on a sigh. Bending his head, he nipped at first one taut peak and then the other before commanding her to continue unwrapping the treasures before him.

"Does it hurt?" he asked. "Does binding them hurt?"

She had unwound almost all of the material, and he

could see angry red marks where her skin had been pinched.

"Not until I take it off. Then it hurts a bit where the material was too tight."

He frowned and moved her hands away, finishing the unwrapping himself. The material fell to the floor, and he stared at the erotic picture before him. He bent toward her, softly kissing each place where the bindings had left a mark, and then trailing his tongue around one dark rosy peak, and barely...barely touching the very tip with his tongue.

Linney held her breath, waiting for him to take her in his mouth, but instead, he slowly trailed his tongue to her other breast, repeating the ritual. Impatiently, she wiggled on his aroused length, innocently massaging him to a new hardness. He groaned at her movement.

"Does that hurt?" she asked, concern in her voice.

"It doesn't hurt," he growled, opening his eyes and smiling at her. "It just feels so good."

"Am I doing it right?"

"My love, there is no right or wrong. It is you and me, and we are together, so everything is right. You must do what you want to do. Touch me. Explore anyway you want. I will not rush this for you."

"I have no clothes on."

"Yes, my love. That is something I am noticing with a great deal of pleasure."

"My point is, you still have your breeches on, and I do not. It's not fair."

"As you wish, my lady." Avery stood up, dumping Linney unceremoniously back onto the bed. She sat up and watched as, with his back to her, he unbuttoned and pulled off his tight riding breeches. She was admiring his muscled buttocks when he turned back to face her, now fully aroused. She gasped.

"I have seen statues of naked men before now," she confided in a whisper, unable to avert her eyes. "They are not like you. None of them was…like you are."

"Thank you, my love—at least, I think that was a compliment." He sat back down on the bed and pulled her onto his lap, her knees straddling his hips and her mound snug against his huge erection. "Those statues show men who are not ready to make love to a beautiful woman, but I am. Do you know what happens when a man and woman make love, Linney?"

"I have read things," said Linney, studying him with a frown. "And I…have seen pictures I wasn't supposed to see." Avery was caressing her breasts again, and she found it difficult to concentrate. "I know that the man's member goes into the woman, but I'm not sure how…or where, and I'm certain yours is too big." She wrinkled her brow in concern and looked up at him.. "Does that mean you and I cannot make love?"

"No, my darling. It simply means we must go slowly. Women are surprisingly flexible." He kissed her, taking advantage of her pouting lips. "Have you ever seen the big belly of a woman with child? Your body will accommodate me just as it will accommodate a growing babe."

"How clever! I have always thought women's bodies vastly superior to men's—even though they might not be as strong in some ways. They do seem to be much smarter."

"I won't disagree. And women's bodies are definitely more beautiful." He circled a nipple with his forefinger. "And more agile. They are also extremely sensitive and can bring pleasure to both the man and the woman. Shall I show you how?"

"Yes, please," whispered Linney.

Avery moved his legs apart, which spread Linney's thighs wider. He cupped her mound and trailed his finger through her curls, seeking her wet heat. Running his finger along her opening, he inserted a finger and groaned when he felt her hot wetness. "Oh, God, Linney. Can you feel how wet and ready you are for me? You feel like liquid silk."

"Will that make it easier for you?"

"It will make it easier for both of us, my love, but first I want you to experience a woman's pleasure all for yourself, so I'm going to stroke you here...like this. And here...and here, like this."

Linney caught her breath and closed her eyes.

"Does that feel good, love?"

"Oh, yes, Avery. It feels...it feels so... I don't know..."

Avery continued to stroke between her legs as he took one nipple into his mouth.

Linney moaned. "Avery...I can't...I don't know what to do."

"Just relax, darling. Just let the feeling come and relax into it." He pushed another finger into her, gathering her wetness and using it to stroke down her slit again and again, teasing the swollen bud at her center. He took her other nipple into his mouth to suckle.

"Avery, please. I don't know how to do this." Linney clutched at his arms and arched her back, her hips pressing rhythmically against him. Her breathing was fast and broken.

"You're doing just fine, my love. Now look at me, Linney," he whispered, continuing to stroke her with her own wetness. "Open your eyes and look at me. That's it. Now, just let the feeling come."

Her eyes were wide with passion and fear and pleasure as she verged on her first-ever climax.

"Come for me, my love. You're almost there. That's right, just let the feeling come."

She called his name and he felt her contract around his fingers as he stroked her through wave after wave of pleasure. And afterwards, he held her close to his heart until she stopped trembling and finally relaxed in his arms.

****

Linney opened her eyes slowly, overwhelmed with sensation. Avery was all around her. His scent, his strong arms holding her, his lips pressed against her hair, the beat of his heart under her cheek. She nuzzled the soft tawny hair on his chest and then pushed back so she could see his face. He was watching her. His eyes were dark and his mouth curled up a tiny bit, giving him a smug look, as if he was very proud of a recent accomplishment.

"That was lovely," she said, letting her breasts caress his chest as she put her hands around his neck and pressed against him to whisper in his ear.

"Shall we do it again?"

Linney's eyes widened in surprise. "Can we? That would be wonderful, but…"

"But what?"

"I don't think you had the same…uh…feeling that I did. Can we do that for you?"

Avery smiled at her concern for him. "We can. In

fact, you can start by touching me." He guided her hands downward.

"What do I do?"

"Anything you want."

Sliding her hands down his shaft, she encircled him with her fingers, squeezing gently.

"It's quite hard," she said, with the effect of making him even harder, "but here it's like velvet." She ran a finger around the tip and smiled at the bead of liquid that appeared. "It seems you are wet for me as well. Shall I use this to stroke you?"

Judging from Avery's response, the idea was quite welcome. She smoothed the moisture over and around the tip and down the length of him. "Would this be better?" She fluttered both hands up and down over his velvet hardness and then tightened her grip. "Or this?"

Avery groaned and put a hand over hers to show her his preference, and together they stroked him to a hardness he could no longer bear.

"Linney, I need to be inside you. Now. I need to be inside you, now." Turning, he laid her down on her back and rolled on top of her. Kneeling on the bed, he straddled her thighs. "I want to feel you around me, Linea."

Linney nodded, her eyes wide with anticipation and worry.

Taking himself in his hand, Avery positioned himself at her entrance, stroking her opening even as he began to push himself inside. He heard her sudden intake of breath and felt her tense. He looked into her eyes, dark green with passion, but also fearful.

"Relax, darling," he whispered. "We won't do this until you are ready."

It took all his control to stop and hold himself barely inside her entrance, letting her learn the feel of him. He leaned forward, inching his way inside her as he kissed her lips and explored her mouth with his tongue. When he moved his lips to her breast, he also moved his finger to stroke the swollen bud that was the center of her pleasure. Feeling her relax, he pushed himself in farther until he reached the barrier that told of her virginity. He withdrew slightly and smiled as he felt her clench to hold him.

"No," she said. "Please don't leave. Not yet."

"Believe me, darling. I'm not going anywhere. But it may hurt for just a bit when I push all the way inside you."

Concern showed immediately on her face. "Will it hurt you?"

"Oh, my love. It won't hurt me, and it will only hurt you for a moment or two. It will be easier if you're relaxed, so right now I'm just going to kiss you and tease your breasts until your nipples ache for my mouth. And I'm going to stroke you here…and here… Don't think, Linney. Just relax."

Avery kissed, and suckled first one nipple and then the other and then covered her lips, letting his tongue tangle with hers as his fingertips continued to caress the hard, sensitive peaks of her breasts. Eventually her tension dissolved and he felt her relaxing beneath him. He withdrew completely and leaned forward to whisper in her ear. "Hold on tight to me, Linney." As soon as she put her arms around his neck, he thrust deeply. She cried out, but he swallowed her cries with kisses as he held himself motionless deep inside her.

She was tight, as he knew she would be, and he felt

himself swell in the knowledge that she was now his. He kissed her lips and her nose and her eyelids. "Linney?"

She opened her eyes slowly, and he was humbled by the love and trust shining there. He wiped at a single tear and furrowed his brow. "Does it still hurt?"

She smiled at his obvious concern. "Not as much now, and it feels good to have you there."

"It's about to feel even better," he whispered.

He waited another moment and then started moving slowly within her. He withdrew slightly and chuckled when she again clenched to hold him inside her.

"There's more, my love. Never fear. There's more, I promise. We're going to make you come again."

Slowly he started to move inside her, grinning at her gasps of pleasure. He repeated his movements, again. And again. And again. He pulled out almost entirely, and then, giving rise to his primal instincts, he plunged back in, each time harder and deeper.

He put his hand down between them and stroked her as he had before. He smiled as she tried to protest, whispering his name and trying to be coherent, and he smiled at the flush that stole up her breasts and throat. Her eyes were wide with amazement. "I love watching you watch me make love to you," he said.

His thrusting grew faster and more determined. "Look at me, Linney," he said gruffly. "Open your eyes so I can see you. I'm going to come inside you and I want you to come too. You're almost there. I can feel that you are. You're ready, sweetheart, come for me. Now."

His command sent Linney over the edge of

pleasure, convulsing and contracting around him as he thrust again inside her, pushing deep and holding himself there as he reached his own climax and poured himself into her at last.

****

Avery collapsed to one side, wincing at the pain in his shoulder but pulling Linney close in his embrace. She snuggled against his chest with a sigh. After a few moments, he roused himself and whispered her name. "Linney?"

The only response from his true love was a slight purring as she slept, completely relaxed, in his arms. "I will never let you go again," he mumbled, pulling her closer as he kissed her hair. "You're mine, Linney. I belong to you and you belong to me."

They had much to discuss, but for now it could wait. Somehow he managed to pull the bedclothes over them both, and then he, too, fell into a relaxed, dreamless sleep.

Chapter 31

The sun was already up when Avery awoke to the unparalleled satisfaction of having a beautiful woman asleep in his arms.

As if sensing his wakefulness, Linney struggled to open her eyes. He watched carefully as the layers of memories came back to her—desperately hoping they would not be tinged with regret. He knew the exact moment she remembered it all, because she met his eyes and smiled her beautiful smile—one that spoke of secrets shared between lovers and the promise of more to come.

He grinned back at her, harkening back happily to her cautionary words about never assuming she was like other ladies. "Good morning, my lady."

"Good morning, your grace."

"Did you sleep well?"

"I was in your arms. Need I say more?"

"Never," he whispered, kissing her lightly on her slightly sunburned nose.

With Herculean strength, he extracted himself from the cozy nest they had created and tried hard not to think about the warm, barely awake temptress he left behind. He walked stark naked to the basin, aware that Linney lazily followed his progress with a kind of smug possessiveness that made him smile and seriously rethink his decision to leave their bed.

Finally however, she, too, braved the brisk morning temperature, darting about the room to collect her clothes and then disappearing behind the dressing screen.

As Avery sat down to pull on his boots, the buckets standing by the door triggered memories of the earlier events of last evening and, like one of the pails filled with cold water, the reality of it all hit him again. His fury—at what might have happened to her, at the risks she had taken, at the irresponsibility of her actions, all of it—returned with a vengeance, and he fought to maintain a composure he did not feel.

"Linea, we need to talk."

Linney reappeared from behind the screen dressed in boots, tight breeches, a short chemise, and holding her shirt and several strips of muslin in her hands. "What would you like to talk about?" she asked, bending over to pick up a strip of dropped muslin.

Avery struggled to keep his mind on the topic at hand and not on the way the tight breeches shaped her bottom. "Are you ready to explain what you're doing here?"

Linney straightened and her eyes flashed at his tone. "I believe I explained everything last night, but if you'd like to talk, you can explain why you would be sending messages to a barmaid when you claim to love me?"

"Did you honestly think I wouldn't recognize you immediately? I saw you in the yard and decided to teach you a lesson. I wanted to shock you—scare you so you would understand how dangerous this little escapade of yours was. Do you understand how much trouble you could have gotten yourself into? What on earth possessed you to do this? And how was it that you were on a mail coach in the first place?"

"I booked passage on it at the Blackbird Inn outside London."

"And how did you get to the Blackbird Inn? Please tell me you had your father's coachman take you there."

"Of course I didn't. I hired a hackney cab. I'm not a child, Avery. I knew what I was doing. I disguised myself as a boy because no one would question a youth traveling by himself. Mary's brother is about my size, so I borrowed clothes from him. Mary's other brother told me where I could catch the mail coach, and Mary packed a bag of food for me. I had plenty of money for the cab and for the coach—at least I did until someone took it."

"You were robbed?" Avery sat down on the bed in a daze.

"I believe the correct term is pickpocketed. Mrs. Pearson said there's a man who rides the mail coaches when he needs money and he picks pockets. She said all the locals know him, and the travelers think he's just a nice old man. He forgot his Bible and his hat in the coach and I offered to retrieve them. When I gave them to him, he said 'thank you' and patted me on the back and shook my hand a lot. I think that's when he got his hands on my money."

"I expect that's not all he got his hands on," muttered Avery. "So what was the rest of your plan?"

"After spending the night here, I was going to take the Birmingham-bound mail coach to Eastland."

"And when you finally found me, what were you going to do?"

Linney swallowed slowly. "I was going to ask you

why you wrote to everyone except me. I was going to ask you if you ever really loved me and if so, why you stopped. I was angry and hurt because I thought you no longer wanted me. I had to do something. I was just so worried and frightened." She whispered as she hung her head. "I still am."

It suddenly dawned on Avery that all the doubt and anger and fear he'd been experiencing when he thought Linney no longer loved him was simply the inverse of what she had been going through—except that she didn't have the freedom to get on a horse to come and find him. At least not as herself.

"I did write to you, Linney. I wrote at least five times over the week, and I never heard anything back from you."

"Did you receive the letter I sent to you? Mother allowed me to write because I told her how worried I was and that I had this strange, awful feeling you needed me. She told me about a similar feeling she'd had for my father, so she let me write to you even though I'd received no letters from you."

"No, I didn't receive anything from you," said Avery. He frowned as he tried to figure out the mystery, but his mind kept returning to the partially nude woman in front of him. Linney was trying to wrap the strips of muslin around her chest to bind her breasts and doing a rather poor job of it.

"Did you truly think anyone would mistake you for a boy?"

She stopped her task to glare at him. "I think most people don't notice anything other than their own lives, so yes, if they were expecting to see a boy, then that's what they saw. It was only because I had to bring up so much water for you and because I took off my coat that you noticed."

Avery laughed out loud. "My love, you are delusional. My friend saw through your disguise the minute you disembarked from the mail coach the day before yesterday. And yesterday afternoon, when he pointed out the two 'lads' in the courtyard, the first thing I remarked was that I saw no lads, only lasses. Is the other girl your companion?" Hope springs eternal, he thought to himself.

"No," said Linney as she turned back to her task. "We met the night we arrived. Mrs. Pearson let us trade chores for meals and a place to sleep in the barn. We each figured out that the other was in disguise. She's delivering some letters to someone in London. She seems quite nice."

Up to this point, Avery had been more interested in watching Linney don her masculine disguise than in listening to her explanation, but something she said flagged his attention.

"What did you say?"

"I said she's going to London and she seems very nice."

"You said something about delivering letters?"

"Yes. That's why she's going to London. I guess she doesn't trust the post—I can certainly understand why. I'll never trust it again."

"What's her name?"

"I didn't ask. We were both rather tired last night, and then this morning, after I showed her how to put her knee in a gentleman's private area, I—"

Avery was pulling on his coat, but stopped in his tracks. "After you did *what?*"

"I showed her how to protect herself by kneeing a gentleman—actually, I don't think you can call him a gentleman if you needed to—"

"Linney!" roared Avery. "Explain yourself."

"She saw me do it to that bully from the blacksmith's shop, so she asked me to show her how to do it, and I did."

"Did he hurt you? The bully from the blacksmith's, did he hurt you?"

"I think the question you might want to ask is did I hurt him," sniffed Linney. "And the answer is 'yes.' "

She paused thoughtfully in her toilette. "I think I understand a little more about why that works so well," she said, stuffing her newly braided hair under her cap as she made her way toward the door.

"Where do you think you're going?"

"I have to get back to the barn and help with the horses. The first coach will be here soon."

Avery grabbed her around the waist and pulled her back into his arms. "You're not going anywhere, Miss Braddock. I'm keeping you in my sights at all times from now on. I will pay off your debt to Mr. Pearson. Consider it a betrothal present."

Linney blushed. She turned and put her arms around his neck and gave him a kiss on the cheek. "What a lovely present, Avery! No wonder I adore you." She started to straighten his half-tied cravat, but stopped all of a sudden. "Wait. I can't just leave my friend to do all the work by herself."

"I am more than happy to pay for her as well. We'll go and fetch her from the barn and she can join us and His Grace The Duke of Camberton to break our fast. Are you ready?"

"Yes, I am. Isn't it wonderful? Men have such an advantage over women when it comes to getting dressed." She checked the looking glass to make sure her hair was completely covered. "If I were at home, I'd only be in my stays by now, and Mary would be scolding me for fidgeting while she put up my hair."

"I plan to have a word or two with Mary about several things before our wedding," muttered Avery, dropping a kiss on his fiancée's cheek as he patted her bottom, "but any time you'd like to wear this costume—without the bindings—when we are private, you have my enthusiastic permission."

Linney took a step out of his embrace and looked up at him. "Your permission? About what I wear? Will you regularly be making decisions about my wardrobe, your grace?"

Not about to fall into that particular trap, Avery replied, "Only about those items of clothing I plan to remove as soon as humanly possible, my love. Shall we go down?"

Grudgingly admiring his evasion, Linney grinned and preceded him out the door and down the stairs.

Chapter 32

"Who are you?"

Eve looked up suspiciously at the stranger blocking out the sunlight in the doorway to the barn.

"I'm looking for you," said Hill, coming toward her with an outstretched hand to help her rise.

"The innkeeper's wife said I could stay here," said Eve jumping up and backing away from the stranger. Where was her friend who knew how to incapacitate threatening gentlemen? Did Eve remember what she'd learned?

"Yes, I know," said the man. "She told me where I could find you. You're to come with me."

I don't think so," said Eve. "I'm fine right here, thank you. Besides, I have chores to do—which you would know if you had really spoken with the innkeeper's wife. Go away." She was hoping to avoid a scene, but if he came any closer...

Hill took another step toward the girl. "There's no need to be frightened. My friend has already paid Mr. Pearson for you. I'm here to take you into the inn with me."

"Sir, I don't know who you are or who your friend is, but you should get his money back from the innkeeper because I'm not going anywhere with you. And if you come one step closer, I'll..."

"You'll what?" Hill smiled at the ridiculous picture

of this petite female in boys' clothes threatening a man of his stature. He really should introduce himself, but once he did, she'd commence simpering like every other marriageable young lady in England he'd met since he inherited his title. He was actually enjoying a conversation with a young lady for the first time in several years.

He took another step toward Eve and, before he knew what was happening, he fell to the ground in agonizing pain, his hands moving instinctively to protect his testicles from further damage.

Eve stood there for a minute, beaming with pride at her accomplishment. Then, remembering the second part of her lesson, she ran toward the inn, leaving the Duke of Camberton groaning and writhing on the ground. Her bunkmate was just coming out the front door of the inn.

"I did it!" cried Eve, running toward Linney. "A man came into the barn and tried to make me go inside with him, and I told him to leave me alone, but he kept coming closer and closer, and then I did it. I kneed him in his private parts."

Linney traded apologetic looks with Avery, who had just come out the door behind her.

"Eve?"

"Avery?"

"Are you hurt? Did you say somebody threatened you?"

"That would be me," said a pained voice coming from the door to the barn. Hill, still slightly bent over, held on to the frame of the doorway for support, his clothes dusty from his time on the ground.

Avery strode over to help his friend.

"I did as you asked, and the chit slammed her knee into my balls."

Eve put a hand over her mouth in horror. "The *duke* is your friend? The one who paid Mr. Pearson?"

Linney watched in confusion and then turned to Eve. "How do you know Avery? Did he call you Eve?"

"Yes, I'm Lady Genevieve Richards. My mother and I are staying at Terra Bella. Who are you?"

"I'm Miss Linea Braddock, Avery's betrothed—well, not officially."

"Yes, officially," grunted Avery as he helped Hill inside to the private dining room. "I believe we agreed on that last night, Miss Braddock. Did you forget?"

Linney blushed scarlet, but smiled sweetly up at Avery. "No, your grace. I did not forget. But it seems I'm still waiting for a proposal."

Hill interrupted what looked like it could become a lengthy discussion. "Miss Braddock, it's an honor to meet you, but if you don't mind terribly, might we continue this discussion while we are—or at least while I am—sitting down? And Lady Genevieve? I'll ask you to keep your distance, if you please."

Hill moved to the side and gestured for the ladies to go in first, but his bow was not noticeably different from his currently stooped position. Linney and Eve tried not to giggle as they swept past him and made their way into the dining room as grandly as if they were having tea with the Queen.

Chapter 33

It didn't take long to sort it all out once all the parties explained their roles in what Avery referred to as the ducal debacle.

When Linney realized Eve was the inestimable Lady Genevieve from Avery's letters to his aunt, she was wary at first. But when Eve produced the letters from Avery that Lady Tangier had pilfered, tears ran down Linney's face as she embraced her new friend.

"I was so afraid he didn't love me anymore," she whispered so only Eve could hear.

"You are all he talked about," Eve replied. And then she tactfully engaged the gentlemen in conversation, leaving Linney alone with her overdue love letters.

Later, as the four sat down at table for breakfast, Linney said to Eve, "I can never thank you enough for what you did."

"You would have figured it out once you got to Terra Bella," said Eve. "You were almost there." She looked at Avery and added, "I am so ashamed of my mother, Avery. I don't understand what she thought to accomplish by stealing your letters."

"I believe her intention was for you to marry me," he replied. "At least that was her plan behind her accusation that I seduced you."

"And did you seduce her?" The quiet question

261

from Hill held more than curiosity, so Avery did not dismiss it lightly.

"Eve has become like a sister to me," said Avery to the world at large. "She attended to my father when I was not there, and I value her friendship immensely."

A nod from Hill confirmed receipt of the underlying message.

"I can't fathom what you must think of my mother, Miss Braddock," said Eve.

"Please call me Linney."

"Then you must call me Eve."

"And once the swelling subsides and I ascertain that I am not injured for life, you may both call me Hill," said the Duke of Camberton.

"Are you sure all of that swelling is from your injury?" muttered Avery to Hill behind his mug, as the ladies filled their plates from the buffet. "Perhaps some of it can be attributed to your interest in the lady herself?"

Avery had seen how Hill watched Eve's every move, and now that he was united with his own love, he was not above a little matchmaking.

"Shut it," grumbled Hill. "I haven't forgotten that it was you who sent me to fetch her in the first place."

"Just think of what a story you'll have to tell your grandchildren."

"You're assuming I'll still be able to sire an heir after this."

Avery laughed at Hill's discomfort. "It serves you right for not listening to the lady." He got up to fill his own plate and then returned to sit beside Linney. "You know, the thing is, I still don't have the ring."

"I'm sure you can find a ring before you take your

vows," said Hill.

"Yes, but it won't be the proper one," said Linney. "Avery thinks we cannot be married without the Easton engagement ring."

"That's not exactly what I said," said Avery. "And you won't get out of marrying me that easily. What I said was I *wanted* to give it to you when I asked you to marry me just as it has been given by all Easton heirs before me to *their* fiancées."

"So are you saying you would marry me even if you didn't have the ring?"

"Try and stop me."

Linney flushed with delight. Looking up at Avery, she said softly, "I know how important the ring is to you, Avery."

"You are infinitely more so, my lady," he replied.

"But surely you will have time to retrieve it from Terra Bella before you announce your engagement," said Eve. "You should have it, Linney. It is truly the most beautiful ring I have ever seen. And it would look so perfect on your hand."

Complete silence followed Eve's words.

"*You've* seen the ring?" asked Avery.

"Mother showed it to me—it's beautiful."

"Eve," said Avery slowly, "the ring is missing. When did you last see it?"

"Mother showed it to me right before you arrived. The night your father died. I thought you knew she had it. She said your father gave it to her for safekeeping. It's in a lovely little enameled box. I remember the duke telling me he was having it brought from London to give to you."

"When I asked your mother about it, she said my

father showed it to her, but then he took it back and she never saw it again. She denies ever having it."

"Then she's lying. When I saw the ring, it was on my mother's hand. She must have hidden it somewhere."

"I've had Olsen and Mrs. Chapman and Merton searching everywhere in the castle," said Avery, "including your mother's room—but they found nothing."

"It must be there somewhere." Eve was very close to tears. "Avery, I'm so sorry."

"It's not your fault," said Avery. "We just have to figure out what she's done with it. It must be somewhere in the castle. My father would more than likely have put it in the hidden cupboard in his dressing room. He showed it to me once when I was a boy and told me it was where he kept his treasures." Avery laughed. "I remember telling him at the time that it was a rather small cupboard and he must not have very many treasures. He laughed and said that's what the secret passageways were for."

"Did you look in the hidden cupboard in the duchess's rooms?" asked Linney, who had been following the conversation with great interest.

Three pairs of eyes looked at her in surprise.

"You've never been to Terra Bella, my love," said Avery, furrowing his brow. "How do you know there's a secret cupboard in the duchess's rooms? *I've* never heard of it."

"Well, you wouldn't have, would you? It would be something your mother would pass down somehow to the next duchess. Terra Bella is built in the same style as Glenhaven, one of the castles I studied and did architectural drawings for. The family wing of Terra Bella was added at about the same time Glenhaven was built, and the popular design at the time was to make the rooms for the mistress be mirrors of the master's rooms in the placement of elements such as fireplaces, doors, windows—things like that. Since there's a hidden cupboard in the duke's rooms, chances are good there's a matching hidden cupboard in the duchess's rooms. And if there's a secret passageway for the duke, then there's probably one for the duchess as well."

"I just can't believe my father would tell someone outside the family about the hidden cupboard," mused Avery.

"Maybe he didn't have to," said Linney. "Maybe he simply acknowledged that there was one. Hidden spaces are usually in plain view or simply hidden behind a tapestry or paneling or even a piece of furniture. The success of their secrecy is that no one knows they exist. However, if you know where to look, they're relatively easy to find."

"And my mother seems to be quite good at 'finding' things," said Eve sarcastically. "Perhaps she saw the duke opening the cupboard when he thought he was alone."

"Merton did say my father…uh…entertained Lady Tangier in his rooms a few times," said Avery. "I can have Olsen check for a hidden cupboard in the duchess's room. He knows about the one in my father's rooms. Your mother probably assumed I would have her rooms searched, so she hid it. I have a feeling that if Eve and I said we were going to marry, the ring would magically reappear."

"I'm very sorry, your grace," said Eve with a

twinkle in her eye, "but I won't marry you just so you can find your ring."

Avery pretended to be hurt by Eve's words and dramatically put his hand to his forehead. "You wound me to the quick, my lady. I hope someday to find another who might look favorably upon my suit."

"How do you know all of this about hidden cupboards and secret passageways, Miss Braddock?" asked Hill, looking a little annoyed with Avery's antics and teasing familiarity with Eve.

"Please call me Linney, your grace. I did some drawings for my father in his role as solicitor for the Society of Antiquarians of London. They preserve and protect historical sites and artifacts and often need technical drawings of an item or property to catalogue their assets."

"Yes," said Hill. "I know of them. Before he died, my own father was a member of their organization."

"Well, several years ago, the draughtsman they hired to do some drawings became ill and was unable to complete the project he was working on. My father needed the work done quickly and asked if I could help him. He took me to the site of the project so I could do my initial sketches, and he gave me the measurements the other draftsman was using. It was like building the house all over again. I loved it. But there were a couple of places where the outside measurements didn't match those on the inside—even after allowing for the thickness of the walls. I asked my father about it, and we visited the site again. When we investigated, we found twin hidden passageways—one going from the master's bedroom and one from the mistress's bedroom. They merged into a single passageway before going down a set of stairs and exiting through an outbuilding."

Linney smiled at her memory. "We tried to walk through the whole passage, but it became very cramped. I got farther than Papa, but part of the underground tunnel had collapsed, so I had to go back. We finally figured out that the passageway paralleled the main hall and then descended to an outside building on the other side of the walled kitchen garden."

Avery stared at Linney as if he'd never seen her before. "You continue to amaze me at every turn, my love."

Linney took a very proper sip of her tea before setting it down and dabbing her lips with her napkin. She smiled up at him, gazing through her lashes. "I have many facets you have yet to uncover, your grace. I believe I have warned you multiple times about the folly of assuming I am like other ladies. You do so at your own peril."

Avery laughed and the others joined in. He took Linney's hand and brought her fingertips to his lips. "I apologize again for my shortsightedness, my lady. You are brilliant as well as beautiful." He turned her hand and kissed her palm, whispering softly so only she could hear, "And I look forward to uncovering all of those facets."

Distracted by that thought—and his body's obvious agreement—Avery missed Hill's question.

"I beg your pardon?" he said, taking note of his friend's bemused grin.

"I asked if you knew of any out buildings on the grounds of Terra Bella that might be the endpoint for a secret passageway."

"I can't think of any, can you?" Avery sat back in his chair. "We've been all over the castle and the grounds, but I can't recall—"

"Wait a minute," said Hill. "Do you remember that time old Cuthbert came after us for stealing the cook's pork pies, and he chased us out behind the kitchen?"

Avery grinned. "How could I forget it? He had a pitchfork! I honestly thought we were both about to be skewered."

"Remember we dodged into the summer kitchen and went down into the cellar and hid behind some barrels in the corner? You called it—"

"The apple room! Yes. We must have waited in there for hours before deciding it was safe to come out."

"And do you remember the wall inside, beside the barrels?"

"Yes, we were in there so long that the whole place is burned into my brain. It had a door that seemed to go right into the side of the hill. We tried to open it, but it made too much noise, and we didn't want Cuthbert to hear us."

Linney laughed at the picture of the two dukes hiding from a servant armed with a pitchfork, and traded grins with Eve, who seemed to be thinking the same thing. "Did you ever go back and explore the door?" she asked.

"That was about the time we seemed to be getting into a lot of trouble," said Hill, winking at Avery. "Right after that we were both sent off to school."

"In a castle as old as Terra Bella, there could be several different hidden spaces—secret passageways, hidden closets, hidey holes—in addition to the cupboards," said Linney. "The spaces were often used by the master—or the mistress—for clandestine visits from secret lovers." She smiled at Avery.

"I'll have them all sealed shut," said Avery with a frown.

Linney continued. "Originally they were used to hide priests, or as a way to escape a fire or marauding enemy soldiers."

"It's definitely something to investigate when I return to Terra Bella," said Avery. "Maybe there is a hidden passageway. I just wonder why I never heard of it."

"But you said your father showed you the secret cupboard and told you the rest of his treasures were in a secret passageway," said Linney.

"He was teasing me."

"But maybe he was telling you the truth when he teased," suggested Eve.

"When you say it that way, it does sound like him," admitted Avery.

"You could try looking for information about the secret passages in his will," offered Hill. "When I became duke, there were scores of old documents about the lands and estates."

"That's certainly possible. I've not had a chance to read much of anything," said Avery. "Perhaps there is mention of a secret passageway and maybe I will be able to find the ring before we're married."

"Speaking of marriage, your grace, might I point out that there is another, rather important, aspect to this entire conversation?" Linney slowly set down her cup and saucer and, smiling sweetly, turned to Avery. "At the risk of repeating myself, I would like to remind you that there can be no *wedding* until there is a *proposal*. And, as that is something you have yet to accomplish, I see no reason to talk further about a ring or a wedding." Linney cocked her head at Avery in challenge.

Narrowing his eyes, Avery studied her face for a moment. "Very well, then," he said, pushing back his chair. Taking her hand in his, he knelt before her on one knee while Hill and Eve looked on, smiling broadly.

"Miss Linea Priscilla Braddock, I love you more than life itself, and I promise to cherish you to the end of my days if you will but say you are mine. Will you please do me the very great honor of becoming my wife, my beloved, and my duchess, now and forever?"

"Oh, Avery," whispered Linney, tears catching in her throat, "do you even have to ask?"

"Actually, my love, I do. You have been quite clear on the topic, and as such, I will require a response in front of these witnesses before I release your hand."

Linney blushed while Eve and Hill laughed at Avery's determined face.

"Yes, your grace. I will be honored to marry you."

Avery leaned forward, and Linney bent down to meet his lips and seal their betrothal with a kiss.

Still holding her hand, Avery came to his feet. "Might I also hope that the two of you might stand up with us? It will be a very small affair because I am, of course, in mourning, but Linea needs a bride's maid and I need a best man."

"Of course," replied Eve looking at Linea's smiling face.

"It would be my honor," said Hill. "Except...must Lady Eve and I stand very close to each other?"

Everyone was laughing when Avery glanced up

over Hill's head at the doorway of the private dining room and frowned. "Is that Edgewood?" he asked over the ladies' chatter.

Hill turned to confirm the sighting. "It is. What the devil is he doing here?"

"It can't be anything good," said Avery, standing. "Will you ladies excuse me for a moment? It seems I have a message from my brother."

Chapter 34

"Is that Camberton?"

"Good morning to you as well, Edgewood. Yes, the Duke of Camberton is having breakfast with my fiancée and our friend, Lady Genevieve Richards. Would you care to join us?"

"We need to get to London as soon as possible. Whit has been beside himself. We received word that you were gravely injured and Camberton was dead. Whit would have come, but he did not want to leave his duchess. The kidnapping rumors persist—specifically the one about the Frenchman wanting to abduct Vivian just to destroy Whit. Is that Miss Braddock? In breeches?"

"Yes," said Avery. "Don't ask. Come sit for a minute and get something to eat. I'll see to fresh horses for us. We have just been sorting out the events of the past few days—starting with Hill—that is, Camberton—and I being ambushed by the Frenchman and his thugs. That's most likely where your faulty intelligence originated."

Edgewood grunted but followed Avery to the table where Hill rose to welcome him. Avery introduced Linney and Eve to the earl who surveyed their disguises with raised eyebrows. "I'm not certain whether to shake hands or kiss fingers," he said with a bow.

"If you are going to scold us, my lord," said Linney

with a mischievous grin, "I'm afraid you'll have to queue up behind these two gentlemen, who seem to believe we have been somewhat cavalier in our plans of action."

"I still claim it is only because they cannot comprehend all the intricacies of the problems we faced," said Eve. "They are, after all, only men."

"Not at all, ladies," said Edgewood, "I was actually thinking to recruit you both. Your disguises are first rate."

"Good God, Edgewood," groaned Avery. "Do *not* encourage them."

Linney exchanged smiles with her cohort. "We did succeed in accomplishing our intended goals, did we not, Lady Genevieve?"

"We did, Miss Braddock. And we managed to protect ourselves in the interim." Eve smiled sweetly at Hill, who took a step away from her.

"So it was your goal to carry water and muck out the stables?" asked Hill.

"Of course not," said Linney. "That was only a means to our respective end goals."

"And what was your goal, Miss Braddock?" asked Edgewood. "As I understand it, your parents are under the impression you are with your cousin, and your cousin and her new husband were under the impression you are with your parents—until Vivian received your note, of course."

"Certainly one of my goals was not to worry any of them any sooner than was necessary," said Linney, "but my primary goal was to find Lord Hammond—or rather, the Duke of Easton—and either make him marry me or tell me to my face that he no longer wished to do so. And to that end, I am well on my way to achieving my goal, am I not, your grace?"

"You are, my dearest," confirmed Avery. "Edgewood, before I see to the horses, congratulate me. I'm to be married."

"That's excellent news, Avery, congratulations! Miss Braddock, are you certain you have not been coerced into a *mésalliance*? I would be very happy to engineer your escape if you but say the word."

Linney laughed and gestured for Edgewood to take Avery's seat. "Thank you for your concern, my lord, but I am right where I should be."

"And you, Lady Genevieve? Do you need rescuing from this pair of diabolical dukes?"

Eve smiled and then sighed. "I'm afraid the only person I need rescuing from is myself, my lord. Achieving *my* goal seems to have landed me in rather vexing circumstances."

"If I can ever be of assistance—"

"Trust me when I say the lady is capable of taking care of herself," said Hill, grimacing while both ladies giggled.

Edgewood explained the general nature of his visit and his orders from the Duke of Whitley. When Avery returned, the two men stood and made their goodbyes.

"Ladies, it has been a pleasure," Edgewood said, bowing. "I promise that their graces will return for you by this time tomorrow."

Eve busied herself at the buffet while Avery said goodbye to Linney. "If I can, I will call on your father while I'm in London and procure a special license so we can be married as soon as I return. I love you. I hate leaving again—especially so soon after...our night together."

Linney smiled and pressed her lips to his, relishing the feel of his arms around her. "It's different this time," she whispered. "This time I know you love me and will be back to marry me. The anticipation makes the eventuality that much more wonderful. But do be careful, my love, and travel safely."

Reluctantly, Avery put Linney away from him. His next words included Eve. "Mrs. Pearson has arranged for two rooms and said she would help you with a bath and clothes. We will be back tomorrow, and then we can decide what to do next. Much depends on what Whit has to tell us."

And just like that they were gone.

Chapter 35

"A bath sounds wonderful," said Eve after the gentlemen left. "I have straw in some very strange places."

"I'll see if Mrs. Pearson has found us some clothes," said Linney. "I can help you wash your hair, if you like." She stood to leave, but at the last minute turned back to the table.

"Eve, before we change from our disguises, might I interest you in one last adventure?"

"What do you have in mind?"

"The mail coach to Eastland leaves in twenty minutes," said Linney. "If we take that coach to Terra Bella, could we not look for the secret passageway that Avery and Hill mentioned? If it's there, as I suspect it is, we could follow it to see if it goes to the duchess's rooms and see if we can find the missing ring. I know Avery said he doesn't need the ring to marry me, but I also know it would mean a lot to him if he had it."

"Oh, absolutely," said Eve. "I feel horrible that my mother took the ring in the first place, and I would love to find it for you and Avery. Are you sure there's room on the coach? Sometimes they do fill up."

"I'll check, and I'll see to the tickets. Why don't you bundle up some food for us and ask Mrs. Pearson for some candles. We'll have to hurry."

Twenty minutes later, two lads were on their way

to Terra Bella atop the Birmingham-bound mail coach. The road was well traveled in most places, but huge ruts near the bridges caused much jouncing of the passengers—especially those riding up top.

"Hold on up there, lads," called the driver as they bounced over an especially egregious section of road.

"Bloody idiot's going to break an axle," predicted the gloomy porter who rode on top with the girls and had almost no natural padding to cushion his ride.

"He seems to be making good time," observed Linney with a half-smile.

"That's the problem. He's determined to beat his best time, and a day like today—what with the dry roads and a light load—don't come often. We'll get to Eastland before dark, for sure, but we might not be in one piece."

And sure enough, by the time the sun was starting to set over the western hills, Linney and Eve had not only arrived at the Lion and Compass Inn in Eastland, but had managed to catch a ride with a delivery wagon to the castle.

"It's a lovely village," said Linney. She took a sip from the flask of water Mrs. Pearson had provided for their expedition.

"Everyone I met here was so nice," said Eve. "They all loved the old duke, and they all love Avery. They will be so pleased that he wants to continue doing the work his father began."

"I forget you spent so much time with Avery's father," said Linney. "How long have you and your mother been here?"

"A little more than three months," said Eve.

"Do you know the building that Avery and Hill

talked about?"

"I've seen it on my walks, but I've never been inside. It's like an extra kitchen, with a root cellar for storage—at least I think that's the one they meant."

"I'm hoping we can find the passageway before it gets too dark. Then I can use the candle to go up the passageway to the duchess's rooms. Do you think you can sneak into the castle and help me figure out where the duchess's rooms are from the inside?"

Eve giggled. "It's fun to think that we're sneaking into what will eventually be *your* rooms, isn't it?"

Linney grinned. "I hadn't thought about it like that." Then she frowned. "I have vowed not to do any more counting of my chickens before they hatch, so I'm not going to even think about being married to Avery until it's done."

"Do you love him very much?"

Linney was quiet just for a moment. "I do, but 'love' doesn't seem to capture everything I feel for him. Sometimes it scares me. I've never really been in love before—I've had silly crushes—but nothing like this. It's different with Avery. Everything seems so easy and right, and yet so momentous and exciting."

"Did you always feel that way about him?"

"Actually, I think I did, but I was too afraid to admit it at first. Mainly because I didn't know whether he shared my feelings, and also because he had such a scandalous reputation. But when we were apart, my heart just ached not knowing how he was and wondering why he didn't write. I was so angry with him and so sad, and I kept trying to figure out what I'd done wrong or where I'd misunderstood what he said to me. Somewhere, deep down in all of my different feelings, I think I knew he loved me the same way I loved him."

"I'm so happy for you," said Eve, "and I have to admit, I'm jealous—not that I love Avery," she said quickly. "I mean, I do love him, but not like that. He's like a brother to me, but I'm jealous of his love for you and yours for him. I hope I feel that way about someone someday."

"Here now, lads," called the driver of the wagon. "Off you go. I've got to be getting home to the missus."

Linney and Eve jumped down from the wagon and waved their thanks. Then they started down the lane to Terra Bella.

"Will you have trouble getting into the castle without seeing anyone?" asked Linney.

"I don't think so. I should be able to avoid everyone except maybe Olsen, and he would help me. My mother's maid might be a problem, and, of course, if my mother is in her rooms, then I'll have to figure out a way to lure her away."

"Will she be very angry with you?"

"Most likely. She was furious when I told her I had no intentions of marrying Avery—she probably had apoplexy when she learned I was gone."

Chapter 36

"You made good time," called the Duke of Whitley from the doorway of the inn where the men planned to get fresh horses.

"If you don't mind my asking, your grace, what the devil are you doing here?" asked Edgewood, scowling. "We were to meet at the Blackbird."

"There's been a change of plans," said Whit, holding Avery's horse as he dismounted. "Come inside and eat while I talk. Two fresh horses, please, Rogers. These gentlemen will be leaving as soon as they've finished eating."

"What's this all about, Whit?" asked Avery as the four men entered a private room at the back of the inn.

"I didn't want to wait with the latest news, so I decided to meet you halfway. The Frenchman is on the move. He was sighted just yesterday near Eastland— actually near Terra Bella itself."

Avery uttered an oath.

"We knew he was close by because of his attack on Avery," said Hill, "but I'd hoped he'd moved on. Do we know any more about what he wants there?"

"The most obvious reason is still revenge for the thwarted effort to kidnap my duchess, but it seems there's a new plot that involves Avery directly. Your father's death was part of it, Av, I'm sorry to say. Our sources say that the lady your father was traveling with works for Jones and was tasked with the death of the duke. For some reason, it was important to the Frenchman that you inherit as soon as possible."

"Lady Tangier is a French operative?" Avery didn't hide his surprise.

"I'm not sure about *that*," said Whit. "We have no evidence she worked for Napoleon, just that she has a connection with Jones. It's possible—in fact, it's more than likely—that Jones is now working for no one but himself. We still don't know everything, but the reason I decided to meet you here is we heard Jones is putting his plan against Avery into action. And, like the coward he is, his revenge focuses not on the men involved but on their women."

Whit paused for a moment and then continued. "Avery, the day before yesterday, my men foiled a kidnapping attempt on the Furies—two men in the middle of the park in broad daylight. If Charlotte hadn't started pummeling one of the men with her parasol and reticule, and if the girls had been anything other than thrilled to join in on their defense, they would have been taken."

A deadly calm came over Avery as he listened to Whit. What kind of deranged man took out his revenge on three little girls? He would find this man and he would make sure he never threatened anyone again. As Whit continued, a cold fear crept up his spine.

"We managed to round up both of the perpetrators, and, after extensive interview sessions, were able to extract bits and pieces of the Frenchman's plan—it's a bit crazy, but it seems his goal was to leave your family without an heir. So first he had your father killed, and now he is after you. What's more, he knows of your connection with Miss Braddock and is adamant that there be no possibility of an heir there either."

Avery didn't try to demure. After last night, there was the distinct possibility Linney was carrying his heir. He'd made no attempt to prevent such a circumstance because there was no doubt in his mind that they would marry soon.

Whit continued. "The Frenchman has had someone following Linney in London, but when she left town they lost the trail. Yesterday a man accosted her maid and demanded she reveal Miss Braddock's whereabouts. She refused to tell him anything and called for help. Luckily her brother was close by at the time and gave the man a good beating. From the note Linea sent to Vivian, I knew she was on her way to Terra Bella, so I sent Edgewood to see if he could find you. With this new information, it's imperative that you find her and keep her safe."

"She and Lady Tangier's daughter are at an inn in Aylesbury. They're safe enough there, but I'll go and bring her back to London anyway. I don't want to take any chances. As long as she stays away from Terra Bella until Jones is apprehended, she'll be safe."

"So far we've been lucky in that the men Jones has hired seem to have little loyalty. They are willing enough to give him up with some encouragement and a few threats. But Jones himself seems to be completely out of control which makes him extremely dangerous. And unfortunately, right now he seems to be after Linney."

Avery stood and exchanged looks with Hill. "Is there anything else, Whit? I'd like to get back to the inn tonight."

"Just be careful—both of you. Jones has nothing to lose. He's not likely to be rational if you come up against him. I'd like to question him, but don't take any chances. If your only choice is to eliminate him, then do so. And Camberton? There's a good chance Jones has found out you provided some of the intelligence we used to rescue the codemaker. See to your family—especially the women—until we have this madman in custody."

"My sister is in Paris, so it's just my mother," said Hill, "but I'll make sure she's safe. What about Eve? Is she in danger as well?"

"Eve?"

"Lady Genevieve. Lady Tangier's daughter," said Avery.

Whit glanced quickly at Edgewood, who shrugged and shook his head. "I've not heard anything about her," he said. "I don't think she's part of the scheme, so perhaps her mother's association with Jones keeps her from harm. As long as she is not aligned with either of you, she's most likely safe, but if I were you, I wouldn't assume anything."

Chapter 37

It was in the gloaming that Linney and Eve arrived at the first outbuilding on the back side of Castle Terra Bella. Lighting their lantern, the girls quickly slipped inside the old building and crept down the stairs. They were immediately met with the pleasant smell of apples.

"The apple room," whispered Eve with a grin.

"They said it was the wall against the hill, beside the barrels. Over here." Linney led the way toward the back of the building and around a stack of three wooden barrels on their sides.

"There it is," said Eve. "What if it's locked?"

"Then we go back to the inn and let Avery find it later," said Linney shrugging her shoulders. "Let's try it."

Expecting a stuck latch and rusty hinges, Linney was pleased when the smaller-than-normal door opened easily, showing only a yawning blackness beyond. "Someone knows about this door," she said. "The hinges have been oiled."

"At least we don't have to worry about getting fresh air into the passageway," said Eve.

"Not so far, no. Are you ready?"

"Just about. Help me pull this dress on. I should be able to slip up the back stairs without anyone noticing me, and I'll get to the duchess's rooms in about twenty minutes. If mother is there, I'll figure out a way to get her to leave, and then I'll go back and look for a door."

"Knock twice on the outside wall and I'll know you're alone. I don't know if I'll be able to hear you, but we can try. Be careful, Eve."

"You too," said Eve. Leaving the candle and flint for Linney, she took the lantern and walked quickly toward the servants' entrance of Terra Bella.

Chapter 38

"Where have you been? I've been waiting for almost an hour."

Lady Tangier's heart stopped at the unexpected but not unfamiliar voice. She quickly closed the door to her room behind her. The sun had set, but she could make out the dark figure of a man standing in front of the fireplace where the flames had died down to bright coals.

"I've been in Eve's room, trying to find something," she said, taking what she hoped was a calming breath.

"And did you?"

"Did I what?"

"Did you find what you were looking for?"

"No," she said shortly, crossing the room to sit down at her dressing table. "As a matter of fact, I did not, and I was just going to write you a letter to that effect."

"I am heartened to know you have finally decided to communicate with me. I've heard nothing, and I've been waiting for several weeks now." Jones sauntered across the room to stand behind her, placing his hands on her shoulders and moving his thumbs to massage the back of her neck.

"You did not send word that the duke had survived the attack. Why?" His fingers tightened around her throat, making it difficult for her to speak.

"You were playing a game of your own, were you not? Without my permission." The fingers tightened more as he leaned down to whisper in her ear. "I should snap your pretty neck."

She tried to breathe, but the fingers pressed too tightly against her windpipe.

"The next time you disobey me, I will." He released her and lazily crossed back to the fireplace. He smiled when he saw her put her fingers to her throat where his hands had been.

"I am here to check up on you, my dear. I am concerned you may have forgotten your objective."

"I accomplished my task," said Lady Tangier defiantly, standing up and crossing the room to him. "The old duke is dead and Lord Hammond is the Duke of Easton."

"Agreed," said Jones, leaning against the mantel as he regarded her. "Which beggar's the question, why are you still here? I have reports you are engaged in another scheme—one that is not part of your mission for me."

"Why do you care? I did what you asked. You're taking a great risk to come here. Did anyone see you?" Her petulant tone brought another smile to his lips.

"Of course no one saw me. I entered the same way I entered the boudoir of the new Countess of Tangier many years ago—through a secret passageway."

"How did you find out about that?"

"Ah, so you know it too. I thought you might." Jones pushed away from the fireplace and circled slowly until he again stood behind her. She started to walk away, but he caught her roughly by the waist, pulling her back against him and grinding his aroused body against her backside. He boldly fondled her breast with one hand while he sent the other snaking down her leg and rucking up her skirt on its way to more intimate destinations.

Bending slightly, he whispered in her ear, "All castles have secret passageways, my lady. It's simply a matter of finding them and making sure the entrances are well lubricated." Under her gown, his long finger lazily stroked along her slit before plunging in deeply. At her gasp, he murmured, "Ah, yes. Entrances must be well lubricated so they will open easily. It seems yours is ready to be entered, my lady." He teased her with several more strokes before abruptly pulling his hand away and laughing at her frustrated moan.

"I regret I haven't time right now to explore that particular passage further, my dear. Now, why don't you tell me about this new scheme of yours, and I will decide whether or not I approve."

Lady Tangier jerked out of his embrace and turned with her hand drawn back to slap his face.

He easily caught her arm, twisting it back behind her as he pulled her up against him. "Now, now, my lady. That would not be wise." He crushed his mouth to hers in a punishing kiss until she finally stopped struggling. He released her arm and tipped her chin up, looking into her eyes. "That's better, my sweet. You know I will never stay away from you for long. I never could—even when you married that old coot. As I recall, you were always ready to welcome me into your bed—especially once you found out that the only thing stiff about the earl was his collars. He barely had enough iron in his rod to avoid pissing himself, so it was mine you used for pleasure and for procreation.

How *did* you manage to convince the earl that the child you carried was his when he couldn't even consummate the marriage?"

Laughing, Jones set the countess away from him and turned back to the fireplace. "Now tell me your plan."

Shaking out her crumpled skirts, Lady Tangier pouted. "Why should I tell you anything?"

"Because if you don't I will slit that lovely throat of yours." His pleasant tone only made the threat more ominous.

"I had hoped to marry the duke before he died," she said. "As his widow, I would have a settlement and a place in society. But he refused to marry me—even after I seduced him. After the attack, he took forever to die, and by then Lord Hammond had arrived. It was then that I realized I could also have a happy future as the *mother* of the new Duchess of Easton. I decided to make it look as though Easton had compromised my Eve so he would be forced to marry her."

"You mean *our* Eve, don't you, my dear?" Jones pondered her words for a moment. "I am not unhappy with that plan—especially the part where my grandson becomes the Duke of Easton. It would be a different kind of revenge, but it is not unappealing."

"Well, it's not going to happen now," snapped Lady Tangier. "Eve left yesterday for London, and she took Easton's letters to the Braddock chit with her."

"What?" bellowed Jones. "Why did you not destroy them? You must find Eve and get the letters back. You cannot allow her to—"

The knock on the door froze them both.

"Mama?"

Lady Tangier looked up fearfully and then pushed at the man who both frightened and excited her. "You must go," she hissed. "She cannot find you here."

"Mama? Are you in there?" The knock sounded again and the latch rattled.

Jones laughed at Lady Tangier's panic and kissed her leisurely on the mouth before opening the door to the secret passage.

"*Au revoir, cherie*. Do not fail me," he warned, and then he slipped through the open door and into the tunnel beyond.

Chapter 39

Linney could barely see the rough-hewn walls as she made her way through the tunnel. She had given Eve the lantern and kept the candle to light her own way, but the single flame barely penetrated the thick darkness. Beneath her feet, the floor of the passageway was uneven, but smooth and free of debris.

The passage progressed just as she had thought it would—she could picture her progress as she walked by narrow cracks of light and enticing smells that signaled an exit to the kitchen. She was relieved to realize she could hear voices from the rooms quite clearly. Soon the narrow tunnel began to climb—not stairs, as such, but rather a mixture of steps here and there along with rather steep inclines. Linney knew she was moving up to the next floor, and she was fairly certain the tunnel followed the course of the back stairway—after all, no one would notice that the servant's staircase was not as wide as the outside dimensions implied.

She continued slowly along the passageway, trailing her fingers along the wall to help maintain her balance in the darkness. It was possible that the tunnel ahead was blocked for any number of reasons—incomplete construction, deterioration, or even items that were stored there from generations past. It was also possible the tunnel simply came to an end around the next bend.

The only thing she knew for certain was that the way out was behind her.

Every so often, she felt an indention where the wall was carved out to hold a sconce. Sometimes she felt a little shelf under the sconce. Raising her candle, she saw a flint and stone on the shelf. Remember that, she reminded herself. If her flame blew out, the darkness would be absolute.

The passageway continued to climb. Linney was almost certain she'd reached the level where the bedrooms for the duke and duchess were located. Then, just as she was beginning to wonder if she'd misjudged her progress, she saw cracks of light that indicated a door to a lighted room. But which room?

Moving as quietly as she could, Linney crept closer to the outlined door. She could hear muffled voices talking on the other side. A woman's voice sounded angry. Was that Eve's mother? A man's voice replied, but Linney couldn't quite make out what either one was saying. She moved closer and put her ear to the wall.

The woman sounded defensive. "...as though Easton had compromised my Eve...marry her."

"You mean *our* Eve, don't you?...not unhappy with that...Easton...different kind of revenge..."

The man's voice grew louder. It was still unfamiliar, and yet the accent reminded Linney vaguely of someone she knew. The woman mumbled something, and then the man bellowed, "What?"

Then the woman's voice again "...for London...Easton's letters to that Braddock chit."

Linney heard a knock at the hallway door. The voices in the room were immediately quiet.

"Mama?"

It was Eve.

"…go! She cannot find you…"

Linney heard Eve knock again and call, "Mama, are you in there?"

Linney heard footsteps from the room coming closer and then heard a slight scraping sound. Someone was opening the door to the hidden passageway!

Terrified, she snuffed her candle and crouched under the little shelf in the small alcove beside the door. She flattened herself as much as she could against the recessed wall and held her breath as the door opened fully to reveal the silhouette of a large man.

"*Au revoir, cherie*," said the man. "Do not fail me."

He closed the door and stood there. He was so close that Linney could easily have touched him. She waited for him to leave, but then she realized that, like her, he was listening to the conversation in the room.

She willed her heart to thump more quietly as she prayed the man would neither burst back into the room to harm Eve nor light a candle and discover she'd been spying on him.

Closing her eyes, Linney concentrated on breathing slow, shallow breaths without making a sound.

Chapter 40

The ride back to the Dog and Pony was agonizing. Avery and Hill rode flat out whenever possible, but sometimes the main road was crowded with other riders and carriages, requiring caution and causing delays. The two men were tired, but fear urged them on. And even though his head told him Linney was safe at the inn, Avery's heart bade him go faster.

The summer days were long, so they managed to reach the Dog and Pony before the sun had started to set in earnest. Avery barely allowed his horse to stop before dismounting and striding toward the doorway.

Mrs. Pearson looked up at his entrance. "Your grace," she said. "We didn't expect you until tomorrow. Couldn't keep away from her for that long?" The woman started to smile but switched quickly to concern as she noted the grave look on his face.

"What is it, your grace? Is something amiss?"

"The ladies, Mrs. Pearson. Are they upstairs?"

"Actually, they are not. They didn't tell me all the details, but they said they would be back before you gentlemen returned, and then they bought tickets on the mail coach that stops in Eastland."

"Eastland? When did they leave?"

"Not an hour after you gentlemen left this morning."

"We'll need fresh horses, Mrs. Pearson. Is your

husband about?"

"I've already got them, Avery," called Hill, striding into the inn behind him with a grim look on his face. "Pearson says the ladies were still in their disguises."

Avery shook his head as he turned to walk out. "Maybe that's good," he muttered. "Maybe that will keep them safe." He looked up at his old friend. "She's going to be the death of me yet."

Chapter 41

The moon had risen by the time Avery and Hill rode down the lane that led to Terra Bella. Bathed in the moonlight, every building looked ghostly, and the mist rising from the low spots gave the familiar landscape an otherworldly feel.

"Do you think they're inside the castle?"

"No," said Avery, "I think they tried to find the hidden passageway in the apple room, so let's start there."

Tying their horses in a nearby copse, Avery and Hill proceeded on foot toward the old stone building where they had sought refuge so many years ago. Leaving Hill as a lookout, Avery slipped inside and descended the steps to the cellar. At the back of the room, beside the barrels, he saw the door that seemed to lead into a wall—just as it was all those years ago. He could see that the door was slightly ajar. He moved closer, but froze and retreated behind a stack of barrels when he heard a low whistle from outside where Hill kept watch.

A light appeared at the top of the stairs, and as Avery watched, Eve came down the steps with a lantern in her hand and headed toward the hidden door. Hill entered quietly behind her and nodded at his friend. In one move, Hill grabbed Eve and put his hand over her mouth and his mouth to her ear. Eve's struggles quickly ceased as she recognized her assailant. She was still in Hill's embrace when Avery came up behind them.

"Is Linney in the passageway?" he asked in a low whisper.

"I think so," said Eve. "But she should be back any minute. I was going to take the lantern and see if I could help her find her way out. She only has a candle."

"Do you know where the passage goes?"

"I think it's as she said. I think there's a door to the passage in the duchess's rooms. Mother was in her room, and I thought I heard her talking to someone—a man. I knew I had to get her out of the room before Linney got there, so I knocked on her door and made up a story about Merton needing to see her. I was supposed to knock twice on the wall when the room was empty, so Linney would know which one it was, but I didn't get a chance because Agnes came in just as Mother and I were leaving. I decided just to meet Linney back here—I thought for certain she would have returned by now. Maybe I should take the lantern and go in after her."

"No!" said Avery and Hill together.

"You stay here with Hill," said Avery. "Give me the lantern, and—"

He stopped and they all listened. There were footsteps coming from the hidden passage. Hill pulled Eve with him behind one of the big barrels and covered the lantern while Avery moved closer and stood behind the stack of barrels, hoping to see Linney appear in the doorway. The door opened wider and a figure emerged—someone much bigger than Linney. Avery watched in horror as the figure stood up straight and the moon illuminated the face of the man who—not two days ago—had pointed a pistol at his head. The Frenchman. Cold dread entered his heart. Where was Linney?

In the moonlight, it was clear that the Frenchman was again dressed for the evening, although this time his neck scarf was undone and one lace cuff looked badly torn. Avery failed to understand why a man would be dressed for an elegant evening when he was riding great distances through woods and fields. He waited until he heard the man go up the stairs and out the door, and then made his way back to Hill and Eve.

"Who was that man?" asked Eve. "Did you recognize him?"

"Unfortunately, yes," said Avery. "That was the Frenchman. Napoleon's spymaster—at least he used to be. His only job these days is revenge—specifically revenge on me by harming Linney. At least he didn't have her with him, so he's not abducting her. Which means either she somehow avoided him, or…"

He couldn't put words to his other thought. If the Frenchman had encountered Linney in the secret passageway, she was more than likely dead. The Frenchman was vicious, cruel, and extremely efficient at eliminating anyone he considered to be a loose end. Jones knew about Linney's connection with him, and in his quest for revenge, the man would not hesitate to kill her.

"I'm going in to find her," said Avery, taking the lantern from Hill. "Wait here in case Jones returns."

Chapter 42

Like the Frenchman, Avery had to stoop to enter the passageway, although once he was through the door, the tunnel accommodated his height. The floor was uneven but smooth, as if it had been used a great deal.

"I don't know why I'm the only one in the world who knows nothing about this bloody tunnel," he muttered to himself, holding the lantern up high. "Evidently every Tom, Dick, and Harry's been using it to get into the castle—*my* castle, where I've lived my entire life—but there's no need to tell me anything. I'm just the damn duke, that's all."

He was angry—at his father for not telling him about the hidden passageway—and he was furious at Linney for again going off without considering the consequences of her actions. And at himself for being so careless with her a second time.

Most of all, he was terrified of what he would find in the tunnel.

As he rounded the first turn, the passageway began to climb, with a step here and there and a steady incline. Just as the tunnel leveled off, he heard footsteps coming toward him. He quickly blew out the lantern and moved to one side of the passageway, his other four senses trying to compensate for the lack of light.

He smelled roses before he heard her rapid

breathing, and only seconds after that he grabbed her, feeling his way to her waist and pulling her against him, surrounding her with his embrace and smothering her gasp and scream with his lips. He felt her melt against him, and though he desperately wanted to ensure she was unharmed, it was several minutes before he could convince himself to let her out of his arms. At last he released her, but he held tight to her hand, refusing to let her go entirely.

"What in bloody hell were you thinking?" he hissed.

"Would it be possible for you to berate me after we are out of this passageway?" Linney whispered back. "I am positive I heard someone else farther up in the tunnel, and given my recent failures at espionage, I would greatly prefer not to encounter that person here."

Without another word, he started back down the passageway, holding her hand as they made their way back to the entrance in the dark. In less time than it had taken him to find her, they were back in the stone building with Hill and Eve. Still not saying anything, Avery led the foursome outside to the grove of small trees where their horses were tethered.

In the light of the moon, Avery turned to search Linney's face. "Are you hurt? Did he see you?"

"I don't think anyone saw me, and no, I'm not hurt, just frightened and very glad to see you."

Taking a deep breath, Avery adopted the demeanor of his profession and continued his questioning without emotion. "You said there was someone else in the tunnel?"

"Yes. I think there were two people in there. A man and a woman."

"A man came out a few minutes before I went in to find you. Did you see him or recognize his voice?"

"No, I didn't see him, but if it was the same man who was in the duchess's rooms with Lady Tangier, he had a very proper British accent."

"Yes, that's him. The Frenchman. Monsieur Jones. Napoleon's spymaster. He's British and he's been betraying his country and killing his countrymen for years. And now he's after you."

Avery wanted to scare her. He wanted her to know how much danger she had been in—and still was.

"Me? Why would he be after me?"

"Because he's after me," said Avery. "And he knows the best way to hurt me would be to harm you. And because he's a cruel, ruthless madman who would stop at absolutely nothing to get his revenge."

"Was the woman in the tunnel Eve's mother?" asked Hill.

"No, it wasn't Lady Tangier," said Linney. "The woman sounded more like a servant. Did she come out as well?"

"No, just Jones, and now you. Where were you when you heard him?"

"I was near the duchess's rooms, and he was in the room talking to—I assume—Lady Tangier. Then I heard Eve knocking on the door and calling to her mother. That's when the man came into the passageway."

"How did he not see you?"

"There's a carved-out alcove area and a little shelf right beside the entrance to the duchess's rooms. When I heard the passage door opening, I blew out my candle and tucked myself into the alcove under the shelf as much as I could. The man stood outside the entrance forever—I could hear him breathing, and I could easily have touched him. I was terrified that he might smell the candle or hear me breathing, but then there was a noise farther up in the passageway and he went toward it. I stayed where I was, and that's when I heard the other woman's voice. She sounded like she was pleading about something. I heard a scuffling noise, and then I heard the man's heavy footsteps coming back— at least I assumed it was the same man. He passed right by me. The buttons on his frock coat hit my face. I thought for certain he would see me, but he didn't."

Linney didn't notice Avery's grip on the lantern tighten as she told her story.

"I waited a little while longer to see if the woman would also come by, but no one ever did. Perhaps she left through another door into the castle. I finally decided to find my way out, and that's when I ran into you. You nearly scared me to death."

"That makes us even, then. Monsieur Jones is the one who arranged for Vivian to be kidnapped, and he has been seeking revenge against Vivian and Whit as well as against Edgewood, Camberton, and me. His favorite form of revenge is to make men suffer by hurting the women they love. That's why Whit has had Vivian in the country since their wedding. And that's why you were supposed to stay at the inn. What were you thinking, Linney?"

When she started to speak, Avery held up his hand. "No, don't answer that. Please, just don't say another word."

He turned to Hill. "I'm going back in the tunnel to see where it ends. Under no circumstances is she to move from this spot. See to it, Camberton."

"Yes, your grace."

He turned back to Linney. "You. Stay. Here. I mean it, Linea. Do not move from this spot. I'll have your word on it."

"Yes, your grace," said Linney, meekly. "I promise."

It seemed like she held her breath for hours while Avery was gone, but in truth it was only a matter of minutes. He returned with the grim news that there had, in fact, been another person in the passageway. He'd found the body of Lady Tangier's maid, Agnes. Her wounds indicated she'd been strangled.

****

Some hours later, after the Duke of Easton had informed the household of his return, after Hill left to check on his mother, after Lady Tangier was summarily moved back to the guest wing—which, Avery made clear, she should plan to vacate within the week—and after ensuring Linney was made comfortable in the duchess's chamber by the placement of a deep, copper bathtub in front of the fire, Avery knocked softly on the door that connected the two suites. He, too, had made good use of a hot bath, and, with the help of Olsen's valet services and two shots of his father's single-malt scotch, had finally started to relax.

"Come in."

Avery opened the door to find his fiancée in a lacy white nightgown and robe, brushing out her hair to dry. In the glow of the firelight, her long, white-blonde locks were golden. The light from the flames silhouetted her figure, making her night clothes all but transparent to his eyes. His mouth went dry at the vision she created.

Mentally shaking himself, he cleared his throat. "It occurred to me that I never welcomed you to Terra Bella."

Linney smiled. "Thank you, your grace. Perhaps if I had arrived in the normal way, you might have had that opportunity."

She put down the brush and went to take Avery's hands, drawing him back toward the fire. "I owe you an apology, your grace. You are right. I didn't think at all about the consequences of Eve and me coming here, and I am so sorry. It was a foolhardy idea, and it endangered not just my life but Eve's as well, and of course yours and Camberton's when you came to our rescue. And while I know it doesn't excuse my actions, I did want you to know that I did what I did because I wanted to bring this to you."

Turning to the dressing table, she picked up a small enameled box and handed it to Avery. "I have not looked inside," she said, "but I'm hoping it contains the ring that means so much to you and your family."

Avery took the box and opened it, his face displaying no emotion.

"Linney," he said, closing the box again, "the Easton engagement ring is only a symbol. There are other, more valuable pieces of jewelry I will give to you as my duchess, but I wanted you to have this ring so you would know how much I love you and so you might feel part of this family that I love. In my fervor, I made it into something much more than that, but Linney, the ring is worth nothing to me if I don't have you to wear it."

Linney pulled his arms around her and slipped her

own around his waist. "Does this mean you will forgive me for leaving the inn and worrying you?" she said into his chest.

"I will think about it, but right now I'm trying to think of a way to make you promise not to go running off again—at least until we're married and the Frenchman has been apprehended. Maybe I should lock you up here in this room."

"Will you be locked up in this room with me?"

"Absolutely." He smiled down at the green eyes that held such passion and love.

"Then I promise," she whispered, brushing her lips against his and settling in for what promised to be a very pleasant stay indeed.

Author Note

The Elgin Marbles, a collection of Classical Greek marble sculptures, were originally created under the direction of Phidias for the temple of the Parthenon and other buildings on the Acropolis in Athens. The Marbles were removed and—depending on your point of view—either stolen or saved by Scottish nobleman, soldier, politician, and diplomat, Thomas Bruce, the seventh Earl of Elgin. Elgin gave them to the British Museum in 1816 (not 1815 as I have intimated) where they are still the subject of controversy between the museum and the nation of Greece.

Continue the Dukes in Danger series
with Edgewood's story …

The Duke's Defense

by

Carolina Prescott

Dukes in Danger:
A Haversham House Romance
Book 3

Chapter 1

Haversham House, New Year's Eve 1815

"*Why* am I here, your grace?"

"I take it you mean in addition to celebrating my half-brother's wedding to my wife's cousin and welcoming the coming new year?"

"I had other plans. I do have a life, you know."

"Don't sulk. I know about your life. You would have spent the holidays alone or with ghosts from Christmas past."

Tonight, the newly married Duke of Whitley—known to a select few as the Crown's brilliant spymaster—had an insufferable air of contentment about him that the Earl of Edgewood found rather tiresome. The once coldly condescending Ice Duke was now something of a domesticated beast. These days he tended to save his infamous stare—a look that brought all manner of enemies, as well as friends, to their collective knees—to heap contempt upon anyone who would inconvenience his duchess, who, in the spirit of the Christmas season, was great with child.

There was no use telling Whit that he was not the first man to be waiting for the birth of his offspring, just as there was no use telling him that other men, too, had wives who glowed and seemed even more beautiful in the graces of pregnancy.

1

Edgewood found it all rather off-putting and more than a little annoying. "I wasn't alone," he countered.

"Scotch whiskey—no matter how old—does not count as companionship."

"I wasn't referring to the whiskey, although now that you mention it, that might be the better choice. I was referring to—never mind. I have no need of reprimands from you, so I ask again. *Why* am I here?"

"I need the Duke of Marsden to arrange an extraction."

"The duke is unavailable. He also has a life."

"One hears rumors to the contrary. It seems no one has seen or heard from the duke since his rather token appearance after the death of his brother."

"My point exactly. He's not available to do any of your dirty work."

"This particular extraction is actually quite civilized compared to some of the duke's other excursions. In fact, it is only because it requires a journey to Paris that it even qualifies as such. The party being extracted is quite willing to leave, and the party in possession of the package is just as eager for the operation to take place, having plans to relocate his own family to more hospitable environs."

"If everything is running so smoothly, why do you need the duke? It sounds like a simple matter of documents and transportation."

"Just so. Except that the white terror is raising its flag throughout France, and the Royalists have been somewhat indiscriminately executing those who served Napoleon—especially his generals."

"Fine. So you need someone to spirit one of Napoleon's generals out of France. I'm assuming this general was the one who proved so valuable before Waterloo?"

"You know how I feel about assuming anything, but yes. In this you are correct."

"Still, it sounds like a relatively straightforward mission. Why do you need the duke?"

"It is not the general who is in need of the duke's escort. It is the general's mistress. In order to maintain the charade that is their cover, I have need of the duke's rank along with his innate air of superiority and insufferable arrogance." Whit hesitated for moment. "I also need his skill and experience. This *should* be a simple mission, but considering the current state of affairs in Paris—throughout the country, really—and in light of some intelligence I have only recently received, it has the potential to become perilous."

Edgewood hesitated, but just for a second or two. "Nevertheless, as I told you. The duke is unavailable."

"The mission also has a personal connection for me," said Whit.

Edgewood raised an eyebrow. "Really? How personal?"

"An old friend. I've known her since she was born. The lady has done some work for us over the past few years, but now it's time for her to come home. I need someone I can trust to fetch her."

"Fetch her? You make her sound like a bone, which, I must say, doesn't bode well for the appeal of this mission or offer much incentive to save this damsel in distress."

Whit laughed. "If I were you, I would be careful about saying things like that in front of her. You might find your family jewels handed to you on a plate."

Edgewood shifted uncomfortably at the implied threat. "Why me? You have plenty of men—and women, for that matter—whom you can trust."

Whit watched the dancers whirling about in their sparkling ensembles, laughing and talking in anticipation of the new year—now just minutes away. When he finally answered his friend, Whit spoke clearly and said perhaps the only words that would ensure his friend's complete and total cooperation.

"It's Henrianna, Edgewood. She's in danger."

A word about the author...

Carolina Prescott writes historical romance. She's been a fan of romance ever since reading Victoria Holt's *Mistress of Mellyn* as a teenager—one spunky governess and one brooding hero later, she was totally hooked.

Carolina Prescott's affinity for history and her quest for that inevitable happy ending make writing historicals a wonderfully logical career choice. She divides her time between an apartment in the trees (and a block from Starbucks®) in Northern California and her native North Carolina, where she has a home with lots of room for family, visitors, and a very understanding Brittany spaniel.

Visit Carolina at:

carolinaprescott.com

Thank you for purchasing
this publication of The Wild Rose Press, Inc.

For questions or more information
contact us at
info@thewildrosepress.com.

The Wild Rose Press, Inc.
www.thewildrosepress.com

CPSIA information can be obtained
at www.ICGtesting.com
Printed in the USA
FSHW020459100921
84685FS